FOUL POLE

Carolina Waves Series Book 6

TINA GALLAGHER

Galsalla Press

Foul Pole: Carolina Waves Series Book 6

By: Tina Gallagher

Published by Galsalla Press

Copyright © 2021

Cover Design: Qamber Designs

Editor: Jeannine Luby

To Anjannette…my Anjannette may have your name, but she'll never compare to you. No one does. You're an amazing person and I'm so honored to call you my friend.

Thank you to my amazing readers who gave this series a chance.

Chapter One

LEO

I SHIFTED into a reverse warrior pose, fighting to keep my balance as every muscle in my body protested the movement. Blinking, I crinkled my nose in an attempt to divert the sweat that somehow still managed to trickle into my eyes even though I'm looking up at the ceiling.

The curses ricocheting through my brain mocked the incense-and-serenity vibe in the studio. But seriously, this is bullshit. I've been through every cardio, strength, and flexibility training Major League Baseball has to offer and haven't struggled or sweat this much. I've already done all these poses on the other side of my body and am definitely feeling it.

At least this hell is almost over.

"Exhale and come into an extended side angle pose by placing your right forearm on your right thigh. Then extend your left arm and hover it over your ear."

I followed Clay's directions, breathing through the

discomfort as he had me flow through triangle and half-moon poses.

"Step back to downward dog and you can rest there for a few breaths, or if you'd prefer, move into child's pose."

Oh trust me, I'd *prefer*.

I lowered onto my knees and, reaching my arms forward, rested my forehead on the mat, thanking every supernatural power in the universe that this torture is almost over. I could have stayed like that forever, but once again, the taskmaster shouted out a command.

Okay, he told me what to do in a soft, calm voice, but either way, he was making me move.

"Shift to a seated position with your legs straight in front of you."

My knees cracked as I moved onto my ass and stretched my legs out. The back of my right calf settled into the wet spot my sweaty forehead had created and I shifted it slightly to the left.

"Inhale and straighten your spine then bring your arms straight out to the side and up over your head, reaching toward the ceiling. Draw your spine up and inhale, keeping your torso long. As you exhale, lean forward from your hip joints, not your waist."

My hamstrings, hips, and lower back protested as I did what he told me. I breathed deeply, compelling my muscles to give in to my will. But as I've learned in the past week of classes, it will take more than determination to make things happen.

"Don't grit your teeth. Keep your face and jaw relaxed and with each inhale, lengthen your spine and with each exhale, fold deeper. Imagine your belly coming to rest on your thighs, rather than your nose coming to your knees. Keeping your feet flexed, grab hold of either your toes or your ankles."

My toes? Yeah right.

I glared up at Clay, my jaw clenched. His raised brow and muted smirk would have made me laugh if I had the energy and enough breath. Despite my sneers and groans, it's the first time in a week that he's dropped his professional demeanor during our private sessions.

"Keep your neck a natural extension of your spine, don't look up or down."

I looked forward again and slicked my hair back off my face before grabbing my ankles.

"Keep breathing and if you're able, deepen the stretch with each exhale," Clay said.

Sweat dripped off my chin and immediately soaked into my shorts, forming a blotch that got larger with each subsequent drop. He had me hold that pose for what seemed like forever before saying the words I've been waiting for since this torture session started.

"Release your hold on your ankles and come back to a seated position. Now, with your core engaged, exhale and slowly lower your back to the mat. Rest your hands at your sides with your palms facing up and put your feet mat-length apart. Close your eyes and transition into Savasana, allowing your body to be just as it is and yourself to be whole and complete, simply lying there, breathing."

My body felt heavy as I eased onto the mat and my muscles relaxed. I closed my eyes and listened to the soothing background music and focused on regulating my breathing until it settled into a slow, comfortable rhythm.

In my opinion, this is the best kept secret of yoga. I think if everyone knew the torturous classes ended with this relaxing pose, they'd be packed. The first few times I did this, my mind wandered, thinking about all the things I had to do once I left the studio, not to mention how much pain I was in. But after just four classes, I'm learning to Savasana like a pro.

My mind and body totally relaxed and I enjoyed just lying on my mat breathing. Then a beat pounded into my consciousness. I opened my eyes and looked around, trying to figure out its source.

I spotted Clay through the glass door of his office. He'd started going in there after my first class when I said the thought of him watching me in Savasana was giving me the wiggins.

Sitting up, I twisted first to the right side then the left and shook out my legs. I grabbed my water bottle and finished its contents in one gulp. As I swallowed, I identified the song that had intruded on my Savasana. *Boom Boom Pow* by The Black Eyed Peas is an awesome song, but not something to listen to while in a state of total relaxation.

"You have five more minutes," Clay said from behind me.

"I was rudely interrupted by your music."

"I wasn't playing music." He frowned, then cocked his head to the side. The music changed to a slightly slower tempo as *Sorry* by Buckcherry started to play. "The floors must be finished downstairs."

"What does that mean?"

"The floor was being refinished in the pole dance studio downstairs, which is why there haven't been any classes there this week." He looked at his watch. "Although there aren't usually classes this late on a Sunday. Down there or up here. Which is probably why whoever is down there wasn't too concerned about blasting the music."

I got up and walked across the room to grab a spray bottle and rag off the shelf. Kneeling down, I sprayed down my mat and wiped it clean.

"I appreciate you meeting with me privately."

"No problem. I can't have you in my class distracting everyone with that pretty face," he said with a chuckle.

"Smart ass."

"But seriously, we'll do whatever works for you."

"You're the one with the busy schedule." I sat and slipped on my socks and sneakers, then rolled my mat and stood. After returning the spray bottle to its home, I tossed the rag into the hamper. "I'm free most anytime since it's the offseason. So if you need me to come during the day, I can."

I reached down and grabbed my water bottle and mat.

"Mornings or early afternoons might actually be better during the week. I'll text you tomorrow and let you know about Tuesday."

"Sounds good."

"It's getting easier, right?"

"No comment."

"Well, I see improvement in the few sessions we've had. Your balance is better and you don't seem to be protecting your lower back as much, so it must be loosening up."

"I do feel more loose, but this is harder than I thought it'd be. When the Waves' trainer recommended yoga, I had no idea it'd be so tough."

Clay patted me on the back and opened the door.

"You'll get there."

"I'll take your word for it."

That said, I stepped into the hallway and walked toward the stairs. I was rounding the landing when the unmistakable thump of *Fat Bottomed Girls* pounded out of the open door on the first floor. I jogged down the rest of the way and walked over to peek inside.

Holy shit!

I never believed in falling in love at first sight, but good

Lord, I fell into something the moment I spotted her. With her long limbs, porcelain skin, and platform boots, she looked like some kind of goddess as she climbed the pole. When she reached the top, she released her left hand and extended her arm out to the side and held on by her right hand and her ankles as she spun around and around. With her body away from the pole, she gripped it with her right hand near her thigh then wrapped her right leg around the pole and continued to spin with her right arm extended.

My sister Angie used to have a musical jewelry box with a ballerina inside that would spin around when the top was opened. That's exactly what the woman on the pole looked like.

I watched in awe as she straightened her legs and rolled around the pole then tipped back and hooked her left leg, seeming to hang on by the back of her knee. She arched and grabbed the heel of her right boot as she kept spinning around and around. I was getting dizzy just watching.

She let go of her boot and kicked her left leg back toward her head. And I don't know how it happened, but next thing I knew, she was hanging upside down in a full split.

Hooking her left leg around the pole again, she wrapped one arm behind her and grabbed on. Twisting her body, she straightened her legs until she hung upside down with her back against the pole. She looked like a sexy bat.

Freddie Mercury continued to sing about how fat-bottomed girls make the world go round and I have to agree. Not that the enchantress in front of me has a fat anything, but her bottom is perfectly rounded, especially in comparison to her slim figure and tiny frame.

Releasing her hands, she let her arms hang toward the ground while just her knees held her to the pole. She slid down slowly until her fingertips brushed the floor as she continued to spin. Around and around she went until she finally placed her hands flat on the floor slowing the momentum. Once the spinning stopped, she let her legs fall back until her feet landed against the hardwood floor with a bang.

She stood, whipping her hair over her shoulders and gripped the pole again. Before executing another mind-boggling trick, her eyes widened when she spotted me.

Her sky-high heels added a sexy sway to her hips as she walked in my direction. My mind raced as I tried to think of something to say that would accurately convey how much her performance blew me away. But I didn't have to worry about it because she didn't give me a chance to speak.

"Show's over," she said, and slammed the door in my face.

ANJANNETTE

I PLACED my hand over my chest, as if that would still my pounding heart. When I looked up and saw that man watching me, it took all my willpower to hide my initial panic. Thankfully, I noticed the yoga mat under his arm and realized he must have been upstairs with Clay before I totally freaked out.

Resting my back against the wall, I slid down to the floor. After unzipping both of my boots, I slipped them off and rubbed my feet. For eight-inch heels, they're pretty comfortable, but still squeeze my toes a little.

I heard a knock on the door and stood. Turning the

knob, I opened it a crack and breathed a sigh of relief when Clay Moody stood on the other side of the threshold instead of the Greek god that had been there a few minutes ago. Whether he's Greek or not, that's what I'm calling him since he looks just like John Stamos.

"Hey Clay."

After opening the door, I walked over to my iPad and lowered the music.

"What do you think of the floors?" he asked as he stepped inside.

"They're beautiful. I'm really happy with them."

Picking up my tank top, I shrugged into it before turning around.

"How was your vacation?"

"Relaxing," I said. "It's the first one I've taken in a long time and I made the most of it."

"Do anything special?"

"Nothing fancy. A few friends and I rented a lake house in the Poconos. We hiked, kayaked, and drank way too much."

"Sounds like a good time."

"Yeah, it was." I nodded. "I'm surprised to see you here."

"That's actually why I stopped in. I'm doing private sessions with a friend of mine so I'll be here at different times for the next few months."

"I saw your car in the lot, but didn't realize you were with someone. I hope my music didn't totally kill your session."

"No, he was halfway through Savasana when it started."

"Oh good. Besides the fact I had the music cranked up louder than usual, I left the door open because there are still some fumes in here." He blinked then shifted his eyes toward the door I'd had to open for him. "Your friend stopped by and I slammed it in his face," I explained with a shrug. "Sorry about that."

"No worries. It'll keep him humble," Clay said with a chuckle. "Anyway, I just wanted to stop in to welcome you back and let you know that you may be seeing me here at weird times."

"I'll be sure to keep the music at a decent decibel and the door closed."

He nodded and walked toward the door. "Have a good night."

"You too."

A minute later Keera arrived.

"Guess who I just saw downstairs."

"Clay?"

"No, not Clay." She waved her hand in a dismissive gesture. "When I pulled into the parking lot, I saw Leo Marakis getting into his car, but he pulled out before I could talk to him."

She said the name as though I should not only know who that is, but I should also be impressed. I just looked at her and blinked.

"Leo Marakis," she said again, raising her voice slightly on the last word making the name sound like a question.

I lifted my brow and shook my head.

"Leo Marakis."

She drew out the five syllables, as if saying the words more slowly would magically give me the knowledge she seems to think I should possess.

"You can say the name as slow or loud as you want, but I have no idea who that is."

Keera rolled her eyes.

"Have you been living under a rock? He's the catcher

for the Carolina Waves and one of the hottest guys in professional baseball."

"You know I don't follow baseball or any other testosterone-filled sports."

"They're worth watching for the eye candy alone." Keera's train of thought switched tracks and she seemed to have an epiphany. "Wait a minute." Her eyes widened and she grabbed my hand and squeezed. "He was carrying a yoga mat. Was he in this building?"

Her question was asked with a quiet reverence that made me laugh. She removed her hand from mine and crossed her arms over her chest.

"Look, just because you're a total misandrist doesn't mean the rest of us don't enjoy the company of a hot guy."

This is not the first time Keera has said that exact thing to me. And I'll admit that the first time I heard the word, I had to look up the exact definition of *misandrist*. It's not exactly in my everyday vocabulary.

"I don't despise men," I said. "I just don't have the patience to deal with egotistical pretty boys."

"You don't have the patience to deal with men, period." Keera rolled her eyes at my shrug. "You've got to get back out there sometime. You broke up with Travis the Weasel three years ago. Don't you miss sex?"

I'll admit that at first I did, but for the past couple years, not so much. In fact, all my toys have been collecting dust. Now I channel all my sexual energy into my business. The fact that Peaches & Pole is generating enough revenue to allow me to cut back on my web design business says a lot.

Instead of answering her question, I said, "I'll admit your Leo Marakis is easy on the eyes."

"You saw him?"

"I'm guessing the man you're talking about is the one

Clay just told me he's doing private sessions with. Dark hair and eyes?" Keera nodded. "Looks like John Stamos?" Her eyes widened and she nodded again. "He was watching me freestyle."

"And what did you do?"

"I slammed the door in his face."

"Seriously?" I nodded. "*What* is wrong with you?"

"What would you do if you thought you were alone then looked up and found a guy watching you dance?"

"If he was a muffin like Leo Marakis, I know *exactly* what I'd do." She bobbed her eyebrows.

I grabbed my grip spray and coated the top of my feet, shins, and inner thighs. After placing the cap back on and returning it to the shelf, I turned to face Keera again.

"You and I both had shitty exes and are dealing with our breakups in our own way. Your dick band-aids seem to be working for you, but at this point in my life, casual sex would only make me feel worse."

"I'm not saying you have to go out and throw your cat at every guy you see, but don't you think it's time to put yourself out there again?" When I didn't answer, she continued. "By not dating, I feel like you're still letting Travis have power over you."

Instead of answering, I grabbed a spray bottle and rag and walked over to the pole I'd used. After spraying the rag, I tucked it in my bra and climbed to the top, cleaning the grip off as I slowly slid down. Just for good measure and to give me extra time to collect my thoughts, once I reached the ground, I gave the lower half an extra scrub.

"He doesn't still have power over me. This doesn't have anything to do with Travis. Not specifically anyway."

Other than my therapist, I haven't talked to anyone about this. But maybe it's time. If anyone would under-stand, it's Keera. She had a shitty ex too. I didn't know her when she was with him, but from what I understand, he was just as bad as Travis.

I walked over to the iPad and turned the music back on but lowered the volume. What I'm going to say is difficult enough to admit, I don't want my words echoing through a quiet room. Keera had settled on the floor and I sat across from her and rested my back against the wall.

"After I left Travis, my therapist made me realize that since I started dating in junior high, I hadn't been single for longer than a month. I've been stuck in a cycle of relationships, moving from one guy to the next, always focusing on fitting the mold of whoever I was with at the time. I've given up pieces of myself or ignored my own wants just to make whatever guy was in my life happy."

I shifted my gaze to the side and blinked away the tears that threatened to fall. Drawing my knees up, I wrapped my arms around them before looking at her again.

"Travis was a dick and borderline mentally abusive, but the fact that it took me three years to realize that tells its own story. I made it easy for him to totally bend me to his will. I lost myself in that relationship because I didn't really know who I was."

Looking around the studio, I smiled. Pole is the one thing I wouldn't give up for Travis. At first he thought my dancing was cool but quickly started to resent the time I spent at the studio. After a while, I compromised and only attended classes I taught and trained on my home pole the rest of the time. That appeased him at first, but after a few months, he pushed for me to totally stop again. Thankfully I had one brain cell working and didn't give in to his demand.

"After I finally broke up with him, my therapist suggested that I take a six-month dating hiatus. The fact that I had such a hard time being single at first made me realize how much I needed a break from men and I decided to extend it to a year. And now, I'm happy with myself and my life, my friendships. I know who I am and what I want." I shrugged. "Part of me is afraid that I'll backslide and lose that if I get involved with someone new."

"Not if you're with a good guy," Keera said.

"The fact that I'm a bad picker is a whole other therapy session and the reason I've been taking an extended break from anyone with a penis." I released my knees and shifted to my feet. "But we're here to figure out the end of our routine and practice, not lament on my sexless existence."

Keera stood and walked over to give me a big hug. With her arms still around me, she pulled back to look me in the eye.

She released me and stepped back.

"Why didn't you tell me this before? I would have shut up."

"I didn't tell anyone. It's not exactly something you want to shout from the rooftops."

She nodded and seemed resigned to let the subject drop.

"Now that I've brought down the entire vibe, I need some feel-good music."

I scrolled to an upbeat playlist but just before I hit play, Keera spoke again.

"But you have to admit that Leo Marakis is seriously hot."

Full disclosure, my hoo-ha had perked up for the first time in more than a year at the sight of Leo Marakis. But I'm keeping that to myself. I've shared enough already today.

Chapter Two

LEO

I LOOKED around my empty basement, reminding myself that this whole house is a work in progress. Under my sister Angie's supervision, the first and second floors were remodeled while I was on the road during the season so at least the main living areas are complete. For the most part anyway. But I want to manage this space myself.

Right now it's all white walls and concrete floors, but eventually it will be my man cave. Not that I live with anyone I need to escape from right now, but since I'm on the road so much, it'll be nice to have a comfortable space to decompress in when I am home.

My cell buzzed and I glanced at the caller ID, smiling as I answered.

"I was just thinking about you," I said, then added. "Actually, I was thinking about your girlfriend."

"First of all, she's my fiancée," Trey said. "And second, be careful what you say next."

He tried to sound menacing with that last sentence, but didn't quite pull it off. Trey knows I'd never disrespect Nori or him. He's my brother from another mother and considering I have two brothers and three sisters from my actual mother, I wouldn't have added him to the mix if I didn't want him there.

"I'm standing in my empty man cave, looking at the blank walls, wondering when you're bringing Nori up here to plan a mural and give me some color suggestions."

Trey's fiancée paints the most amazing murals and I'm hoping she'll transform my basement into something spectacular. The walls anyway. I'll be in charge of everything else.

"Come on, the season ended a couple weeks ago. You can admit that you miss me. It can't be easy being in Scranton without me. You're probably sad."

"I lived here without you when I played for the Rail-Riders and somehow survived," I said referring to my years with the AAA Yankees affiliate based in the Scranton area.

His chuckle echoed through the line.

"I haven't been back there since graduation. How is it?"

"Pretty much the same. But you know, I like it here."

Trey Youngman and I met in this city over a decade ago when we both attended Lackawanna College. He was an arrogant prick and the fact that we were not only roommates, but also teammates meant we were with each other almost all the time.

I grew up with a big, loud, nosy family, so I know how to deal with a *lot* of personalities. But he was more than even I could handle at first. Then one day I heard his father yelling at him. I couldn't believe the awful, berating things the man was saying. And I realized that despite the fact he was born with a silver spoon in his mouth, Trey's life wasn't all that easy and it definitely wasn't as perfect as it looked from the outside. One night, I said something to him about that and he opened up about his family. We've been best friends ever since and he was made an honorary member of the Marakis clan.

As if he read my thoughts, he said, "Maybe I projected all the shit I had going on in my life when I lived there on the city. If you like it, it can't be all that bad."

"People say the same thing about you," I said to lighten the mood.

"Nori said that exact thing about me."

Trey's laugh punctuated his thought.

"See, you have me to thank for your *fiancée*."

"That's not totally untrue. If it wasn't for you and Crispin playing matchmaker, who knows if Nori and I would have gotten together?"

"I'm sure you would have figured it out."

"See, that's why I keep you around. You have faith in me."

"Uh oh, you must want something if you're saying stuff like that."

"Nope, just speaking the truth," he said. "But I actually am calling about coming up there. You must have psychically transferred your thoughts to Nori because she texted and wanted me to call you. She just had a commission pushed back so she has a break in her schedule the third weekend of the month. Will you be around?"

"Absolutely. Other than the time I spend with Clay kicking my ass, I'm pretty free."

"How is Clay?"

"He's doing well."

"No lingering effects from the accident?"

"No, and he credits that to yoga."

Clay was one of our teammates in college and he was a

kickass pitcher. Like Trey and me, he was drafted after graduation but during his first season playing Minor League ball, he was in a horrible car accident. He got pretty banged up, but thankfully healed after a few months, for the most part anyway. Unfortunately, his right knee and left elbow suffered some lingering effects and his pitching wasn't as sharp. He played the following season but got lit up every time he took the mound so he hung up his cleats.

"Is he gonna fix you?"

"If he doesn't kill me in the process," I said. "I'll admit, my lower back feels looser than it has in a long time, but seriously, he's killing me. Stretching and holding poses doesn't seem that hard but it is. By the end of the hour, I'm dying."

"Come on, it can't be that bad."

"I'll tell you what, you can come to a class with me while you're up here."

"Challenge accepted," he said. "We'll have to figure out a good bet so that when I breeze through class, you'll owe me something."

"It needs to be something I'll be able to enjoy when I win."

"You wish."

Before I could answer, my alarm chimed.

"I don't have time to debate, yoga calls."

After getting a few more digs in, we hung up and I left the house and headed to the studio. I was just halfway through the fourth song of my 80's playlist when I approached my destination. The box truck I'd been following through town pulled over and blocked the entrance to the parking lot, so I pulled into a space on the street. But not before I spotted a white Honda Pilot that had been in front of the truck turning into the lot. And just my luck, my red-haired goddess sat behind the wheel.

ANJANNETTE

I PULLED into the space next to Clay's truck, happy to see it was the only other vehicle in the parking lot. I've got a lot to do and the last thing I need is to see a certain sexy ballplayer. It's bad enough when he creeps into my thoughts, which he has been quite often since I met him the other day.

My phone rang just as I shifted my car into park.

"Hey."

"I'm stuck in traffic," Keera said. "Like *really* stuck. This highway is bumper-to-bumper and I haven't moved an inch in ten minutes." She let out a long sigh. "So I'm gonna be late."

"No worries."

I grabbed my purse, duffle, and laptop case off the passenger seat and slipped my wrist through the straps. Tilting my head to hold my cell against my shoulder, I opened the car door.

"I came up with some ideas for our routine. While I'm just sitting here, I'll text you what I have in mind."

"Sounds great." I bent my elbow to hold the bags in place and slid out of the SUV then kicked the door closed.

"I'll get there as soon as I can."

After hefting the straps onto my shoulder, I locked my doors, and returned my hand to the phone to give my neck a break.

"Just be safe," I said as I walked toward the building.

"Will do."

I slid the phone into my purse and looked up, then

froze. The Greek god stood there holding the door open for me.

Cheese and rice.

"Hi."

His voice is pure, velvet perfection, just like I imagined it would be.

I'm totally gobsmacked and instead of offering an intelligent response, I looked around the parking lot. As if the fact his vehicle isn't present matters. The man himself *is* and he's even hotter than I remember.

I looked back in his direction and he smiled, displaying straight, white teeth and just a hint of dimples on each side of his perfectly-shaped mouth.

"Are you going in?" he asked.

"Oh um yeah. Thanks."

I stepped forward, turning slightly to avoid hitting him with my bags as I stepped over the threshold. He followed me inside and hovered a few steps behind as I fumbled with my keys and unlocked the studio door. His fresh, clean scent filled my nostrils as I turned to face him and I fought the urge to curl up against his chest and inhale.

"I didn't get to introduce myself the other day," he said. "I'm Leo Marakis."

I looked down at his extended hand and blinked. Just being in his presence has made my libido come to life after its two-year hibernation. I really don't want to know what actually touching him will do, no matter how innocent it may be. But, it would be really rude to leave him hanging, so I reached out and placed my hand in his.

As soon as our palms touched, I felt like I stuck my finger in a socket. I sucked in a sharp breath and let go of his hand, taking a half a step back. Shifting my rounded eyes to his face, I couldn't help but notice his confused look. Whether it's because he'd felt the electric current arc between us or the fact that I dropped his hand like it was a hot potato, I'm not sure. Either way, he composed himself pretty quickly and blew me away even more with his next words.

"I wanted to apologize for watching you dance the other day. I'm not a creep, I swear, but I just couldn't look away." He offered a nervous smile and seemed to consider his next words carefully before speaking. "That was the most amazing thing I've ever seen. At one point, I wasn't sure how you were staying on the pole. It was like you were glued there or something. How'd you do that?"

His warm brown eyes stayed on mine as he spoke and I felt mesmerized. So much so that I continued to silently stare into them, even after he finished speaking. I have no idea how long I just stood there gawking at him, but I'm pretty sure it was longer than is socially acceptable. And while I'd love to say I snapped out of it on my own, the spell wasn't broken until he raised his perfectly-shaped brow.

"Oh. *Oh*, um…" I shrugged then gestured lamely before getting my hands under control by grabbing onto the straps of my bags. "Practice."

"How long have you been dancing?"

Looking up at the ceiling, I did the mental math before meeting his gaze again.

"About eight years."

"That's it?"

"*It?*" I blinked. "I think eight years is a pretty long time."

His low sexy chuckle had tingly vibrations pinging between every one of my erogenous zones. Which seem to have multiplied since the last time they were awakened.

"I've been playing baseball for twenty-five years and have never done anything nearly as impressive as what I watched you do in there," he said, pointing to the open doorway of the studio.

My mouth dropped open. Through the years, I've pretty much heard it all. Comments from guys who have varying degrees of fascination and criticisms from prudes who think I'm over-sexualizing and objectifying myself. But aside from the few men who've frequented the studio, I've never had one show such frank admiration for what I do on the pole.

"Good, you're here." Clay's voice broke the spell between Leo and me before I had to comment. I looked over my shoulder and watched as he descended the last couple steps and walked over to us. "Hey Anjannette."

"Hi."

"What's up?" Leo asked Clay.

"I have a box in my truck and I was hoping you could help me carry it up. It's not heavy, just big and awkward for one person to handle."

"Sure. Just let me run my bag upstairs."

Clay's eyes shifted between us and he nodded.

"I'll meet you outside."

After he left, Leo looked over at me.

"So I just wanted you to know that I wasn't being a perv, I was just really impressed." His mouth slowly curled into a smirk and he added, "Anjannette."

I swear I dropped an ovary at the sound of my name coming out of his beautiful mouth in that low, sexy tone.

"T-thank you."

He took a step closer.

"So do you have a last name, Anjannette? Or are you like Cher or Madonna or Prince and just use one?"

For some reason that question struck me as funny and it snapped me out of the Leo-induced trance I've been in during our whole exchange.

"I'm flattered that you'd mention me in a question adjacent to those greats, but to answer your question, I have a last name. It's Peach."

I held out my hand to formally shake, figuring it should be safe now that I've regained my wits. I've never been more wrong about anything in my life. As soon as Leo's hand touched mine, that spark of electricity zinged again.

"It's nice to formally meet you, Anjannette Peach." His eyes shifted to the plaque next to my door. "Now the studio name makes total sense."

I looked over at the logo and smiled. When I decided to open my own studio, I'd wracked my brain trying to think of the perfect name, but nothing seemed right. Then one taco Tuesday, after way too many Margaritas, Keera suggested Peaches & Pole and it stuck.

But I don't want to discuss that with Leo. I don't want to discuss anything with him. I mean, I do and that fact makes me not want to. He's not only good-looking, he's also charming as hell. Time to shut this down.

"You better go find Clay before he thinks you got lost."

"Oh shit, you're right." He flashed a killer smile. "I got distracted."

I rolled my eyes and chuckled.

"You can leave your bag there," I said. "I only have one person coming here tonight so it'll be safe."

He dropped his duffle bag right next to the stairs. I turned and stepped into the studio and placed my bags on the floor.

"See you around, Anjannette Peach," he said as he walked across the foyer and exited the building.

I closed the door behind me and leaned back against it. Taking in deep breaths, I let them out little by little, trying to slow my heartbeat and calm the myriad sensations coursing through my body. Leo Marakis is potent, I'll give him that. One conversation and I'm more hot and bothered than when I got to second base with some other guys. Which is definitely a problem, especially if he's going to regularly be in this building.

I'll just have to keep my door closed at all times.

My laugh echoed through the empty room at that last thought.

As if a standard door is any kind of defense against that man's charms.

Chapter Three

LEO

"SEE, I told you it'd get easier," Clay said then took a big bite of his burger.

"I don't know about that, but my back does feel better. It's definitely looser and so are my hamstrings." I shoved a handful of fries into my mouth and looked around the diner. "This place hasn't changed a bit." I held up a fry. "And the food tastes exactly like I remember it."

"I've lived in Scranton my whole life. Not much changes here."

After he tortured me, Clay and I decided to grab a bite to eat. Besides the fact I enjoy his company, I figured it would also give me a chance to pump him for information about the sexy redhead renting the studio on the first floor of his building. I'm just waiting for a good time to slip it into the conversation.

"My hometown is the same. I guess that's why I've always felt so comfortable here."

Clay nodded and shoved the last bite of burger into his mouth. He rested his elbows on the table as he chewed and swallowed.

"How are you feeling? Any pain?" he asked, then took a quick drink of water.

"Only when I'm in your studio," I said around a chuckle. "But seriously, no. Not like I had during the season. Now it's just routine aches and pains from catching, and I don't think any amount of yoga will help with that."

"I'll do my best to get you where you need to be for the season."

"I appreciate that."

"Remember you're paying me an obscene amount of money. The least I can do is get you into playing shape."

"I'm just giving you the going MLB rate for a private trainer."

I had pain and tightness in my lower back and hamstrings all last season. The Waves' trainer, Max Rigsbee, managed to keep me in the game with stretching and massages, but it was obvious I needed to do something through the winter to help fix my issue. He recommended yoga and since I was moving to Scranton and Clay has a studio, booking sessions was easy. What wasn't easy was convincing Clay to accept my money.

He wanted to give me a discount and I refused to pay him any less than what I'd give a private trainer. It was only after I threatened to take my business somewhere else that he conceded. There's no doubt in my mind he knew I was bluffing, but I still got what I wanted.

"Whatever you say." Clay shrugged. "But it did allow me to finish the floors in Anjannette's studio sooner than planned. Plus I'll be able to add a salt room to my studio. I didn't think I'd be able to do that for another couple years. So I thank you, my friend."

I nodded and finished my drink, trying to hide my smile. I've been trying to figure out how to bring up Clay's sexy tenant and he's just given me an opening.

"So what's Anjannette's story?" I asked.

"Her *story*?"

"You know, where's she from, what's she do…"

My lame gesture finished the sentence then Clay added the question I really wanted answered.

"Is she seeing anyone?"

"Well sure. I mean, if that's what you want to talk about."

He rolled his eyes.

"You know she's my tenant, not my best friend."

"Don't tell me you don't know anything about her."

"I didn't say that." Clay leaned back and rested his arm against the back of the booth. "She grew up locally and she used to work full-time as a web designer. That's actually how I met her. A friend referred her and she created the site for my studio."

"A web designer?" He nodded. "I guess I can see that."

"Why?"

"It can be kind of artsy. I mean, you'd have to have some sense of design to make things look decent, right?"

"What makes you think she's artsy?"

"Just her whole look." I shrugged. "The way she dresses, the tattoos and piercings. Her whole vibe."

"I didn't realize you spent enough time with her to pick up on her *vibe*."

"Are you gonna bust my balls through this whole conversation?"

"Maybe."

"Dick."

He shifted forward and leaned his elbow on the table.

"But seriously, are you interested in her?"

"Yeah, I am."

"Why?"

"What do you mean *why*?"

He shook his head.

"Never mind the question. It's really none of my business. But I just want to remind you that you're going to be coming to the studio regularly for the next five months."

"So."

"You might want to think twice about going there if you're just looking for a one-night thing."

"I'm not that much of a manwhore."

I'll admit that I haven't lived like a monk, but the women I've casually spent time with weren't looking for anything serious. But I don't need to discuss that with Clay.

He held his hands up in a gesture of surrender.

"Just pointing it out."

"I appreciate that," I said. "And I'm not saying I plan on proposing marriage immediately, but I am interested in getting to know her."

"Well, good luck."

"Why do you say it like that?"

"Anjannette is great. She's just..." He tilted his head from side to side. "She's friendly but closed off too. Even after five years, I don't know a whole lot about her."

"But she's not married or anything, right?"

That's a line I *never* cross. Not only does it go against my morals, I don't need that kind of drama in my life. Besides, my mom would kill me. And yes, even at thirty-two years old, I still worry about disappointing her.

"Definitely not married, and I don't think she's involved with anyone. But like I said, there's a lot I'm not privy to. She maintains my website and rents space in my building. That's about it."

Clay opened his mouth to say something, then closed it again.

"What?"

"I've gotten the impression that her last relationship didn't end well. But that's just based on things she's said and conversations I've overheard." He chuckled. "It's amazing what women talk about when they're together."

"You don't have to tell me about that. I have three sisters and too many female cousins to count, remember?"

"So you speak their language."

"I don't know if I speak it, but unfortunately, I understand it."

"That's a good thing." Clay smirked then nudged his chin toward the door. "Because she just walked in."

ANJANNETTE

KEERA STOPPED JUST inside the door of the diner and I bumped into her.

"What's wrong?" I asked and stepped back.

"Looks like it's our lucky day."

She glanced over her shoulder at me then shifted her eyes across the room. I followed her gaze and cursed under my breath. I've already interacted with Leo Marakis once today. I can't deal with his magnetism right now. I'm too tired. In a weak moment, I may just get sucked right into his vortex.

Leo twisted in the booth and looked over at us. Even though Keera is standing in front of me, his eyes skimmed right over her and met mine. The edges of his mouth curved up into a small smile, just enough for his dimples to make an appearance. I can't tell you how many times I've watched the entire *Full House* series and this man is making every one of my Uncle Jesse fantasies pop into my head.

"Hey Clay," Keera said as she walked toward their booth. "Who's your friend?"

I followed Keera over and heard Clay introduce her to Leo. She shook his hand and admitted to knowing his identity, offering a few flirty comments in the process, making it look so easy.

Leo turned his attention to me.

"Hi Anjannette."

Heat spread up my neck and to my face. I'm sure my cheeks are bright red, but there's nothing I can do about it.

"Hi." The word came out as more of a croak and I cleared my throat. "Hi."

Keera settled into the booth directly across from them and I mentally cringed as I sat opposite her. I'd hoped we could sit in the other room. At least it looks like they're finished eating so hopefully they'll be leaving soon.

"So Leo," Keera said. "What brings you to our fine city?"

"I live here."

"You live in Scranton?"

He nodded. "During the off season anyway."

"So you could live anywhere you want and you chose here?"

"Yep."

"Why?"

"I like it here."

"Again, I ask *why*?"

Leo's laugh is as sexy as the rest of him. Deep, rich, and apparently infectious because we all joined in. Even the waitress chuckled as she walked over to take our orders.

Since I get the same thing every time I come here, it's not an issue that I've been too distracted to look at the menu.

Once the waitress left, Leo answered Keera's question.

"I went to college here and played for the RailRiders for part of a season and always liked the city. It's big enough to be interesting but small enough to keep it from being overwhelming. And the most important thing is that it's two hours away from my family. Which is far enough to give me some space, but close enough that I can easily visit."

"Interesting," Keera said. "Do people know you live here?"

"I haven't taken out a billboard ad or announced it on social media, but my friends and family know." Leo offered a sexy smirk. "And now so do you."

"I'm so honored." Keera rested her hand against her ample chest. "And I promise I won't tell anyone."

"Since you don't know my address, I feel pretty safe."

"I don't know your address *yet*."

Leo let out a surprised chuckle but was saved from having to respond when the waitress returned with our food. My mouth watered as she placed my bacon cheeseburger and fries with gravy in front of me. I only had a granola bar that I found in the bottom of my purse for lunch and I'm absolutely starving.

But as excited as I am about eating, even the food can't distract me from the uneasiness I've been feeling as I listened to Keera and Leo's sexy banter. Will he be her next dick band-aid? My stomach tightened at that thought and I mentally shook it from my head.

Why do I care if he is?

I picked up my burger and took a big bite. Of course, that's when I was spoken to.

"Anjannette, Rick just texted and said he's available to

video the recital. Do you mind if I give him your number so you can discuss the details?"

Shaking my head to answer his question, I chewed, willing the huge bite I'd taken to disintegrate. Of course it didn't. I felt three sets of eyes on me and I placed my hand over my mouth as I continued to both shake my head and chew.

Finally. *Finally.* The pieces were small enough to swallow without choking. I took a drink for good measure.

"Thank you so much Clay. I've planned every single detail of this recital and didn't even think about hiring someone to videotape the performances until a couple days ago."

I'm not going to mention that I was reliving my glory days of winning the Pole Sport Association competition two years ago by rewatching the video of my performance at the time.

He looked down at his phone and his thumbs quickly tapped along the screen. A second later the phone buzzed and he smiled then looked up at me.

"He'll give you a call tomorrow."

"Sounds good."

"Please eat some of these." I slid the heaping plate of fries toward Keera then picked up my fork and speared a few. "I'll never finish them all."

"What's this recital you're talking about?" Leo asked, thankfully before I filled my mouth again.

"My students are putting on a show."

"It's to celebrate Anjannette's first year in business," Keera added.

"That's quite an accomplishment. Congratulations," Leo said, looking way too sincere. "Are you in the show?" I nodded. "When is it?"

When I didn't answer, Keera did.

"A week Saturday at seven-thirty."

He pulled out his phone and turned his attention to it for a second then looked over at me and smiled.

"I have it in my calendar. I'm looking forward to it."

I shoved the fries into my mouth, not sure what to say. The thought of Leo watching me dance is both thrilling and terrifying. There's something about him that throws me off balance and that's something I definitely don't need when I'm spinning around a pole. Or any other time.

Chapter Four

LEO

"WHY DIDN'T you tell me Trey and Nori are coming up to visit?" Angie asked as she burst into the stockroom.

I finished stacking cans on the shelf then turned to face her.

"I didn't know I was supposed to."

I broke the empty box down and tossed it into the corner then looked over at her and chuckled. Angie is all about the graphic T-shirts and the one she's wearing now sums her up perfectly. It says *Not Fragile Like a Flower. Fragile Like a Bomb* with corresponding illustrations.

"Nice shirt."

"Don't try to distract me from the fact that Trey, Nori, and probably Crispin are going to visit and you weren't going to invite me."

She crossed her arms over her chest and thrust her bottom lip out in the pout that's gotten her whatever she's wanted for as long as I can remember. As the youngest of six, Angie rarely had to follow the same rules as the rest of us.

"You already took over my house here. I'm not taking the chance that happens in Scranton too."

"Ha, ha, ha. Very funny. I was there most of the summer dealing with renovations, remember?"

"And I appreciate that. It's the reason I was able to move into a nearly-perfect house once the season ended." I walked over and kissed her forehead before bending down and bundling the flat boxes I'd tossed onto the floor. "I'm just busting you."

"Don't try to be nice after you totally forgot about me."

"As if anyone could forget about you."

I walked past her and headed outside to toss the cardboard into the recycling bin. Angie followed and stood in the doorway as I opened the dumpster and threw the garbage bags that had been resting beside it inside. After closing the lid, I turned to face her and rolled my eyes when I saw her holding up her cell, most likely taking pictures.

"Someday I'm gonna make a bunch of money selling my collection," she said, confirming my suspicions.

One of her favorite things to do is take pictures of me doing random or embarrassing things. Every once in a while, she sends me a mockup of a photo in a fake newspaper with some bizarre headline. And for my thirtieth birthday a couple years ago, she made me a video. I have to say, she has some pretty interesting shots.

"If someone actually offers you money for a picture of me throwing garbage into a dumpster, you go for it," I said, knowing she'd never do it.

We walked back inside and I locked the door behind me.

"Where is everyone?"

"Nicky left earlier to go pick up a new slicer. I sent Mom and Dad home and said I'd close up."

I grabbed a broom and walked around to the main part of the deli and started sweeping. I could do this routine in my sleep. Other than using the slicers, my parents had my siblings and me working here since we could walk and talk.

"You know you could grab a broom and do behind the counter," I said to Angie, who sat perched on a stool right next to the cash register.

She wrinkled her nose and I thought she was going to ignore me, but was pleasantly surprised when she stood, grabbed a broom from the closet, and started to sweep.

"I can't believe you still help out here."

"Why?"

"Leo, you're a professional baseball player. You make millions of dollars a year. Why would you work in the family deli?"

"Mom and Dad refuse to retire," I said as I stood and emptied the dustpan I filled with the dirt we'd collected into the garbage can. "Me working here is no different than any of you guys helping out."

We put the brooms and dustpan back into the closet and I took off my apron and tossed it in the hamper.

"It's a lot different," she said. "Nicky works here full time. The rest of us all still live nearby and pitch in when necessary. You have to travel to be here."

"I come to visit anyway. Might as well help out while I'm here."

She wrapped her arm around my waist and pulled me close for a side hug.

"You're one of the good ones, Leonidas Marakis."

I gave her a final squeeze and pulled away far enough to open the door and let her walk out in front of me.

"I wouldn't even have my career if it wasn't for the sacrifices Mom and Dad made and the support they gave me through the years. They don't want money or fancy vacations or even a new house. The only thing they want is me here, being present, occasionally helping out." I dug the fob out of my pocket and unlocked my car door. "So that's what they'll get."

"Just make sure to live your life. You bought a house in Scranton to give you some space. Coming here all the time certainly won't give you that."

"Something going on with you?"

Angie's always been funny and energetic and sassy, but I've noticed an underlying sadness and discontent recently that seems more obvious every time I see her.

"I'm just…I don't know." She shook her head then shrugged. "Maybe I'm having an early midlife crisis or something. I just feel like I need a change."

I leaned against my car.

"What kind of change?"

"I'm not sure."

I clicked my fob again and relocked the car doors.

"Let's go get a drink at Murray's and talk about it."

We walked out of the parking lot of the deli and took the sidewalk to the bar two doors down. I held the door open and followed Angie inside. A few patrons sat at the bar but all the tables were empty. After grabbing a couple drinks, we settled into a booth in the corner.

"What's going on?"

"I was up for a promotion at work and didn't get it."

"Oh wow. I'm sorry."

She took a drink and looked around the bar before meeting my gaze again.

"The thing is, I'm not even sure I wanted the job, so I

don't know why I'm upset about it. It was just the next step, you know?"

"I thought you liked your job."

"At first I did. Being a graphic artist seemed like a great way to be creative and have a real job." She used air quotes with the last two words. "But now it's just boring. What I do is anyway."

"So find something else."

"Anything else will just be more of the same."

"You're so talented. Maybe just focus on the art. Don't worry about having a real job," I said, mimicking her air quotes. "Look at Nori. I never would have thought someone could actually make a living painting murals, but she's killing it. You know I'll help you out if you need me to."

"I appreciate that, but I already live in your house. I can't expect you to financially support me while I sort out my shit."

"I know I bust your ass about living in my house here, but I really don't mind. I'm very fortunate to make a great living doing what I love. I'd be an ass if I didn't share that with my family. Besides, Mom and Dad weren't the only ones who supported me with baseball. You all did, even if it was grudgingly."

Angie smiled at that last sentence. She hated being dragged to my games and forced to sit through tournaments.

"It wasn't so bad once I got older."

"Yeah, that's because you started crushing on all my teammates. What a nightmare."

"For you maybe. I kind of liked it." She offered a saucy smirk. "Speaking of teammates, how's Clay doing? Is he as hot as ever?"

"Can't say that I noticed if he's hot, but he's doing

well. The yoga studio is thriving plus he owns the building it's in and rents out the space on the first floor."

"What's in there?"

"A pole dance fitness studio."

"That's so cool. I've wanted to try that forever. Maybe I can drag Nori to a class when we're there." She smiled and wiggled her eyebrows. "And while I'm in the building, maybe I'll have a chance to catch up with Clay."

I'm not sure what makes me more nervous, my sister lusting after my former teammate or her spending time with the woman I'm lusting after.

Then again, she could definitely do worse than Clay. And, despite being my pain-in-the-ass little sister, Angie is my biggest cheerleader. Maybe she'll put in a good word for me with Anjannette.

It could end up being a win-win. Or a total disaster. Either way, it gives me a reason to talk to her again. Maybe I'll even ask her out for coffee or something equally harmless. I finished my beer and set the glass back on the table with a thud.

"I'll find out the class schedule and let you know."

ANJANNETTE

I CLIMBED to the very top of the pole and settled into a pole sit while Keera did the same directly below me. We sat like that as the pole made a full rotation then fell back into a straddle, an inside leg hang, and finally a jade split. The studio sped by as we spun round and round, waiting for the beat that would signal for us to start our next move.

When I heard it, I pulled back up into a pole sit before

squeezing my thighs tight and arching into a layback while Keera eased into a split on the floor. Once I spun around to the right spot, I placed my palms on the floor, loosened my grip on the pole, and let my legs fall back. My heels clacked against the floor as I landed into a split directly across from Keera. We threw our hands in the air in time with the final beats of the song.

My arms still in the air, I looked over at Keera, and saw the smile on her face mirroring my own.

"That felt perfect!" she said.

"Yeah, it did." Grabbing onto the pole, I pulled myself up and stood. "Let's find out."

I walked over to my iPad and pressed the button so it stopped recording. Keera had shifted against the wall and I made my way back to her side and sat next to her. Holding the iPad so both of us could see, I started the video and watched with a critical eye. Other than a couple places where we were a tiny bit out of sync, I'm pretty happy with it.

I handed the iPad to Keera and she played the video again while I removed my boots.

"I think this is good," she said. "What do you think?"

Before I could answer, I heard a knock on the door. I stood and walked over with a gut feeling of who was on the other side. Sure enough, Leo Marakis stood across from me as I opened the door.

"Hi Anjannette."

"Oh, hi Leo."

"Hi Leo," Keera yelled from across the room.

He peeked his head in and returned her greeting.

"I apologize for interrupting but I wanted to ask you a couple questions. When I heard the music shut off, I hoped it was safe."

"It's fine. We're taking a break."

"Oh good." He looked down and rubbed the back of his neck before meeting my gaze again. "First, my sister is coming to visit this weekend and is interested in taking a class, and maybe bringing a friend along. Would that be possible?"

"When will she be here?"

"Friday evening through Monday or Tuesday."

"There aren't any classes Friday or on the weekend because the recital is Saturday. But there's a beginner class Monday night at six. Assuming they're beginners."

"They are," he said. "What do you need to save them spots?"

"Just their names."

He followed as I walked over to my laptop and brought up the scheduling program.

"Angie Marakis and Nori Somers."

I pulled up the correct date and their names into the class.

"Phone numbers?"

He rattled off his sister's number, then looked up the other one on his phone.

"They're in. Just ask them to get here fifteen minutes before class to sign the new student paperwork."

"Will do," he said. "What do I owe you?"

"Nothing. The first class is free."

"Get them hooked with a freebie, huh? Good strategy."

"It's been working well."

I logged out of the computer and straightened to face him. I'll give him credit, his eyes stayed locked on mine during our exchange. That's more than a lot of guys would do considering I'm only wearing pole shorts and a sports bra.

"I was also wondering if you'd like to get coffee sometime."

"Oh, uh thank you, but um, I'm really busy the rest of the week. So no. But thank you for asking."

I rolled my eyes at that last sentence. What the hell? Could I sound like more of a dweeb?

"Maybe when things slow down for you after the recital," he said. "Which I'm looking forward to, by the way. I bought tickets off Clay yesterday. My sister and friends are coming too."

"Great," I said, thinking it was anything but.

"Yep," he said with a smile. "I'll let you ladies get back to work. Bye Keera."

"See you Leo."

"See you Saturday, Anjannette."

I nodded and watched as he walked out of the studio. After closing the door behind him, I turned and made my way back to Keera.

"I can't believe Leo Marakis asked you to go for coffee and you said no."

Keera unzipped her boot and eased her foot out then did the same with the other. She stretched her legs out in front of her and wiggled her toes. I sat next to her and picked up the iPad.

"Between last-minute items for the recital, private lessons to get everyone's routines fine-tuned, and regular classes, I don't have time."

"You don't have time for coffee?"

Oh I have time for lots of coffee, just not with a certain ballplayer, who looks more appealing every time I see him. And I really wish Keera hadn't been here when he asked. She'll never let me live it down.

Instead of answering, I tapped the screen of the iPad and started our video again.

"I think our routine is solid. I'm not going to obsess about the two places we were slightly out of sync. This is just a fun recital, not a competition. No one is keeping score."

"You're just going to ignore my question?"

I sighed and set the iPad in my lap then looked over at her.

"Like I said, this week is going to be crazy. I just don't have the time."

"I'd make time for Leo Marakis."

"Then you go for coffee with him."

"Trust me when I tell you, that if that man was interested in coffee or anything...and I do mean *anything*...I'd make time." She leaned closer, her eyes locked on mine. "But he's not interested in me. It's pretty obvious you're the one he wants."

I definitely feel a vibe from him. He and Keera were bantering the other night, but there wasn't any heat between them. But all he had to do was look at me and I swear I nearly got singed.

The man makes me feel so much with a single glance, it's unsettling. Especially since I'm way out of practice. Unfortunately, my libido doesn't seem to care about that, it's determined to take notice of Leo Marakis any time he's near.

I shook that thought out of my head and turned my attention back to Keera, who was patiently waiting for a response to her comment.

"To quote Buffy, 'I don't want to be the one.'"

Chapter Five

LEO

"I REALLY LIKE THIS PLACE," Nori said as she snuggled next to Trey on the couch. "It's so bright and open. You did a great job picking out colors."

I picked her, Trey, and Crispin up at the airport a couple hours ago and brought them back to my house. After giving them the grand tour, we decided to just stay in and order Chinese takeout.

"You know that was all you and Angie."

"Give all the credit to Angie. She asked for my opinion on her ideas, but she's the one who picked them."

"Speaking of Angie, did she send you an update on her ETA?" Crispin asked.

I glanced at my phone.

"No, but she should be here within the hour, unless she hits traffic."

That led to a discussion of my sister and her missed promotion. The general consensus is she should find another job. I didn't offer much to the conversation because Nori and Crispin seemed to know more about the subject than me.

That last thought made me smile.

I didn't even know either of them last year at this time. So when Trey and Nori shared a ride from Fayetteville to Myrtle Beach, they not only found each other, Angie and I also gained some good friends.

"I'm so sorry if I started an argument between you and Angie when I mentioned we were coming here this weekend," Nori said. "I thought she already knew."

"Don't worry about it. It's not like I didn't want her here, I just forgot to mention it." I chuckled. "And it's not like she'd need an invitation. Trey can confirm the fact that my family doesn't wait to be invited to show up."

"That is a true statement. They descended on us in college all the time," he said. "And his house in New Jersey pretty much has an open-door policy."

"Which is exactly why I bought this place."

I saluted them with my beer bottle then took a long drink.

"We've met Angie and Chris. When do we get to meet the others? Especially your older brother?" Crispin bobbed his eyebrows as he added that last question.

"You're in a committed relationship now," Nori reminded him.

"That doesn't mean I can't enjoy a little Marakis eye candy." He glanced at me. "No offense, but now that we're actually *friends* it seems creepy to appreciate your appearance like I used to."

"No offense taken." I patted my hair. "As long as you still appreciate my hair."

I'm not being cocky when I say that I was blessed with a great head of hair. So was my entire family. We could all be in shampoo commercials. Of course, I'm the only one who actually is.

As a hairstylist, Crispin shares my love of my thick locks. When we first met, he begged me...yes actually *begged* me...to let him cut my hair.

His eyes skimmed over my head and he smiled.

"You don't have to worry about that changing. In fact, I'm glad I brought my scissors. You need a trim."

"Yeah, it's getting a little long." I dragged my fingers through my overly-long hair and nodded. "Speaking of hair." I looked over at Nori. "I almost didn't recognize you."

She had fuscia hair when we met, which Trey initially hated. But once they got involved, he liked it enough that when she mentioned going back to her natural color, he talked her out of it. So I was totally surprised to see her show up with blonde hair today.

"Yeah, I was sick of it. Thankfully I have a kickass stylist that got me back to my natural color gracefully." She blew Crispin a kiss.

The food arrived and Angie pulled into the driveway just as the delivery guy was driving away.

"Perfect timing," I said as she stepped out of her car.

She slammed the car door and walked toward me with purposeful strides.

"I quit my job."

I quickly stepped aside when it was obvious she wasn't going to stop to chat after dropping that bomb. Following her inside, I set the bags down on the kitchen island.

"Did something happen?"

Normally I can read her mood, but she seems to be a jumble of emotions right now and I'm not sure which one is prominent.

Trey, Nori, and Crispin joined us. After she hugged the three of them, she took a deep breath.

"I'm starving. Why don't we sit and eat and I'll fill you in?"

We settled around the table and once everyone's plates were full, she told us what happened. The guy who got the promotion she was up for embarrassed her in a meeting by criticizing the work she did for some big campaign.

"I explained that the client wanted something totally different than anything else we'd done for them. I also said that I realized what I created was a little edgy, but the client liked the initial mockups."

"So if the client liked them, what's the issue?" Nori asked.

"He went on to mansplain that in his experience, a client may think they want something different but they really don't. And that if we go with my crazy concept, we'll lose the customer. Then he went on to talk down to me as if I didn't have a clue." She dropped her fork on her plate and put her hands out, palms up. "So I quit." Blinking, she looked around at each one of us before dropping her hands on the table. "Holy shit. I still can't believe I did it. "

"You're better off," I said. "The fact that they passed you up for that promotion shows that they don't value your talent."

Everyone agreed with me and vocalized their own support.

"We can brainstorm artsy career options this weekend," Nori said.

Angie nodded, then insisted we change the subject.

"Speaking of this weekend, what kind of things are there to do in this fair city?" Crispin asked.

"Well, tomorrow night we're going to that pole dance recital at the studio in Clay's building."

"And on Monday night, we're going to a class," Angie said to Nori.

"I've never taken a dance class in my life so that should be interesting."

"Neither have I, but it looks like so much fun and it's supposed to be a great workout."

"I'm sure it'll be fun." Nori chuckled. "I just hope I don't kill myself."

"I'm sure Anjannette wouldn't let that happen."

As soon as the words were out of my mouth, I regretted speaking them. My tone came out too friendly, too warm, too *interested*. And don't think Trey and Angie didn't notice.

My sister looked at me with narrowed eyes as a slow smile spread across her face.

"Who's Anjannette?"

"The woman who owns the studio."

I shoved a dumpling into my mouth and chewed.

"Is there something special about this *Anjannette*?" Trey asked.

That's a loaded question. Mostly because I'm not sure how to answer it. There's definitely something about her, but I'm just not sure what or why I'm so drawn to her.

Trey's witnessed me with enough women through the years, so he'll definitely notice my attraction to Anjannette when we're in the same room. Hell, I knew he was interested in Nori just by the way he talked about her.

I thought about just ignoring his question, but I know that will only make him and Angie make the subject a bigger deal than I want it to be.

So instead, I said, "That, my friend, remains to be seen."

ANJANNETTE

"STOP LOOKING AT YOUR PHONE," Rosa said, her hand poised in front of my face. "You're gonna end up with eyelashes on your brow."

"Sorry. I keep getting texts and I don't want to miss anything."

"They can wait fifteen minutes while I finish your hair and makeup."

I started to shift my eyes to look up at her but stopped myself at the last minute.

"Thank you so much for doing this. With the way my nerves are today, I wouldn't trust myself with a hairbrush never mind liquid eyeliner."

"Relax. Everything is going to be fine."

She pulled back and studied my face then went in with a few more lashes. My natural eyelashes are short and pale so they need a lot of work. But Rosa is a professional and I trust her implicitly.

"I just want everything to be perfect."

"You're the master planner, so I know you've beaten even the tiniest detail into submission," she said with a smirk. "Besides, this isn't your first rodeo. How many recitals did you put together at the other studio?"

"That was different. It wasn't *my* studio."

"It doesn't mean you didn't treat it like it was."

I shrugged as she shifted behind me and started on my hair.

Rosa and Keera and a bunch of the other girls followed me when I opened my studio, and I'll be forever grateful for that. Starting with some students made things a lot less scary.

Although even if they hadn't followed, I would have

ventured on my own anyway. Like my relationship with Travis, my time at the other studio needed to come to an end. It was time for me to use my skills and experience to build my own dream instead of someone else's.

True to her word, Rosa had me show-ready in less than fifteen minutes. I stood and checked myself out in one of the mirrors I'd propped against the wall. Clay had graciously offered me use of the unoccupied space directly across from the studio for people to get ready.

"You're a miracle worker." I shook my head and watched the curls she'd created bounce back into place. "The only way I get this much curl in my hair is if I use hot rollers. And even then, I'm lucky if they last an hour."

"These will definitely last through your performance," she said with a smile.

The door opened and a few of my students walked into the room. I took in a deep breath and blew it out.

"Looks like this party is really getting started."

I walked across the hall and into the studio and immersed myself in last-minute details. Before long, people started to arrive. Much to my surprise, we "sold out" a week ago, so all the chairs should be full. Anyone who buys a ticket tonight will be designated to the standing section.

As my pre-show playlist sounded in the background, I checked the actual show's music for the hundredth time, making sure it was all in order. I'd just gotten to the bottom of the list when Keera sidled up next to me.

"Your hottie is here."

"He's not my hottie."

"Then how do you know who I'm talking about?" she asked with a knowing smirk.

I rolled my eyes and made the mistake of looking over my shoulder toward the door just as Leo walked into the studio. His eyes scanned the room before shifting in my direction and locking onto mine. I sucked in a startled breath at the heat that engulfed my body just from that.

A man stepped behind him and said something, pulling his attention from me just long enough to break the spell. I closed my eyes and took in a few calming breaths in an attempt to slow my pounding heart.

"Wow."

I'd forgotten Keera was standing right next to me. Which is absolutely bizarre since we'd been speaking just a second before Leo entered the room.

I set the iPad back onto its dock, surreptitiously making sure my nipples aren't visible through the thin material of my wrap dress.

Looking back at Keera, I raised my brow.

"Wow what?"

She shook her head and laughed.

"I don't think I can find the words to explain."

Leo and his friends sat in the row of chairs in the back against the back wall. A few people approached to talk to him and at first I wondered why, but then remembered he's a bigtime baseball player. The man he's with seems to be getting a lot of attention too.

"Who's that guy with Leo?" I asked Keera.

"Trey Youngman." At my deadpan look, she explained. "He's a pitcher. Formerly with the Yankees. Now with the Waves."

She raised her voice on the last word of each of those sentences turning them into questions. I shrugged. When it comes to professional athletes, I only know the really big names. Even then, I probably wouldn't have a clue if I actually met them.

I'm more of a *Buffy, Outlander, Lord of the Rings* kind of girl. Now if David Boreanaz, Sam Heughan, or Jason Momoa walked into the studio, I'd know them for sure.

"I'm guessing the girl with the long, dark hair is his sister," I said.

"Yeah, they look a lot alike. The other one is Nori Somers. She's engaged to Trey. I've seen her in pictures with him."

I looked at the man in question. He and the tiny tattooed woman look as different as Leo and me. Before my mind could delve into that comparison, I turned to face Keera, putting my back to them.

"Do you want to go check on Sophie to make sure she's ready?"

"Sure. While I'm over there, I'll get into my costume so I can come over and introduce Mel while you strip."

I'm wearing my first costume under my dress so it will only take me a minute to change and come back for my doubles routine with Keera.

"Sounds good." I grabbed the microphone. "I'm going to let everyone know we're going to get started in about five minutes."

"You should be so proud of yourself." She hugged me then pulled back with a big smile on her face. "What you've done here, the community you're building, is amazing."

I waved my hand in front of my eyes and blinked away the tears her words had caused.

"Don't make me cry. Rosa will kill me if I ruin my eye makeup."

With a laugh, she made her way across the studio and out the door.

I turned on the mic and announced that the show would be starting. Soon every chair was full and the standing-room-only section was as well.

Rosa's husband Mason volunteered to play DJ for the night and he settled into his designated seat in the corner.

Rick the videographer was in place and I spotted Sophie lingering in the doorway ready to start her routine.

I'd like to pretend my tight stomach, pounding heart, and excess energy are all in response to the excitement of the studio's first recital, but I'd be lying. The sexy man who's barely taken his eyes off me since he entered the room is definitely the root cause of some of those reactions.

But that's something I'll need to evaluate at another time.

Doing my best to ignore him, I stepped into the center of the room to start this show.

Chapter Six

LEO

I CLAPPED throughout the last number with the rest of the audience, unable to keep the smile off my face. Each dance leading up to this finale was amazing and the best part is that all the performers looked like they were having a blast.

Anjannette and Keera had danced together wearing mile-high patent leather boots and I'm still not sure how they did what they did without kicking each other in the head or losing an eye. It was pretty impressive.

"This is spectacular," Angie said then bumped me with her shoulder. "Seriously, are you watching this?"

"I'm wat–holy shit, did you see that?"

Instead of answering me, she let out a loud catcall and clapped harder.

I'll admit that my initial reason for attending this recital had more to do with seeing Anjannette than watching the show, but I've really enjoyed myself. While they're not my normal hangout, I have been in strip clubs, so I've seen women dance on poles. But not like this.

Half the time I had no idea how the dancers stayed on the pole. And other times, I thought for sure they were going to crash to the ground, but I'm happy to say that never happened. Any drops or tumbles were part of the choreography.

As the song came to an end, some of the dancers hung from the top of the poles and the others dropped to splits at the base. Everyone in the audience jumped out of their seats and gave them a standing ovation.

The dancers took their bows, then circled together into a group hug. Anjannette walked over with the microphone in her hand and joined in for a second before stepping into the middle of the floor. The room got quiet as she began to speak.

"I want to thank you all so much for coming tonight to support both the dancers and the studio. Peaches & Pole has been a dream of mine for a long time and I'm so happy to finally make it a reality. But I couldn't have done that without all of you." She looked over at all the students and smiled. "You've turned this studio into everything I'd hoped it would be. A positive environment where people can come to have fun, get fit, and feel empowered. It's been a magnificent first year and I'm looking forward to seeing where we all go from here."

Her blush was visible even in the dim lighting as Keera approached with a huge bouquet of peach roses and handed them to her. She fumbled with the microphone to thank everyone again, then Keera took it off of her.

"You made this place what it is. Thank you for being you."

Anjannette clutched the flowers to her chest as Keera

pulled her into a big hug. Tears streamed down her face as each of the students did the same.

"This was fun. You did good, Leo," Angie said. "Even if we're only here because you're crushing on the sexy redhead," she added with a snarky smirk.

That's definitely not something I want to admit or discuss, especially with my little sister. So instead of answering, I changed the subject to food.

"What do you guys want to do for dinner?"

"What are our options?" Crispin asked.

"We could go to the diner if you're in the mood for greasy food." I looked at Trey. "Clay and I ate there a couple weeks ago and the food is exactly the same. The place hasn't changed one bit."

"Oh wow, I haven't thought about that place in years."

"But now that you have, you want a burger and gravy fries, right?"

"I'm more of a cheese fry guy."

"How could I forget? I think you ate them every day for two years."

"Not every day, but close," he said. "I'd be up for that."

I looked at Angie, Nori, and Crispin who seemed less than enthusiastic about the prospect of diner fare.

"Or we could go somewhere a little less casual."

Keera approached before I could expand on that thought and offer suggestions.

"Hi Leo, thanks so much for coming, and for bringing your friends."

The last part of the sentence was directed at Trey.

I introduced her to everyone and she congratulated Trey and Nori on their engagement, which surprised me at first. But she knew who I was, so it stands to reason she'd know him too. Plus Trey's engagement was all over the news.

"Your dance was ah-mazing," Crispin said.

She batted her eyelashes at him as her smile popped a dimple in her right cheek.

"Why thank you kind sir," she said in a fake Southern accent as she curtsied. "I don't want to be a total fangirl here, but I can't believe Leo Marakis *and* Trey Youngman are in this building."

Trey elbowed Crispin in the side.

"She sounds like you when we first met, using our full names."

"Yeah, I totally fanboyed at first," Crispin said, then looked at Keera and smiled. "Then I got to know them and realized they're nothing special."

"Burn," Angie said and stood and leaned across me to give him a high five.

"Hey, you're supposed to stick with family."

She stuck her tongue out at me and sat back down.

"I didn't come over here to start a family feud, just to see if you guys wanted to come out to eat with us. Some of us are going to Poor Richard's."

Her eyes shifted to me and she smirked and bobbed her eyebrows.

"Poor Richard's like on *The Office*?" Crispin asked.

"Well yeah, but it doesn't look anything like it did on the show," Keera said.

"Now I'll fanboy." He looked at Nori. "Remember they used to have that *Office* tour and I wanted to come but by the time we got our shit together to actually plan it, they stopped doing it?"

"I remember," Nori said. "But now's your chance." She looked at us. "That is, if you guys all want to go there."

"I'm game." Angie pointed her index finger then shifted it between Trey and me. "That one will do whatever you want and this one *definitely* wants to go if a certain studio owner will be there."

Keera and my sister shared a conspiratorial smile.

"She absolutely will be there."

It seems there's going to be some matchmaking going on tonight. I guess that's karma biting me after all the behind-the-scenes planning I helped Crispin with to put Trey and Nori in each other's company.

Honestly, I don't mind. Anything that puts me in Anjannette's immediate vicinity is fine with me. I just don't know how she'll feel about it.

ANJANNETTE

"SO HOW SORE will I be after class Monday?" Angie asked.

"I'm guessing at least a little bit, even if you are in decent shape since you'll be using different muscles. If nothing else, you'll probably get some pole kisses from trying to climb."

"What are they?"

"Oh sorry. Bruises. Until your skin gets used to being smooshed against a pole, they're bound to happen."

I answered more questions from both Angie and Nori about the class and what kinds of things they'll be doing. Which is fine by me because it gives me something to focus on besides the hot guy sitting beside me. And when I say *hot*, I mean it literally and figuratively.

He's throwing so much body heat, I feel like I'm sitting next to a radiator. Not that I'm complaining. I'm always freezing, so it's definitely welcome. It's his magnetism that's unsettling.

I didn't know Keera had invited him to join us until he walked into the restaurant. I'd managed to sit far away from him, but as people left and our party dwindled from twenty to seven, we consolidated to one table and now he's next to me.

"So Leo," Keera said. "How did you end up taking yoga classes with Clay?"

"I had some lower back tightness last season that was causing issues everywhere else. The team trainer recommended I take up yoga to see if I could loosen things up. Since I was moving here and I knew Clay had a studio, I gave him a call."

"Is it working?"

"Yeah."

The single word sounded more like a question and before I could stop myself, I commented.

"You don't sound too convinced."

"Have you ever taken one of Clay's yoga classes?" His sexy smirk left me speechless, so I just nodded. "Then you know what I'm talking about. They're not easy, but I'm happy to say, I do feel better afterwards."

"Isn't it weird taking a class by yourself?" Keera asked. "I like the energy of other people around me."

"Not really. I'm used to working with personal trainers, so the one-on-one thing doesn't bother me." He took a drink of water then added. "The only thing that did freak me out was the fact that he was sitting there during Savasana. I felt like he was staring at me."

I'd stare at him too, especially if he had his eyes closed and I could look my fill.

"Yeah, that'd bother me too." Keera scrunched her nose. "I'd probably just skip it."

"There's no way in hell I'd skip it. Savasana is the best part of yoga class as far as I'm concerned."

"So you just deal with it?"

"After the first couple sessions, I told Clay he was giving me the wiggins so now he goes into his office."

Holy shit, the man speaks Buffy.

I gasped then reached over and squeezed Keera's wrist.

"You okay?" she asked.

I nodded and loosened my grip before slowly releasing her.

"I'm gonna go to the ladies' room."

I stared at her, conveying with every fiber of my being that I wanted her to join me.

"Okay." Keera blinked. "I'll go with you."

She looked over at Angie and Nori, but thankfully they didn't want to come along.

I power-walked across the restaurant and let out a sigh of relief when I burst through the bathroom door and found it empty.

Keera walked in behind me and rested her hip against the sink.

"What are you freaking out about?"

"The man speaks Buffy!"

Folding her arms over her chest, she raised her brow.

"Isn't that a good thing?" I shook my head. "Why?"

"Because." I searched for a rational explanation but came up short. "He's too sexy and charming and nice."

"Yeah, I can see how those things would be problematic."

"You know what I mean."

"Based on what you told me about your past, I get why you're less than thrilled about being attracted to Leo. But honestly, my gut is telling me he's a good one."

I turned to check my makeup in the mirror. Running

my pinky under my right eye, I cleared away a tiny smudge of eyeliner.

"He can't be as perfect as he seems. There's just no way."

"Well, he's definitely all the things you said and the way he interacts with his sister is sweet. Plus he's ridiculously good-looking."

I turned to face her again.

"I'll admit he's a snack, but is it possible he's really *that* nice?"

"First of all he's not a snack, he's a whole freaking buffet," she said. "And he speaks Buffy. How much better could he get?" I didn't have an answer, so I just shrugged. "I know you're gun-shy, but it's not like you have to move in together tomorrow. Just go out for coffee when he asks you again and take it from there."

I tilted my head back and focused on the ceiling and mentally formed my sentence before looking at Keera and speaking it out loud.

"I don't date well. I always end up going from zero to inseparable in the blink of an eye."

"But you're older and wiser now."

"As much as I'd like to believe that, I don't trust myself."

"You're so different than you were even a couple years ago. Stronger. More confident."

"It took me three years to find myself. What if I'm like an addict and just one date knocks me off the man wagon? Or puts me back on it?" I frowned. "I'm not sure which is right."

"You'll be fine." Keera put her arm around my shoulders and pulled me into a side hug. "Besides, you've got to get back out there sometime and Leo really does seem sweet."

She released me and opened the door. I preceded her out of the bathroom and we made our way back to the table. Leo's eyes locked on me when I was halfway there and my entire body broke out in goosebumps.

I can't deny the chemistry between us. He's been watching me all night, both at the recital and at dinner and his gaze feels like a caress. It amazes me that the man hasn't laid a hand on me, yet every erogenous zone is on full alert. I'd like to say it's because I haven't had sex in three years, but I'd be lying. It's just him.

As we sat back down, Keera asked Crispin about his salon down in Myrtle Beach. Trey and Nori were quietly talking, caught up in their little love bubble. I pretended to be interested in what Crispin was saying, but didn't hear a word. All my senses were too focused on the man sitting next to me.

"Anjannette."

Leo said my name so softly, I thought I'd imagined it. But he repeated it a little louder

and I turned to face him. I felt like my eyes were open too wide, but when I tried to correct that, it seemed like I was squinting.

The corners of Leo's mouth curled into an adorable smile as he watched me essentially trying to figure out how to look at him. I blinked repeatedly to reset my look and rested my elbow on the table before meeting his gaze.

"Congratulations on your first recital and your first year in business."

"Thank you."

Leo opened his mouth to speak, but before the words came out, Angie said, "I hate to break up this party, but I think I'm gonna head back to the house. I'm exhausted."

"We'll catch a ride with you," Trey said.

Everyone besides Leo and me stood, ready to leave. I

have a feeling they're all conspiring to give the two of us time alone.

I looked around the table then my eyes scanned our party.

"Don't we have to wait for the check?"

"I took care of it while you and Keera were in the restroom," Leo said.

"What do I owe you?"

"It's my treat," he said.

"Oh, I can't–"

"Consider it a thank you for a fun night. I really had a great time."

Leo's leg brushed against mine as he stood and again, my traitorous body broke out in goosebumps. At least he'd actually touched me this time.

"Thank you," I said as I stood.

"I'm looking forward to class on Monday," Nori said as we walked out of the restaurant. "I was so fascinated watching all the performers tonight. I can't wait to get started."

"If you like it, we'll have to get a pole at the house." Trey's bobbing eyebrows punctuated his lusty smile.

"Let's take it one step at a time," she said. "You know how uncoordinated I can be. I'll probably end up looking like Carrie on *The King of Queens* when she took pole dance lessons."

"You climb up and down ladders all day," Crispin said. "You can't be *that* uncoordinated or you would have broken your neck by now."

"Thanks for putting that out into the universe," she said.

Leo held the door open and Nori and Crispin paused their banter as we all filed out of the restaurant.

"Where are you parked?" When I pointed to my car at

the opposite end of the lot, he said, "I'll walk you to your car."

"I'll see you Monday," Keera said as she pulled me into a hug. "Stop overthinking," she whispered in my ear before releasing me.

"We'll just catch a ride with Angie," Trey said.

Leo nodded and looked down at me. "Ready?"

I nodded and led the way to my SUV. As we approached, I fished my keys out of my

purse. The lights flicked as I pressed the button to unlock the doors.

"Thank you for a great night," Leo said.

"I'm glad you enjoyed it."

He tucked his hands into his pockets and watched as Angie pulled out of the parking lot before turning that dark gaze back to me.

"Now that it's all over, I was wondering if you'd want to grab that cup of coffee we discussed," he said. My eyes widened again and he added, "I'm also open to lunch or dinner if you are."

Despite my conversation with Keera, my first inclination is to say no, but when I opened my mouth to speak, that's not what came out.

"I'd like that."

He looked as surprised by those words as I felt. But he also looked pleased, which made me inexplicably happy.

"Great. How about lunch on Monday?"

"Sounds good."

He pulled his phone out of his back pocket.

"What's your number?"

I watched his thumbs tap against the screen with each number I spoke. My phone vibrated and I pulled it out of my purse.

"Got it," I said as I added him to my contacts.

"How about if I pick you up at twelve-thirty?"

"That works for me."

"Text me your address when you get a chance."

"Oh uh…" I nibbled at my bottom lip as I chose my next words.

"Or I can pick you up at the studio if you'd prefer."

I smiled.

"That sounds great."

"So, Monday at twelve-thirty at the studio?" I nodded. "Great. It's a date."

I opened my door and sat behind the wheel.

"I'll see you Monday," I said.

He waited until I clicked my seatbelt into place before resting his hand against the door and leaned down just enough to look me in the eye.

Flashing a sexy smile, he said, "I'm really looking forward to it."

That said, he closed the door and I watched as he walked toward his car. And I have to

say, the man has a specular ass. Must be from all that time he spends squatting behind home plate.

I squeezed my thighs together to curb the tingling his mere presence had generated. It's amazing how alive my body feels around him. I can't imagine what it will be like when he actually touches me.

I shook my head to clear that last thought, but it wouldn't budge from my mind. After years of not feeling anything, now I feel too much. But also not enough.

As I pulled out of my parking spot, my mind wandered to my bedside table and took a mental inventory. It might be time to dust off a toy or two.

Chapter Seven

LEO

I TURNED into the parking lot and spotted Anjannette standing on the front stoop. Wearing skinny black jeans, a gray V-neck sweater, and black boots, she looked like a model posing for a photo shoot leaning against the brick building scrolling through her phone. She glanced up as I pulled into the spot closest to the entrance.

"Hi," I said as I stepped out of the truck.

She placed her phone in her purse and walked down the steps.

"Hi."

"You look great."

"Thank you."

I opened the passenger door and she blinked up at me. Stepping back, I opened it wider, gesturing for her to get inside. She placed her foot on the running board and stepped up before shifting into the seat. I closed the door as she clicked her seatbelt into place.

Jogging around the back of the truck, I slid behind the wheel.

"I thought we'd go to Cooper's unless you're in the mood for something else. It's relatively close and since it's such a nice day, we can sit on the deck if that works for you."

"That sounds great."

I smiled over at her before shifting into drive and pulling onto the street.

"Did you get to relax yesterday as a reward for putting on such a great show?"

"I did and it was glorious. It was my first full day off in over a year and I made the most of it reading, watching TV, and napping on the couch."

"It was definitely well-deserved. The show really was great."

"Thank you. Everyone worked really hard and I'm so happy they all did so well."

"It seems like a great group of people."

"It is. I'm very fortunate."

I turned into the parking lot at Cooper's and pulled into a space then glanced over at her.

"I'm guessing the studio's aesthetic is by your design more than chance."

Her wide eyes were still on me when I got out of the truck. She'd opened her door by the time I rounded the truck and I grabbed onto the handle to hold it in place as she stepped down.

As we walked through the parking lot, I was again amazed at our size difference. Her long legs make her look much taller than she is, but the top of her head barely reaches my chin. Add in her tiny frame and slender figure and I feel like the Hulk next to her.

When we approached the hostess, I requested an out-of-the-way table on the deck. She led us to a cozy spot in the corner and said our waiter would be over shortly. It was pretty obvious she recognized me, but she didn't say anything. Which is somewhat of a relief.

I enjoy talking to fans, but I'm never sure how the conversations will go, especially with females. Once I was on a date and our waitress told me that I'm on her freebie list. I had no idea what to say to that so I just offered an awkward smile. And even though I offered no encouragement, she continued to flirt throughout dinner and my date got mad at me. Like it's my fault I'm on some women's approved list of celebrity one-night stands.

"I haven't eaten here since my college graduation." I chuckled at the memory.

"What happened?"

"We ordered the shark bite appetizer and Angie woofed a bunch of them down but then freaked out when she found out they were actually made of shark."

"What did she think they were?"

The waiter approached before I could answer.

"My name is Daniel and I'll be your server today. Can I start you off with a drink?"

"I'd like water with lemon," Anjannette said.

"Just water for me."

"I'll bring that right over," he said. "And I just want to say what a pleasure it is to meet you, Leo. I played ball at Lackawanna and you and Trey are legends."

"It's nice to meet a fellow Falcon."

I held out my hand to shake his.

"Also, I've asked Caroline to block out these tables," he said pointing to the two tables across from ours. "That way you won't be disturbed while you eat."

"Thank you. I appreciate that."

He nodded. "I'll be back with your drinks."

I looked over at Anjannette, ready to pick up our shark bite conversation, but she spoke before I did.

"Is it weird having people know who you are?"

"It definitely takes some getting used to, especially away from the field."

"Have you ever had any issues with fans?"

"Nothing really awful. Sometimes fans of other teams like to talk smack, but it's usually in good fun."

Daniel returned with our drinks and took our orders. When he left, I took the opportunity to shift the conversation away from me and my semi-celebrity status.

"So how did you get started doing pole dance?"

"I went to a bachelorette party at the studio I used to attend and just fell in love with it. I'm not a very athletic person, but the pole and I just clicked. I signed up for classes and a couple years later went through the process to become an instructor."

I asked her questions about what that entailed, happy to keep her talking about herself.

"Was opening your own studio always a goal?"

"Um, no. Not really." She paused, seeming to carefully choose her words. "At first I was happy just teaching but I had a lot of ideas that I wanted to implement, and the owners weren't interested. For years I went through the motions and just did what they wanted. It was their business after all."

Daniel returned with our meals. Once he refilled our water glasses and made sure we didn't need anything, he left us alone again. The man is definitely getting a big tip. Not only did he make sure no one sat at the surrounding tables, but he's also taking care of us while giving us space.

"So what changed?"

She shrugged and looked down at her plate, seemingly fascinated by her crab cakes. I bit into my lobster roll, giving her time to collect her thoughts. Or change the subject. There's obviously a story but I only want to hear it if she wants to share.

I was halfway through my lunch when she spoke.

"A perfect storm of things happened over a couple years actually. I ended a long-term relationship that hindsight has taught me was really unhealthy. Shortly after that, I was laid off from my job. Things at the other studio had gotten tense and I realized that I was more invested in that business than the owners. I was planning events and recitals and recruiting new students, and they were sitting back reaping the rewards."

She set her fork down and took a drink of water. I'm curious about the unhealthy relationship comment, but won't push for details. Not on the first date anyway.

"Around the same time, Clay bought his building. He sent me pictures to add to his website and I thought it was a great space. After making a list of pros and cons, talking it over with Keera and some of the other girls, and obsessing about it for months, I reached out to Clay and we negotiated terms."

"With the way that all happened, it definitely sounds like it was meant to be."

"It seems that way. Some of my students from the other studio followed me, but I also had an influx of new people. So there's a good mix."

"And it's your full-time job now?"

She nodded.

"My severance gave me some extra padding in my budget so I could get the studio up and running before looking for another job. It's done so well that I don't have to do anything full-time. I have a few freelance clients whose websites I maintain and I'm good."

"Good for you." Her eyes narrowed. "What?"

She shook her head and stabbed at a lump of crab meat with her fork and shoved it into her mouth. After she chewed and swallowed, she explained.

"Sorry, bad habit. The aforementioned ex said that phrase all the time and it wasn't usually complimentary."

"Well, mine was," I said, my eyes locked on hers so she could read my sincerity. "I'm glad you're able to fully focus on something you love so much."

The corners of her mouth curled up into a small smile as she seemed to study me.

"I've never met anyone like you," she said.

"Is that good or bad?"

"I'm not sure."

"Maybe we need to spend more time together so you can figure it out."

ANJANNETTE

I'M PLEASANTLY surprised at how much I'm enjoying myself with Leo. He's really easy to be with and, other than the attraction simmering beneath the surface, this has been more like lunch with a good friend than a typical awkward first date. And even though it's been a while since I've had a first date, I remember never feeling totally comfortable whenever I was on one. So this is a whole new experience.

"Can I get you anything else?" Daniel asked. "More water?"

Leo looked at me and raised his right brow.

"No, thank you. I'm good. We should actually get

going soon. I have some things to do at the studio before class."

"Just the check, thanks," he said.

"I'll bring it right over," Daniel said, then left us alone again.

"Angie and Nori are really looking forward to class today. They were talking about the recital all day yesterday."

"I think they'll have fun. We're doing a short routine they shouldn't have any trouble with."

"I have a feeling she's going to want a pole installed at the house after this."

I must have looked confused because he explained before I had to ask.

"Angie lives in my house in Bergen County, which is where we're from."

"That's in New Jersey?" He nodded. "So she doesn't live too far away."

"No, it's just a couple hours from here."

"Is she your only sibling?"

"No, I have two other sisters and two brothers."

My eyes widened.

"You have five siblings?"

"Yep. Five."

"Wow! That's a big family."

His sexy smirk did things to my lady parts.

"Now you know why I bought a house here."

Daniel returned with the check and Leo handed him a credit card without even checking the total.

"Do you have any siblings?" he asked.

"I have a brother, but we're not very close."

"Did something happen between you?"

"No, he's fifteen years older and joined the Navy right out of high school, so he was out of the house by the time I was three. After that, we saw each other maybe once a year. And now that our parents are gone, I'd be surprised if I ever see him again."

"I'm sorry. Both about your parents being gone and your brother," he said, then turned his attention to Daniel who'd approached once again.

"Thank you," he said and handed the leather portfolio to Leo.

"No, thank *you*. I appreciate the private lunch."

"Just ask for me anytime you come here and I'll make sure you get to eat in peace."

Leo finished signing the receipt and handed the portfolio back to Daniel.

"Will do. Thanks again." After Daniel left, Leo looked at me. "Ready?"

I nodded and stood then bent down to grab my purse. When I straightened, Leo was standing next to me, a silly smile on his face.

"What?"

"Nothing." He shook his head and let out a soft chuckle. "Something funny just popped into my head." I raised my brow. "The way you reached down for your purse, I was expecting you to do the bend and snap when you straightened."

First he quotes Buffy and now Elle Woods? Who is this man?

He held his arm out, gesturing for me to walk ahead of him. Some people approached as we were on our way out, but he never left my side as he shook hands and auto-graphed random items that were handed to him.

"Sorry about that," he said as we made our way to the car.

"No worries." I looked up at him. "I guess it comes with the territory."

"Yeah, sometimes."

He opened the passenger door and offered me his hand as I placed my foot on the running board. Goosebumps trailed up my arm when my cool fingers came in contact with this warm skin. His grip tightened to steady me as I stepped up and settled into the leather seat.

"Thanks for being so understanding."

His warm brown eyes held mine captive as his thumb drew tiny circles against the back of my hand. Those two small things gave my body a big reaction and I fought the urge to wiggle in my seat. Instead of answering, I just nodded wondering, not for the first time, why I respond so strongly to him.

Slowly sliding his hand from mine, Leo stepped back and closed my door. I managed to collect myself before he slid behind the wheel.

"It's just strange," I said.

"What is?"

"You seem like just a normal guy."

"I am just a normal guy."

"You're basically a celebrity."

He didn't comment until we pulled out of the parking lot and were driving back toward the studio.

"I wouldn't call myself that."

"Celebrity means that you're well known. You are well known."

"You didn't know me," he pointed out with a smirk.

"No, but lots of other people do."

"I hope that doesn't freak you out too much."

"It doesn't freak me out exactly. It's just different."

"Well hopefully it's not so different that you won't agree to go out with me again."

His eyes shifted toward me as he said that then quickly returned to the road.

Even though he technically didn't ask a question, I answered. Sort of.

"It's not."

The dimple in his right cheek popped with his smile. He really is ridiculously handsome. A whole buffet, just like Keera said. And while he's definitely nice to look at, his personality is most certainly pulling me in.

Over the last three years, I've reflected on my past relationships both alone and with my therapist and I realize how dysfunctional they were. Some of the guys I dated were total jerks and others just took me for granted. My reaction to both of those things was to morph myself into versions of them. Yes, I majored in theatre, but I never imagined I'd use my acting skills in my relationships. But that's exactly what I did. Looking back now, it makes me sick.

Even though I essentially agreed to a second date with Leo, I'm still being cautious. I don't want to fall back into bad habits. It's definitely a "it's not him, it's me" thing.

I can't remember a time in five years of dating that Travis waited for me to walk in front of him. Not even in the beginning of our relationship. He was usually at least ten paces ahead and more often than not in the car when I finally caught up.

Which reminds me…

"I have a question."

"Shoot."

"I've heard you quote both Buffy and Elle Woods. How is that possible?"

"What do you mean?"

"I don't think I've ever known a guy who quoted either."

He turned into the studio's parking lot and pulled into

the first spot then shifted to face me, the corners of his mouth curled into a sexy smile.

"I did mention my three sisters, right?" I nodded. "They basically commanded the TV when we were growing up, especially Angie. I've seen every episode of *Buffy* more than once and I lost track of the number of times I watched *Legally Blonde.* That stuff just stuck in my head and I can't get it out."

His distressed look when he spoke that last sentence made me laugh.

"It's not funny," he said around a chuckle, diffusing the meaning of his words.

"It kind of is." I shrugged. "What other shows are you fluent in?"

"I know who the "other Tucker" is, that on Wednesdays we wear pink, and the perfect date is April 25th."

"*John Tucker Must Die, Mean Girls,* and *Miss Congeniality.* Pretty impressive."

"And those don't even take the *Nickelodeon* shows like *The Wild Thornberrys* and *The Amanda Show* into consideration. Or *Gilmore Girls.*"

"Interesting. So, serious question." I tapped my index finger against my chin. "Are you Team Angel or Team Spike?"

His cocked brow and the glint of humor in his eyes had me anticipating his next words. And they didn't disappoint.

"I don't think we know each other well enough to discuss that."

He delivered the words in such a serious tone, it took me a second for them to register in my brain. But once they did, my laughter echoed through the interior of the truck. When I let out a loud snort, he joined me and we just sat there laughing like two fools for I don't know how long.

When we finally settled down, I placed my hand on my chest and drew in a deep breath. I have no idea when I last laughed like that and I have to say, it felt good.

"Thank you for today. It was fun."

"Would you like to do it again Friday night?" he asked. "Clay told me about a Brazilian steakhouse that I'd like to check out if that sounds good to you."

"That sounds great actually."

"Does seven thirty work for you?"

"That'll be good. I get done here at six thirty so I'll have enough time to run home and change." At his raised brow, I smiled and added, "I'll text you my address."

With his eyes locked on mine, Leo rested his elbow against the center console and leaned closer. I held my breath anticipating his kiss but before he closed the distance between us, Clay pulled into the spot right next to us.

We both watched as he waved as he walked toward the front door, unlocked it, and disappeared inside. Leo's gaze met mine again, but the spell was broken.

One side of his mouth kicked up into a half smile and I watched as he got out of the truck and walked around the front. The door opened and just like before, he offered his hand to help me out. I stepped down and looked up at him.

"I'll probably see you later, but I'll definitely see you Friday night."

His clean scent filled my nose when he leaned down and kissed my cheek. The skin his lips touched tingled, my nipples tightened, and my va-jay-jay clenched. If I respond like that to a peck on the cheek, I can't imagine what kind of reaction I'll have to a real kiss.

Chapter Eight

LEO

"HOW MUCH LONGER?" Trey asked through gritted teeth.

"Relax your face and breathe through it," Clay said instead of answering the question.

Trey muttered something under his breath and I held back my chuckle. He deserves to suffer after making fun of me. We never settled on a wager and honestly, I don't want anything. Just being able to bust his ass is enough.

We moved through the rest of the poses, first on the right side then the left, with Trey grunting and groaning next to me. If nothing else, these classes have taught me how to breathe correctly. I'm even noticing a difference when I run.

"With your legs shoulder-width apart, fold forward," Clay said. "Stay there for three breaths then step back and move into downward dog. Pedal your feet and stretch out your calves and hamstrings and loosen up your ankles."

I felt him move to Trey's side and adjust his pose. At this point, I think I have it down, but that's because Clay fixed my issues at the beginning.

"Walk your hands back out again and lower yourself into a plank. Now rest your knees against the mat then sit back with your legs straight out in front of you."

After doing some side twists and touching our toes, it was finally time for Savasana. I lowered onto my back and felt every muscle in my body fully relax.

"I think I'm dying," Trey whispered, once Clay left us alone.

If that's what I sounded like when I first started taking classes...and I'm guessing I did...I don't know how Clay put up with me. The only positive is that Crispin didn't come along. His complaining would be even worse. Louder, for sure and definitely more creative. But the manager of his shop had emergency surgery and he ended up flying home a day earlier than planned.

I didn't answer, but instead focused on breathing, relaxing, and clearing my mind.

"My fingers and toes hurt."

Once again I ignored him and took in a deep breath, filling my lungs to capacity before slowly letting it out. I repeated that twice more before settling into a normal breathing rhythm.

"I never want to get back up. I'm just going to sleep here. I hope there's no class after this."

And on it went.

If Trey wasn't talking, he was groaning and it got to the point that I couldn't tune him out anymore. I opened my eyes and stared at the ceiling.

"You know you're supposed to be relaxing." I turned my head to look at him. "This is the reward for all that work we just did and you're ruining it by whining and complaining."

I sat up then grabbed my water and took a long drink.

"I'm not *whining*, I'm simply stating that it was a hard workout. I wasn't expecting that."

"I told you. I don't know why you didn't believe me."

"Because you're a wimp." He smirked and finished his bottle of water in one long chug.

"Yeah, I'm a wimp. Who sits behind that plate most every night while your sorry ass is resting on the bench between starts?"

Clay came out of his office before Trey could answer.

"You have at least ten more minutes. I can't believe you're up," he said, more to me than Trey. "I normally have to drag you out of Savasana."

"Chatty Cathy here couldn't keep his mouth shut. I couldn't get in my zone, so I just gave up."

Trey groaned as he stood. I purposely got to my feet as gracefully as possible just to show him up.

"You almost killed me," he said to Clay. "I'm not going to be able to get out of bed tomorrow."

"Make sure you move at some point. You know doing nothing will just make it worse."

"I can't promise anything," Trey said.

"It's your body." Clay shrugged and handed Trey a small tube. "This is arnica cream. Tell Nori and Angie to rub it on the top of their feet and shins. It will help with the bruising and soreness they'll most likely have from climbing today."

"I might need to slather it over my entire body."

"Whatever you need to do." Clay chuckled. "Even though you're in great shape, there are still muscles you rarely use. Those are the ones you're feeling now."

"Hopefully they'll quiet down again so I don't know they're there."

"Or you can keep up with the yoga so they'll get stronger and eventually won't hurt. And you'll be better for it. I swear I'd be a mess if I didn't start doing this. My whole body hurt after my car accident and I knew it was only going to get worse as I aged."

"That was such a tough break." I moved over and sat down on the floor, resting my back against the wall.

"It is what it is," Clay said. "Considering what my car looked like after that guy hit me and they had to use the Jaws of Life to get me out, I'm lucky I wasn't killed. Compared to that, having to shift careers seems pretty minor."

He and Trey joined me on the floor.

"That's a great attitude to have," Trey said.

"It took me a bit to adopt it, but now I'm good. And I really love what I do here. Once I got over losing my dream of playing professional baseball, I was able to focus on another one. Now I have a plan and things are really falling into place."

"It seems like things are going great here," I said.

"They really are. When I bought this building, I didn't plan on renting to anyone until I got the spaces fully renovated, but Anjannette was interested in the downstairs studio, so together we cleaned things up down there, with the understanding that I'd fix the rest in the next year or so. But then you came along and gave me the extra funds to get her floors refinished earlier than expected. I got a great price on that so I have some money left over to start working on the space across the hall from her."

"Will that be another exercise-type studio?" I asked.

"I'm hoping to get a coffee shop or something similar

in there. It would be great for the current clientele and I'm sure the surrounding businesses will utilize it as well."

"That's a great idea," Trey said."

"Anjannette knows someone who might be interested in setting up shop there. Right now, she's working as a baker at a local supermarket, but would like to open up something of her own. So we'll see what happens with that."

"Speaking of Anjannette," Trey said. "How do you think Nori and Angie are doing down there?"

I thought for sure when he said that first sentence, Trey was going to ask me about lunch. Now that he's in a happy relationship, he thinks everyone else should be in one, too.

Clay glanced at his watch.

"They're probably having fun now. She usually puts together a fun dance for the last half of class. The first half is all conditioning. I'm guessing that kicked their butts a little even if they're in good shape. Like you guys with yoga, they'll be using different muscles. Plus, like I said earlier, they'll probably be bruised because their skin isn't used to being pressed against the pole."

"I hope Nori likes it. I'd love to get a pole at the house." He bobbed his eyebrows, then added a smirk when he continued, "And I saw the relief on your face when I asked Clay about class. But don't think I'm not curious about your date today."

"You're worse than my mother," I said.

"Inquiring minds want to know."

I pulled in a long breath through my nose and let it out slowly through my mouth. There's no use trying to put him off because otherwise he'll drive me crazy.

ANJANNETTE

. . .

I TURNED OFF THE MUSIC.

"Great job, group one. Wipe down your poles."

The first six students grabbed rags and spray bottles and cleaned their poles, then moved off to the side of the room.

"Group two, you're up."

Nori and Angie took the two poles in the back. I have to say, so far they've been holding their own. And the best thing is that when they struggled, they laughed at themselves and kept trying.

"Ready ladies?"

They all placed their right hand on the pole, shifted onto their tiptoes, and nodded. I pressed play and the slow beat of *Criminal* by Fiona Apple filled the studio. As her silky smooth voice joined in, I watched as my students started to dance.

While I taught the routine, I called out every move, but now I stood off to the side like a crazy dance mom, willing them to get the steps right. And for the most part, they did. It wasn't perfect and they were a little out of sync, but it was still awesome.

Group one clapped and catcalled as they danced, just like the group dancing had done for them.

They went into their final step around and some fumbled the pirouette, but they all nailed their back leg hook and spun down onto their knees. Reaching their arms forward, they shifted onto their chests, and with their butts still in the air, twerked. That was the last of my choreography, but I had encouraged them to freestyle so I kept the music playing.

Like the first group, some stayed down and did some sexy floor work while others got up and started the routine over again. But they all put their own personality into the moves. It was fun to watch them having fun.

"Yes!" I yelled as the song ended.

That word was barely heard over all the clapping and whistles.

"Clean your poles ladies. Great class tonight."

"That's a fun routine," Keera said as I walked toward the desk.

"I think that's because it's made up of relatively simple moves so they all got it."

"Angie and Nori did well."

"They did, especially for their first class."

I dug through my duffle bag and found my clothes. Keera hadn't said anything else, but I felt her eyes on me as I sat on the stool and slipped into my leggings. I made the mistake of looking at her as I stood and pulled them up into place.

"What?"

"How was lunch?"

I glanced around the room, thankful Angie and Nori were still on the other side.

"Do you think now is the time to discuss this?"

"No one is here right now," she said. "And it's not like you're going to give me any juicy details anyway."

After I slipped my sweatshirt over my head, I said, "There aren't any juicy details to tell. We went to lunch and he dropped me off here." She raised her brow. "It was fun. I'll admit that I had a great time. A better time than I thought I'd have for sure."

She squeezed my arm and let out a little squeak.

"That's so awesome. Did he ask you out again?"

"Yeah, we're going to a Brazilian steakhouse Friday night."

"Ooh, nice." She gave me a quick hug. "I'm so happy

you had a nice time *and* that you said yes when he asked you out again."

"I'll admit that I like him. There's just something...I don't know, something about him pulls me in." I shrugged. "I'm going to take your advice and enjoy myself."

She squeezed me again and gave me a kiss on the cheek.

"He really seems great."

"I'm not sure anyone can truly be as nice as he seems, but we'll see."

Angie and Nori approached as Keera let me go.

"Thanks so much for that," Angie said. "It was so much fun."

"It really was," Nori added. "I'll admit that Angie basically dragged me here, but I'm so glad I came."

"You guys were great."

Angie and Nori were the only totally new people in class so I was able to offer some personalized attention, especially at the beginning.

"That's not what it felt like," Angie said. "I thought I was in semi-decent shape but I couldn't do most of the stuff."

"Same," Nori said. "My job is pretty physical, and between lugging supplies and painting, you'd think my arms would be super strong. But I could barely hold myself up."

"It takes time," I said. "It's not only about muscle, you have to build up your grip and learn technique. You guys both managed to climb a little bit and your pole ups were decent for a first attempt. That's more than some people do in their first class."

"I did have fun with that little routine at the end," Angie said. "I even managed to do all the spins and steps."

"You guys seriously were both great," Keera said. "I hope you come back again."

"I'll definitely sign up for a class next time I'm visiting Leo. In the meantime, I'm going to look for a pole studio at home."

"Awesome," Keera said. "But on that note, I'm going to excuse myself and get ready for my class."

After she left, Angie said, "I do have one question."

I braced myself for it to be something about my date with her brother.

"Do you sell those tank tops?"

"Oh yeah," I said, hoping my relief wasn't too evident in my voice.

"I definitely want one."

"I want one, too," Nori said.

"That's seriously the best tagline ever."

I looked down at my branded top with the words *No ifs, just good butts…* and a peach at the end.

"Thanks. A few of my friends and I brainstormed one night and came up with some good slogans, but this was by far the best."

"I'll take a medium."

"And I'll take a small," Nori said.

People were starting to arrive for the next class so I told them to follow me to my office. All the studio merch is organized on shelves so it was easy to find their sizes. I took their payment and thanked them again then walked them to the door of the office. Angie hesitated before leaving and turned to face me.

"I probably should stay out of it, but I heard part of your conversation with Keera."

My stomach tightened and my lunch threatened to reappear. I looked at her with wide eyes.

"I didn't mean anything —"

She reached for my hand and squeezed then quickly let go.

"I'm sorry, the freaked out look on your face made me realize how threatening that must have sounded. I didn't mean it like that. You told Keera that you're not sure anyone can be truly as nice as Leo seems, but I can assure you that he is. And I'm not just saying that because he's my brother. He's seriously the best guy I know."

What am I supposed to say to that? Before I had to think of something, she pulled Nori into the conversation.

"Tell her, Nori."

"He really is a great guy," Nori said. "You're lucky Crispin isn't here to sing his praises. We'd be here all night."

I still have no idea what to say so I just thanked them. Which, when I thought about it, seemed like a strange response. So I added to it.

"At least I know I made the right decision when I agreed to go out with him again."

Angie's mouth curled into a big smile and I wanted to kick myself for even mentioning our next date. What if she tells Leo? He'll think I'm talking about him. Which I am, I guess, but I'm not the one who started it. But what if he thinks I was pumping his sister for information about him? And why do I care so much?

I closed my eyes and took in a breath to center myself before I totally spiral.

Chapter Nine

LEO

"MY FRIENDS and I just started going out to different restaurants once a month. We'll have to add this place to the list."

"I'm glad you like it."

She looked at me like I sprouted a second head.

"Have you noticed the guys walking around carrying huge skewers of meat? I'm seriously in heaven."

We've been here for nearly an hour and we're both just starting to slow down. Initially we sampled everything, but now we're just taking more of our favorites.

Like filet mignon. When the server carrying a skewer of it approached, we both asked for more. Just as he left, the guy with the bacon-wrapped chicken came by and added to our plates.

"I'm going to go grab some more potatoes from the buffet," Anjannette said.

Since my mouth was full, I just nodded and enjoyed

the sight of her walking away. I've seen her in jeans and leggings and even those tiny outfits she wears when she's pole dancing. But when I picked her up earlier and saw her wearing a sexy little black dress, I almost swallowed my tongue.

For the most part, the dress is plain, but the material hugs her every curve perfectly, while the corset top and mesh bell sleeves add the quirkiness I'd expect from her. With the hem ending a few inches above her knees and sky-high stilettos, her legs look impossibly long.

I enjoyed the view again as she walked back.

"These are so good. You may have to roll me out of here."

Honestly, I think she's eaten just as much as me and for the life of me, I have no idea where she's putting it. But I appreciate the fact that she has a healthy appetite. I grew up in a big Greek family and eating is one of our favorite pastimes. It's how we celebrate, socialize, and mourn.

The last real girlfriend I had a few years ago was always on some kind of special eating plan. When she came to visit me during the off season and we went to my parents' house for Sunday dinner, she barely ate. And let me tell you, there's no better way to insult my mother than not eating the food she prepared.

"I think I'd just carry you instead," I said. "I'm just glad you're enjoying yourself."

"I went to a Brazilian steakhouse years ago down in Virginia, but I don't remember the food being this good."

"Clay actually recommended this place. When I lived here before, I didn't have money to go out to eat a lot, especially to nice places so I'm not really sure what's around."

"You were in college, right?"

"Yeah, I lived here for two years while I was in college then for a few months when I played for the RailRiders."

"I didn't realize you played for the RailRiders."

I nodded.

"I was here from March to July then got traded to the Waves and moved down to Fayetteville, North Carolina."

"Were you happy about that?"

"Honestly, I didn't care where I went as long as I could keep playing ball. But I was concerned I wouldn't get a shot to move up. Xander McCay was the starting catcher and both he and his backup, Jimmy Dominguez, weren't that old."

"So what happened?"

"Xander got hurt so I got called up to fill in."

"And you impressed them so much they kept you there."

"That's partly true," I said, then took a quick drink of water. "I did well so they were definitely happy with me. Unfortunately, it didn't stop them from sending me back to Fayetteville when he got off the injured list."

"Well that sucks."

I smiled both at her words and the fact that she's relaxed enough to say them. Our first date was great, but she was obviously nervous and picking her words carefully.

"It's all part of the game, but yeah, it does suck. But, I kept proving myself in Fayetteville and when X-y's contract was up for renewal, he and the Waves failed to come to terms so he moved on and I got another shot."

"Now let's back things up to college. How did you end up going to Lackawanna?"

"The catching coach was scouting at a tournament I was playing in and I guess he liked what he saw, because he approached me after the game and made his pitch. And I liked what I heard." I chuckled. "Then I had to convince my parents I was better off going to a small junior college in Scranton instead of one of the Division 1 schools that had offered me a full scholarship."

"How did you manage to convince them?"

"My ultimate goal was to play professional baseball. After speaking to Coach Benji, the JUCO route seemed the best way to make that happen. I figured worst-case scenario, if I didn't get drafted, I could just continue on to a four-year school and play. Education is super important to my parents, so once I assured them I intended to graduate with at least a two-year degree, they were okay with it."

"And it obviously worked out."

"Yeah, thankfully."

"I honestly didn't realize people outside of Scranton know Lackawanna College exists."

"The school has an amazing baseball program. Most people looking to play beyond high school know it exists. I went to school with guys from all over...Texas, Kentucky, a few from Puerto Rico, and one from Toronto."

Before she could ask me another question, I switched the topic of conversation to her.

"I know you design websites and own a pole dance fitness studio. Other than that, you're a mystery. Tell me about yourself."

"Well, we've already discussed my family so you know about that. I went to the University of Scranton and graduated with a theatre major and computer science minor. After college, a few friends and I moved to Manhattan to make our mark on Broadway." She looked me in the eye, her right brow raised. "Obviously that didn't happen, so after three and a half years of rejection, I moved back here and got a job designing websites."

"Wow! Theatre and web design are worlds apart."

"I know, but they're both very much a part of who I am. I've always loved computers. Figuring out how to get them to do what I wanted was a fun Friday night for me. On the other hand, my friends and I used to write little plays and act them out when we had sleepovers. And I loved that just as much. As I got older, I joined the theatre club at school and usually ended up getting decent parts in the plays. When it came time for college and deciding what I wanted to major in, theater kept shouting at me. So I went for it." She shrugged and let out a sad chuckle. "Obviously it didn't work out, so at least I had the good sense to minor in something that could actually support me financially." She looked at me, eyes wide. "Sorry, I didn't mean to do a full infodump there."

"No, don't apologize. It's fascinating."

Her cheeks turned pink and she rolled her eyes.

"Hardly *fascinating*."

"It is to me. I'd like to learn all about you."

ANJANNETTE

I'M TRYING to keep things casual here, so the fact that he wants to learn all about me should make me nervous.

But it doesn't.

And the fact that it doesn't actually *does* make me nervous.

I've jumped into every single one of my relationships immediately with both feet and look how well those all turned out. My biggest fear is that I'll backslide after all the progress I've made on myself the past three years.

Thankfully our waiter approached before I had to comment.

As Leo signed the check, I took in his head of thick, nearly-black hair and strong jawline. His plump lips naturally curl up at the edges, making him look like he's always happy.

It's all very attractive.

He's very attractive.

Those things combined with the heat I feel radiating from him, even from across the table, make me want to crawl onto his lap and snuggle against him to soak in his warmth and positive energy.

"Ready?"

I blinked up at him and nodded, forcing my brain to expel those last thoughts.

Just like he did at Cooper's, he waited for me to stand then followed me through the restaurant. As he reached around and held the door open for me, I realized that no one had even given Leo a second glance the entire time we were in there.

"What?"

"What?" I asked as we approached his truck.

"You made a *hmmm* sound."

"As we were leaving it occurred to me that no one noticed you in there."

He opened the passenger-side door and held out his hand to help me inside. I settled into the seat and looked over at him.

"Like I said, I'm not a celebrity." He smiled then lifted my hand to his lips and kissed my knuckles. "People don't always know who I am."

He slowly released my hand, resting it against my thigh with care before stepping back and closing the door.

With my hand flat against my leg, I traced where his

soft lips had touched. The tingles the brush of his mouth caused radiated up my arm in a trail of goosebumps. My hard nipples pressed against the material of my dress, jealous as all hell that they weren't getting any attention. I felt like some simpering heroine of a historical romance novel getting so turned on by something so innocent.

The ride back to my apartment was mostly silent, but not uncomfortable. Aside from trying to get my body under control, I sat back and enjoyed the music playing softly in the background. If the songs I've heard are any indication, I'd say Leo and I have the same taste in music. We just turned into my driveway when the beginning harmony of *Fat Bottomed Girls* by Queen filled the truck.

Leo shifted into park and turned to face me, his elbow resting on the console.

"You know," he said with a sexy smirk. "You were dancing to this song the first time I saw you. So I guess that makes it our song."

He's obviously teasing, but we can't even joke about having a song. So I decided to ignore that last sentence and focus on the one before it.

"I'm sorry I was so rude to you that day."

"I shouldn't have scared you like that."

"Let's just say it was fifty-fifty and forget about it."

"Sounds like a plan."

He flashed a dimple-popping smile. Dammit that thing should come with a warning.

"I had a great time tonight," he said.

I nibbled at my bottom lip and nodded.

"So did I."

Again with the smile. The man is killing me.

"Maybe we can go out again next Friday?"

Friday. That's a week from now. So if I accept, it's not moving too fast, right?

"I'd like that."

"What time do you have to be at the studio?"

"Five thirty."

"That won't work then."

"What?"

"I thought we could go on a fall foliage train ride, but it runs until four thirty. We wouldn't make it back in time."

"A train ride sounds like fun," I said. "Let me make sure Keera will be at the studio that night. If she is, I can go. Friday nights are just for open pole, so as long as she's there to open and lock up, I'm good."

"I'm heading to Bergen County tomorrow morning and won't be back here until Monday, but you can text and just let me know. Or call," he added with another smile.

"Okay, I will."

His eyes locked on mine and I held my breath, certain he was going to kiss me. But he didn't. Instead, he looked down and moved back to unhook his seatbelt.

I took a steadying breath as he got out of the truck and watched as he rounded the front. My door opened and I took his hand and stepped out. He interlaced our fingers as we walked the short distance to my front door.

"Thank you again for tonight," he said and turned to face me, taking hold of my other hand.

"Thank you. I had a great time."

Leaning forward, he touched his lips gently to mine. It was a brief kiss, not much more than a mingling of breath, but its effect zinged through my entire body. I felt myself drifting toward him as he pulled back. His eyes shifted down to my lips before meeting my gaze again, as if seeking permission. There's no doubt in my mind that my eyes screamed "*yes, yes, yes.*"

His kissable mouth curled into a small smile as he placed his hands on either side of my face and took a step closer. With our bodies flush against one another, I had no doubt he could feel my heart trying to pound its way out of my chest.

He moved closer still and, tilting my head to the side, kissed the right corner of my mouth, then the left before nibbling at the middle of my bottom lip. I dug my fingers into his biceps and squeezed as he opened his mouth over mine and applied a wonderful suction that nearly brought me to my knees.

Oh my-lanta.

The man can kiss.

Leo moved his hands down to my waist and pulled me even closer, then backed me up until I found myself stuck between a door and a hard body. And I do mean *hard*. Not that I'm complaining. It's been a long time since I've encountered a real live penis and his feels more impressive than most. Most I've come in contact with anyway.

I slid my hands up his broad shoulders and twisted my fingers into his hair as his mouth moved over mine. The kiss was hungry, urgent, and hot as hell. He kissed me like he's been waiting his whole life for the privilege, like he couldn't get enough.

Wrapping his arms around my back, he pulled me tighter against him, smooshing my boobs against his hard chest. I shifted slightly from side to side, trying to ease the ache in my tight nipples. He pulled back at my low moan and I dug my fingers into his scalp to urge his mouth back onto mine.

Tilting his head to come at the kiss from a different angle, he urged my mouth open with the press of his lips. I invited him inside and eagerly met every thrust and caress of his tongue. Releasing my grip on his hair, I slid my arms down to loop around his neck and shifted onto my tiptoes to get even closer.

Every fiber of my being focused on Leo Marakis as the kiss went on and on, deep and wet, his tongue stroking mine in a perfect rhythm, our bodies locked in a tight embrace. I've never been kissed so surely or held so possessively before. It all felt new yet somehow familiar and safe.

Leo changed the tempo of the kiss, slowing it down until he kissed my lips softly one more time before pulling back enough to meet my gaze. I loosened my hold on his neck and my heels clicked back against the sidewalk. He took a half a step back and rested his hands on my waist.

"Thank you again for coming out with me tonight."

His gravelly voice sounded even sexier than usual.

"I really had a great time. Thank you," I said, barely recognizing my own husky voice.

My whole body throbbed in time with my rapid heartbeat, both urging me to invite him inside so we could continue what we'd started. But even though it would most definitely be a good time, that wouldn't be a good idea.

Leo leaned forward and kissed my temple before releasing me and putting some much-needed space between us.

"Let me know about Friday," he said with a strained smile.

"I will." Reaching into my purse, I pulled out my keys and turned to unlock the door. "Have a safe trip to New Jersey."

He nodded and put his hands in his pockets, drawing my gaze to the impressive erection tenting his pants. The entire lower half of my body clenched at the sight.

Stand down, vagina.

I reached for the doorknob with a shaking hand and opened the door. Backing over the threshold, I waved, not trusting myself to speak.

"Good night," he said.

I stared at his perfect ass as he walked back to the truck and got inside before closing the door and leaning back against it. Closing my eyes, I took in a deep breath and slowly let it out.

Leo is not going to make keeping my distance very easy.

I reached down and took off my shoes, then walked toward my bedroom, praying that at least one of my toys is fully charged.

Chapter Ten

LEO

THE NOISE in the family room reached a decibel level sure to cause hearing damage. It was beyond what's normal for a Sunday dinner at the Marakis residence. The cause...a re-broadcast of the game when the Yankees beat the Mets to win the Subway Series in 2000.

There was a collective groan when the Mets loaded the bases in the top of the seventh inning with just one out. I took a long drink of beer and looked out toward the dining room. My mom sat at the table holding my cousin Maria's baby girl, Nadia. She's been bugging my siblings and me for years about her lack of grandchildren, and that gets worse each time one of my cousins has a baby. Which seems to happen quite often these days.

"Come on Pettitte," Nicky yelled at the TV as the pitcher gave up a two-run single to left field. The fact that it happened more than two decades ago made me chuckle. "What are you laughing at over there?"

"You know the outcome of this game and you're sitting here screaming at the TV."

"If only we were all as evolved as you," he said.

I flipped him off and he returned the gesture.

"Boys, settle down," my father said in the same tone we've heard our entire lives.

Putting my feet up on the ottoman, I shifted back in the oversized chair, my mind drifting to Anjannette as I half watched the game. Hopefully it's a good sign that she let her guard down Friday night. I really like her and want to continue seeing her. Especially after that kiss. There was definitely chemistry between us since day one, but *holy shit*, that was beyond what I expected.

It took every ounce of my willpower to leave, but thankfully there was enough blood in my brain to reason that if I stayed, it would ruin any chance of something long-term with her. Sure, the night would have been amazing, but I'm interested in more.

As if she read my thoughts, Angie appeared at my side. She's been bugging me for details about my date with Anjannette since yesterday and I've refused to tell her anything. Resting her hip against the arm of my chair, she handed me a plate filled with *milopita*, *loukoumades* and of course, mom's famous *baklava*.

"Thanks." I popped a loukoumas into my mouth and chewed. This fried dough may not be sold at Dunkin' but everyone should try these honey, cinnamon delights. "But I'm still not going to sit here and spill details like a teenage girl."

"I just want to know it went well. I like Anjannette and think you two would be awesome together."

I glanced across the room. Thankfully my brothers are still engrossed in the game. Not that they care who I date, but it wouldn't be beyond them to tell my mother about Anjannette just to shift attention away from them.

And with my mother occupied with the baby, I feel safe to speak freely.

"It went well."

She looked down at me, her bottom lip jutting out.

"Don't think the pouty face is going to get me to say any more. When have I *ever* discussed my dating life with you?"

"Can you at least tell me if you're going out again?"

I picked up the milopita and took a big bite. She crossed her arms over her chest and stared me down as I chewed. Once there was nothing left to grind, I swallowed then took a drink to wash it down, cringing at the mingled flavors of apple, cinnamon, and beer.

"We may be going out Friday."

"*May* be?"

"She's checking to see if Keera can cover the studio."

Angie's face split into a big smile.

"If it's up to Keera, you're *definitely* going." She did that quick clapping thing girls do when they're excited. "Where are you taking her?"

"A fall foliage train ride."

"Ooh, so romantic. My brother has got game."

She held her hand up for a high five then scrunched her nose at me when I left her hanging.

"What is wrong with you?" I asked, only semi-joking.

"Anjannette is the first female that you've been interested in that I've actually liked."

"You never even met most of the females I've been interested in."

"I've never met most of the females you've *spent time* with. You brought the ones you had at least some interest in home to meet the family." She scrunched up her face.

"And some of them were awful. That last one didn't even eat. What was up with that?"

She had other talents that convinced me I was more into her than I really was, but I'm not discussing *that* with my baby sister.

"I admit dating Allison wasn't my best decision."

"Ya think?"

I shifted in the chair to face her, willing to throw her a bone in hopes of ending the conversation.

"I like Anjannette and I'm hoping to spend more time with her to get to know her better."

She did that clapping thing again then wrapped her arms around me and squeezed.

"Who's Anjannette?"

Angie released her hold on me, and I looked over my shoulder and saw my mother standing directly behind me, Nadia still in her arms.

"Are you seeing someone?" she asked when I didn't answer.

I glared at Angie as she stood and shrugged, her smile not looking one bit remorseful.

"You've been hogging Nadia forever," she said. "Give me a turn."

My mother reluctantly handed the baby to Angie then watched wistfully as she walked away before turning her attention back to me. Her raised brow let me know she was waiting for an answer.

"It's very new, so don't start planning the wedding yet. We just had our second date on Friday."

"Leonidas, I'm not *planning a wedding*, I just want to keep up with what's happening in your life since you moved away." She settled into the spot Angie had just vacated and placed her hand around my shoulder. "So tell me about this girl, this *Anjannette*."

My mom's slight accent made the name sound even more elegant.

"There's not much to tell yet. Like I said, we only went out a couple times."

"What does she do for a living?"

I hesitated, debating on what to tell her. Basically Anjanette owns a fitness studio, but when my mother hears the words *pole dance*, that's not the first thing that will come to her mind. But I don't want to lie to her or even omit the fact, because I really am hoping this thing between Anjanette and me moves forward, and eventually the two of them will meet. I'd hate to start things out on a lie, no matter how white or well-intended.

Apparently I took too long to answer, because the corners of her mouth took on a pinched look and her voice was a little more firm when she asked her next question.

"She's not one of those girls after your money, is she?"

"No, definitely not," I said. "She owns a business, a pole dance fitness studio. It's in Clay's building."

"Pole dance?" I nodded. "Like the strippers do?"

"Yes and no. Strippers do pole dance, but this isn't stripping. It's exercise. When Angie, Trey, and Nori were up, we went to the show the students put on and it's amazing what they do."

"She's a nice girl?"

"I think so, yes."

"Does she eat?" she asked. "She's not like that other one, is she?"

"She definitely eats."

I told her about our date at the Brazilian steakhouse and her mouth curled into a smile.

Patting my shoulder, she said, "Then you'll have to bring her some baklava."

ANJANNETTE

THE LAST OF the students left and Keera sat across from me, her feet propped against the desk. She finished her last bite of baklava and groaned.

"That was amazing." Leaning forward, she put her empty plate on the desk next to mine then sat back. "I don't know how you held off eating it until now."

"I may have snuck a bite before class."

"You're lucky I wasn't the one here when Leo dropped it off. I wouldn't have been able to stop at one bite. It would have been gone."

I was definitely lucky because along with the dessert, he also gave me another delicious kiss. And as tasty as the baklava was, it doesn't compare to him. Just thinking about it makes my lips—and other body parts—tingle. The same thing has been happening since our date Friday. After having a long hiatus, my toys have been getting quite a workout the past few days.

The fact that my libido has come back in full force has me both thrilled and scared to death. The chemistry between Leo and me is off the charts. Definitely stronger than anything I've ever experienced before. So as much as I'd love to jump his bones, the tiny rational part of my brain is making me hesitate.

I heard a *thump* and jumped in my seat. Looking over, I realized the noise had been Keera stomping her feet onto the floor. She leaned forward, her elbows resting on the desk and met my gaze.

"What's that look for?"

"What look?"

"The look that tells me you're mentally spiraling about something."

Sometimes it's annoying as hell when people know you too well.

"I'm just thinking about Leo."

"What *specifically* are you thinking about?"

"Sex."

"What about it?"

I picked up a paper clip and unraveled it as I figured out what to say.

"Physically I've been thinking about sex a lot the past week." I looked her in the eye. "A *lot*."

"That's a good thing." She raised her brow. "Isn't it?"

"No, it's not."

"Why?"

"In my experience, sex leads to bad decisions. Or maybe not necessarily, bad decisions, but it tends to make me overlook issues that would be pretty obvious if I wasn't sexblind. Look at Travis. And before him was Mark." Shaking my head, I took a deep breath in and blew it out. "I could keep listing names, but I think you get the picture."

"Anjannette, do you really think Leo's like those other guys?"

"No. I don't know." I shrugged and looked down and bent the straightened paper clip and folded it in half. "But generally speaking it doesn't really matter because I'm still me."

I looked up when Keera placed her hand on top of mine and squeezed.

"Oh honey, you're amazing. Travis took advantage of you at a vulnerable time in your life. Your dad had just died when you met him and your mom a couple years after that. You felt alone and were probably depressed. He's a narcissistic prick who took advantage of those things. That's his shortcoming, not yours."

"But I should have realized—"

I stopped speaking when she held her hands up.

"Look, all that happened, but it's in the past now. You've been working on yourself for three years and the change is obvious. You're older now, wiser and stronger. And definitely more confident. At some point you have to trust yourself and take a chance again. And in my opinion, Leo is the perfect guy to do that with. For chrissake, he brought you baklava." She reached out and squeezed my hand again. "Just relax, get out of your head, and let nature take its course."

She sat back in the chair and rested her feet against the desk again. I tossed the ruined paper clip into the garbage can and tipped my head back, my eyes closed.

"Friday is our third date."

"Huh?"

I looked over at her.

"Friday is our *third* date."

"And?"

"You know what third dates are usually all about."

"The question remains."

"While everything you just said is true, I don't know if I'm ready to have sex. Mentally and emotionally anyway. Physically, my body is screaming for it."

"I still don't understand what the issue is. If you're not ready, you're not ready. Just don't do it. Is he giving you signs that he's expecting something?"

"No. In fact, he's the one who left Friday night. I was on the verge of inviting him in when he ended the kiss and said good night."

She shifted her chair forward and rested her forearms on the desk, leaning closer.

"Anjannette, this is not a real issue. Other than your body and mind disagreeing about your readiness to have sex, there's nothing to worry about here. If things turn sexy and you feel comfortable, go for it. If not, kiss him goodnight and go inside. Stop worrying about it."

I nodded, knowing she's right. I also know that even though that's true, I'll still obsess. After what I've learned about myself and my past relationships these last three years, I think that's totally understandable.

Keera stood, drawing my attention to her.

"Look, if you're that conflicted, talk to Leo. My gut feeling tells me he's looking for more than a casual thing and no matter what you say, I *know* you are too. At this point, you're not gonna pop your cherry with just anyone."

I opened my mouth to point out that my cherry was popped a *long* time ago, but Keera interrupted.

"You don't take a three-year respite from men and jump back into it like you didn't miss a beat. Like I said before, you're a different person now. You're basically revirginized."

She spoke that last sentence so matter-of-factly, I burst out laughing because the topic is so ridiculous.

"You're right," I said once I settled down. "Not about the revirginized thing, but about the fact that things are different now. I can't do what I did in the past and expect a different result. I'm going to tell Leo that I want to take this slow. At least if he's not interested, I'll know sooner rather than later."

"I don't think you have anything to worry about." She smiled. "The man speaks Buffy

and brings you baklava, Anjannette. I'd say he's pretty much perfect. Give him a chance."

Chapter Eleven

LEO

I GLANCED over at Anjannette before shifting my attention back to the curving country road. For most of the half-hour ride she's been staring out the passenger-side window, seemingly lost in thought. The scenery is much more picturesque now that we've left the highway, but I doubt it's that or the lingering fall foliage that's holding her attention. My attempts to pull her into a conversation at the beginning of the ride were met with one-word answers so I gave up and listened to my 90's playlist while I focused on the road.

We're grabbing lunch before the train ride and according to the nav system, the restaurant is only ten minutes away. I'll give her that much longer to sit with her thoughts. After that, I'm going to have to find out what's on her mind. We'll be together for the rest of the afternoon. Spending it in silence will make for a long day.

After following the road for a few more miles, I turned

onto Main Street, found a spot right in front of the restaurant, and pulled in. I turned off the engine and looked over at Anjannette, who continued to look out her window. Without the music and hum of the engine in the background, the silence in the truck felt oppressive.

I removed my seatbelt and shifted to rest my elbow on the console.

"Anjannette?"

She turned her head in my direction, but didn't meet my gaze. Instead she focused on her left hand as she twisted the silver ring on her middle finger around and around. I gave her a second to look at me or at least say something and when she didn't, I repeated her name and waited until she finally looked over at me.

"What's wrong?"

She blinked and shook her head, offering a forced smile.

"Nothing."

"You've been quiet since I picked you up and it's pretty obvious something is on your mind. I wish you'd just be honest and tell me what it is." When she stayed silent, I asked, "Did I do something to upset you?"

"No." Her eyes widened and she shook her head. "No, you haven't done anything. I'm sorry, I didn't mean to be a downer. I'll be better the rest of the day, I promise."

She unbuckled her seatbelt, grabbed her purse off the floor, and started to open the door. I put my hand on her arm, stalling her movement. Releasing the door handle, she dropped the purse onto her lap, and rubbed her forehead.

"Just tell me. We'll both feel better."

Shaking her head, she nibbled her bottom lip, and focused on the dashboard before meeting my gaze.

"It's silly and I'm sorry I've let it ruin our day."

"It hasn't ruined our day and if it's bothering you, it's not silly."

Letting out a sigh, she shook her head again. I wasn't sure she was going to answer and was relieved when she finally did.

"This is our third date."

"Yeah?"

"Our *third* date."

I raised my brow.

She put her hands over her face and peeked over at me through her fingers.

"Are you going to make me spell it out?"

"I guess I am because I'm not sure what this being our third date means beyond the fact it's the third time we've gone out together."

Dropping her hands onto her lap, she looked over at me and sighed. Focusing on my chin she said, "I'm talking about the third date rule. You know, it's customary for people to have sex on the third date."

Her face practically matched her red hair and I would have smiled at how adorable she looked if the subject wasn't so serious. I was trying to figure out what to say when she continued.

"I know it's kind of expected, but..." Trailing off, she looked down at her hands and twisted her fingers together. "It's just not something I'm ready for just yet." Meeting my gaze again, she added, "Full disclosure, you're the first guy I've dated in three years." She let out a nervous chuckle. "Actually that seems more like a reason for why I *would* be ready to have sex." She shook her head. "But I'm not." Her eyes widened. "I'm sorry. I didn't mean to babble. Honestly, I wasn't even going to bring it up."

"I'm glad you did because you need to understand something." I reached over and placed my hand over her white knuckles. "I'm not expecting anything from you today or any other day. Whatever happens between us will happen because we both want it to, not because some idiot wrote an article in *Cosmo* making a rule that it has to."

Holding her gaze, I leaned closer.

"I like you, Anjannette. Really like you. And I'm most definitely attracted to you, but you don't have to worry that I'm going to try to push you into doing something you're not comfortable with. This isn't high school and I'm not some horny teenager ruled by his hormones." She looked confused by my words, but also a little bit hopeful. "We're not on a specific timeline here. I'd like for us to spend time and get to know each other better, but I don't want you to be afraid that there are strings attached to that." I chuckled. "Don't get me wrong, I'm hoping to experience more amazing kisses like we shared the other night, but it can stop at that if you're not ready for more."

Her lips curled into a small smile.

"You're not at all what I expected, Leo Marakis."

"Is that good or bad?"

"It's good," she said. "Definitely good."

I traced my fingers along her jaw and pulled her in for a quick kiss. Our lips lingered and

the temptation to deepen it was strong, but considering the conversation we just had and the fact that we're sitting in my truck on Main Street, I fought the urge and pulled back.

Nudging my head toward the windshield, I smiled and said, "Come on, let's go grab some lunch. We have a train to catch."

ANJANNETTE

. . .

AFTER A LIGHT LUNCH, we walked a block to the quaint station and boarded the train. Leo had purchased tickets for the first-class car and it definitely lives up to that label. The cream-colored walls and ceiling are perfectly accented with rich golds and greens, with the dark wood trim making it look even more elegant. He gestured for me to sit and I settled into the plush seat next to the window. With its high back and sides, the bench offers a modicum of privacy.

"This car is gorgeous."

He looked around and nodded.

"Have you ever gone on a ride from this station before?"

Shifting his body slightly toward me, he settled his arm across the back of the seat.

I shook my head.

"I went on a train ride at Steamtown years ago with my parents, but not here."

"It's a first for both of us then."

His sexy smile had butterflies rioting in my stomach and I placed my hand over it to settle them. Like I said, Leo is not what I expected. Professional athletes have a certain reputation, but he doesn't fit that mold at all. He doesn't even fit the stereotype of a man with his good looks. Yes he's sexy and charming, but he's also very sweet, thoughtful, and attentive. It definitely makes for an attractive package. I planned on keeping things casual, but he's not making it easy.

The train lurched forward, pulling me out of my thoughts.

"Here we go," Leo said as he leaned a little closer to look out the window.

The view of Main Street moved by slowly at first, but was quickly a memory as the train picked up speed. Soon we were surrounded by a breathtaking landscape painted in rustic reds, oranges, and golds. The colors are a little past peak, but still spectacular.

His arm was still draped over the back of the seat and initially I resisted the urge to lean back against him. But that seemed silly, so I shifted sideways and rested back, settling my shoulder into his armpit. Leo moved closer, repositioning me against his chest, with the top of my head just under his chin and wrapped his arm around my waist.

The train chugged along, its rhythm a soothing serenade as we made our way through the countryside, past fields and farms and a river decorated with fallen leaves.

"This is so beautiful," I said, glancing back at Leo. "Thank you for inviting me."

"Thank you for saying yes."

Again with the panty-dropping smile. The man really should come with a warning label. Before I got too pulled in, I turned my attention back to the scenery rushing past the window and soon my mind drifted back to our discussion in the truck earlier. That was both the most satisfying and embarrassing conversation I've ever had. I've never talked about sex with the guys I've dated, I've always just done it. Which in hindsight I realize is pretty pathetic.

"You okay?"

"Mmm Hmm. Why?"

"You stiffened, like you got stuck by a pin or something."

I thought about telling him I bumped my foot or some other white lie, but that's what I would have done in the past. And I'm trying to change and move forward, be more honest about my feelings. Maybe someday have a *normal* relationship instead of repeating the same mistakes.

Besides, something tells me that Leo would know I was lying.

"I was just thinking about stupid things I did in the past."

"Wanna talk about it?"

"No, I just want to enjoy the day," I said.

He kissed the top of my head and rested his chin against my temple. I pushed any thoughts out of my head and just focused on this moment with this amazing man.

"So what's it really like playing professional baseball?" I asked.

"Amazing. Exhausting. A dream come true," he said. "I don't remember a time when I didn't love the game. My mom said I used to sit on my dad's lap and watch the Yankees games with him when I was toddler. She said it was the only time I sat still."

"It's incredible that now some toddler is probably sitting on his father's lap watching you play."

"I never thought about that, but yeah, I guess it is."

"So you're a Yankees fan?"

"Growing up in New Jersey, it kind of went with the territory."

"I know you said you just wanted to play somewhere, but would you have preferred staying with the RailRiders and eventually moving up to the Yankees?"

He shrugged.

"A few years ago, I may have said yes, but not now. I'm pretty happy playing for the Waves."

"What do you like about it?"

"The owner, Mr. Hanover, runs a great team. He doesn't put up with prima donnas, no matter how good a player is. It makes a big difference with morale and gives the team a family feel. For the most part, things are tension-free and we're all friends, or at least friendly. Which definitely makes things less stressful."

"I guess it's kind of like getting along with your coworkers."

"It's exactly like that," he said. "I know it's a game, but it's also my job. And the other guys technically are my coworkers. The season is long and we spend a *lot* of time together. It helps that we all like each other, or at least respect each other."

"What's exhausting?"

"The schedule. We play a hundred and sixty-two games between April and September. That doesn't include spring training or the postseason. Add in all the travel and it takes a toll. But I wouldn't want to do anything else and I know how fortunate I am." He kissed my temple. "Especially considering the fact that I'm sitting here with the most amazing woman in my arms, on a train ride through some awesome scenery."

I tilted my head back and smiled up at him.

"You're pretty smooth, Marakis."

"I try."

He leaned down and placed his mouth on mine. It was as sweet as the one we shared in the truck, but this time he didn't immediately pull back. Instead he licked at my bottom lip asking for entry. I eagerly opened my mouth, allowing him to slip inside.

Our tongues twisted and twirled together as he took my mouth in a slow, steady kiss, its leisurely rhythm enhanced by the slow rocking of the train as we chugged along the tracks.

Chapter Twelve

LEO

"WAKE UP SLEEPYHEAD."

Clay's voice pulled me out of a very satisfying Savasana. I opened my eyes and looked up, blinking him into focus.

"I think I dozed off that time." Shifting to sit, I grabbed my water and took a long drink then rested the bottle on my thigh. "I guess it was bound to happen."

"I would have let you go, but you said you wanted to talk to Anjannette before her class starts. You have another forty-five minutes or so before her students start arriving. And I'm assuming you'd prefer to see her before they get there."

I couldn't help the smile that spread across my face.

"Ugh! You look just as sappy as Trey."

"Sorry," I said, feeling anything but.

Truth be told, my Savasana had been so enjoyable because as my mind drifted, a memory montage of our last couple weeks together played through my head like a dream. Since the train ride and our little sex talk beforehand, things have been great. Anjannette has been much more relaxed and doesn't seem as nervous about spending time with me.

"I'm guessing things are going well."

Clay raised his voice on the last word, turning his sentence into a question.

"Yeah, they are." I dragged my fingers through my sweaty hair. "She's really amazing."

I stood and went through the process of cleaning and rolling up my mat.

"There must be something in the water at First Allegiant Bank Park. It seems like whoever plays for the Waves ends up getting married."

"We're just spending time together and enjoying each other's company. I didn't say anything about getting married," I said, although the word didn't make me cringe as much as it normally would.

"They were just talking about it on ESPN. First Dan McMullen, then Jack Reagan, and no one ever thought he'd get married. They were followed by Cal Chase, Dale Montgomery, Jimmy Chavez, and Rusty Russell." He waved his hand. "And I'm sure there are more, but the one who convinced me that something is in the air down there is Trey. Who would have ever thought he'd settle down?"

"Not me, that's for sure." I grabbed my duffle and slung it over my shoulder then stepped into my slides. "But he and Nori are perfect together, even if they look like total opposites."

"Kind of like you and Anjannette," he said with a smirk.

"I have noticed the similarities, but Anjannette and I

are just starting out here." I opened the door and a faint beat floated up the stairs. "Tomorrow at two?"

"Yep. See you then."

I jogged down the stairs and gave a quick knock, then opened the door and peeked into Anjannette's studio. And holy hell.

She sat in a perfect L-shape with her legs straight out in front of her, which in itself isn't necessarily impressive, but the fact that she was using just her arms to pull herself up the pole was. I stayed quiet until she reached the top and settled into what I now know is called a pole sit.

"I'm in awe."

I leaned against the door jamb and flashed a smile. Her eyes widened then they met mine and she returned my smile, adding a little sass to hers.

"Want to give it a try?"

With the same controlled movement, she made her way back down to the floor.

"I think I'll leave that to the professionals."

She stood and walked over until she stood directly in front of me.

"Oh come on." She squeezed my bicep then flexed her arm. "If I can do it with these piddly things, you can for sure do it with those guns."

Leaning down, I gave her a quick kiss then rested my forehead against hers.

"Why do I think you're setting me up?"

She shrugged. "No idea."

I straightened.

"Okay, I'll give it a try." I set my duffle on the floor and slipped out of my slides. "But you have to promise not to laugh."

"I can promise no such thing."

"That's not very nice."

I walked across the room and sat on the floor with my legs straddling the pole. Anjannette stood next to me, arms crossed over her chest.

"Get closer to the pole." I moved forward just a fraction. "Closer." She chuckled when I looked at her, my brow raised. "The closer things are to the pole, the easier it is, if you get my meaning."

Oh I got her meaning, but I'm not really thrilled with that idea. Call me crazy, but cramming my balls against cold metal isn't my idea of a good time. But the challenging look in Anjannette's eyes kicked my competitive spirit into high gear and I scooted my butt until the boys nudged against the pole.

I wrapped my hands around the pole and pulled, trying to lift myself, but they kept slipping and I went nowhere. After wiping my palms on my sweatpants, I gripped the pole tighter and tried again, with the same result.

"Okay, what am I doing wrong?"

She walked over to the table in the corner and picked up a bottle then returned to my side.

"Here, try this. It'll help with your grip."

I held out my hands and she added a drop of liquid to each and I rubbed them together.

"Are you sure I need to be this close?"

She stopped me when I went to wrap my hands around the pole again.

"Give it a minute to dry," she said. "And yes, it's harder if you're further back, plus unless you're totally controlled, you'll smash into the pole as soon as your butt leaves the ground."

"I definitely don't want that to happen."

She put her hand over her mouth after I said that, but not before I saw her smile.

Placing my hands on the pole again, I pulled and this

time felt my ass leave the ground, but barely. Tightening my grip, I pulled harder, and moved a fraction of an inch higher.

"Now let go with your bottom hand then reach up and grab the pole as high as you can." I looked over at her, doubt written all over my face. "You can do it."

"I appreciate your confidence in me, but I'm not feeling it."

I forced those words out through gritted teeth then immediately followed her directions, moving as quickly as possible. And it worked. Sort of. Gripping the pole tight again, I pulled myself a little higher.

After repeating the process a couple more times, I barely eked up two feet off the ground. Anjannette had looked so graceful and fluid as she pulled herself to the top of the pole, but I look awkward and strained. I barely recognized the tense, red-faced man in the mirror.

My muscles protested and my hands started to cramp. Before I strain something and reverse all the good the yoga has done, I relaxed my legs and placed my feet back on the floor.

"Now I'm even more impressed by what you did," I said. "Shit, that's hard."

"You have the strength to do it, you just need to get the technique down. If it's something you wanted to do," she quickly added.

I wrapped my hands around her waist and pulled her against me.

"Maybe I'll have to spend more time here so I can practice."

She looped her arms around my neck and smiled up at me.

"I do offer private lessons."

"Do you think you can fit me into your calendar?"

"For you I'll make room."

I leaned down to kiss the sexy smirk off her lips, but as usual, once my mouth touched hers, all bets were off. We stood in the middle of her studio, our bodies plastered together, as her tongue met mine stroke for stroke. Pulling back just enough to turn my head and change the angle of the kiss, I opened my mouth over hers again. She dug her fingers into my hair and moaned.

I've always enjoyed kissing but admittedly, usually a means to an end. But it's different with her. I could kiss her sweet mouth forever just for the sheer enjoyment of the act. There are other things I'd love to do to her as well, but that will have to wait until she's ready.

ANJANNETTE

WITH OUR MOUTHS still locked together, I loosened my grip on Leo's hair, dropped my arms around his neck, and pulled up onto my tiptoes, desperate to get closer. My breasts smashed up against his hard chest was the sweetest torture. If his answering moan was any indication, it was for him, too.

He cupped my ass with his big hands before sliding them to the back of my thighs to lift me up. I wrapped my legs around his waist and held on as he spun me around and set my back against the wall without missing a beat in the kiss. The man is an excellent multi-tasker, not to mention a master kisser. He seriously should get some kind of award.

The kiss went on and on, hot, wet, and deep, as his hips

held me in place. Neither my pole shorts nor his thin sweatpants provided much of a barrier to his impressive erection. A desperate groan vibrated through my chest as I tightened my thighs and he pressed right against my throbbing clit. It wouldn't take much to push me right over the edge.

I banged my head against the wall as I pulled my head back, abruptly ending the kiss. His eyes locked on mine, at first full of confusion, then with understanding. This is not the time nor the place for this, especially not with my students arriving for class soon.

He released his hold on my ass and I slowly let my legs slide down until my feet rested firmly against the floor again. Leo held onto my waist until I was steady, then stepped back.

I fought to keep my eyes focused on his face. There was recently a meme circulating on Facebook celebrating gray sweatpants season but what Leo has going on right now is a million times better than any of those pictures.

"Sorry about that."

His hoarse voice sounded even sexier than usual. Instead of focusing on that, I shook my head.

"About what?"

"I wanted to stop in and invite you to dinner Friday night." He gestured toward the wall I'd just been plastered against. "And as amazing as it was, *that* wasn't part of my plan here."

"It's fine. Really," I added when he shook his head. "In case you didn't notice, I was a very eager participant. Unfortunately, I have a class starting shortly."

He nodded and rubbed the back of his neck, his eyes shifting over to the wall. After taking in a deep breath and letting it out, he looked back at me.

"I was hoping we could get together Friday night. But

instead of going out, I'd like you to come to my house and I'll cook dinner for you."

"You cook?"

"I can make a few things that are edible."

His sexy smirk set my lady parts tingling again and I crossed my legs to nip that in the bud.

"Um sure, yeah, that sounds nice. What can I bring?"

"Just yourself. I'll take care of everything else."

"Are you sure?"

"Positive." He leaned down and gave me a quick kiss then took a giant step back. "You have open pole until seven, right?" I nodded. "How about if I pick you up at seven-thirty?"

"Oh, that's okay, I can drive myself. That way you won't have to leave in the middle of cooking dinner."

Plus I won't have to rely on him to take me home.

"Are you sure?"

"Yep."

"I'll text you my address." He slipped back into his slides and picked up his bag. "See you Friday."

"See you then."

I sat on the floor, my back against the wall Leo just had me pinned against. But before I could fixate on what just happened, Keera walked through the door. She looked over at me with a knowing smile.

"Your lips look just as swollen as Leo's. Hmmm." She tapped her index finger against her chin. "Interesting."

"I'm surprised to see you. I thought you had to work late."

She sat on the floor across from me and put her hands flat on the floor behind her and leaned back.

"Yeah, there's a training class going on and I was supposed to stay and lock up after everyone leaves. But

Simon is there doing some after-hours system updates, so he said he'd do it."

"You know he has the hots for you, right?"

"No, we're just friends."

"That may be true, but I'm pretty sure he wants more than that."

"Well regardless, we're just friends." She shook her head. "I'm done with relationships. They're too much of a pain in the ass. I like my life the way it is now." Sitting up, she crossed her legs and leaned slightly forward, resting her elbow against her knee. "The dick band aids keep me happy."

"Do they?"

"It's much less complicated. Not to mention less stressful."

"If you say so."

She rolled her eyes.

"Don't tell me you're going to be one of those people in a relationship who thinks everyone else should be in one, too."

"No, I just think Simon is really nice. Sweet. Different than all the other guys, which is probably a good thing." Then something she said registered. "Besides, I'm not really in a relationship so your theory is shot."

Shaking her head, she let out a sarcastic chuckle.

"Anjannette." Her eyes met mine. "Leo is crazy about you and whether you're willing to admit it or not, you feel the same about him. You may not have had sex with Leo *yet*, but you two are definitely in a relationship. "

Yet being the key word in that sentence.

Because over the last couple weeks, even though we technically haven't done more than kiss, things have really been heating up between us. And it's getting harder and harder to stop. More and more often I've been thinking that maybe it's time to end my self-imposed celibacy.

Chapter Thirteen

LEO

"THIS IS DELICIOUS," Anjanette said. "What's it called again?"

"*Skordalia.*"

"What's in it?"

"Potatoes, almonds, lemon juice, and garlic. Lots of garlic," I said. "*Skordo* actually means garlic."

She slathered a healthy portion onto a pita triangle and took a big bite. I was enjoying watching her eat when my phone timer beeped. Walking to the other side of the kitchen, I turned off the stove and removed the lid from the pot.

"That smells amazing. What is it?"

"*Dolmades,*" I said. "Stuffed grape leaves."

"You made stuffed grape leaves?" I nodded. "Seriously?"

"Seriously."

"How do you know how to do this?"

"Remember that big Greek family I mentioned? This kind of goes with the territory. And my mother believes all household tasks are gender neutral so cooking wasn't just taught to the girls. We all had to pitch in for Sunday dinners and holidays."

She picked up another triangle of pita and added a dollop of *skordalia*.

"This is my last one. I have to save room for grape leaves."

"And *moussaka*. I know you like eggplant but I wasn't sure how you feel about lamb, so I made it with beef instead."

"Is this heaven?"

"Are you sitting in my kitchen quoting *Field of Dreams* right now?"

"Maybe." She dragged out the word, imitating Fat Bastard from *Austin Powers*.

"You just may be the perfect woman."

"No, just a woman with the viewing habits and sense of humor of a twelve-year-old boy."

"Then you're definitely perfect for me."

I figured she'd have another sassy comeback for that, but instead, she blushed and focused her attention on the island countertop. She's definitely not comfortable with compliments. Eventually I'll find out why that is, but until then, I'll just keep dishing them out to her.

"The *dolmades* have to cool for about a half hour. In the meantime, why don't I give you a quick tour?"

She popped the last bite into her mouth and hopped off the stool.

"Lead the way."

"We'll start upstairs and work our way down," I said, leading her toward the stairs, then stepping aside to let her walk up first.

I'll admit my reasons for that are less than gentlemanly. I'd told her we'd have a comfy night in and to dress casual, and she'd actually listened. Her black leggings mold to her perfect ass like a second skin and I watched, fascinated by the hypnotic rhythm of her hips as she ascended the stairs ahead of me.

The show was over much too quickly as we reached the upstairs hallway. Anjannette

turned and looked over the railing down to the living room below.

"This house belongs in a magazine. It's incredible." She pointed toward the floor-to-ceiling windows lining the far wall. "What do they look out to?"

"The back yard. Beyond that are trees."

"The view must be spectacular."

I nodded.

"Yeah, the setting is one of the things that sold me on this house. There are only trees behind it and the houses on either side of me are far enough away so it's private."

"I wish it was still light out so I could see."

"You'll just have to come back when it is."

I leaned down and gave her a quick kiss then stepped back and gestured for her to continue down the hallway. Starting at the far end, I showed her the three guest bedrooms before taking her into my room.

"Oh wow! This is...wow." She looked over her shoulder at me. "I think my entire apartment can fit in your bedroom."

I was going to tell her I doubted that was true, but I've never seen her place so I couldn't say for sure. Especially since I've lived in apartments that were smaller than my current bedroom.

Immediately inside the double doors is a sitting room, complete with a fireplace. One step down is my bedroom and ensuite bathroom. The king-sized bed called to me from across the room. I'd love nothing more than to skip dinner, lay Anjannette out naked on top of the Egyptian cotton sheets, and feast on her instead.

I ushered her out of the room and back downstairs before I could act on that. As much as I want her, we're on her timeline here. She's more important to me than a quick...or not so quick...roll in the hay.

"You've already seen the living room, kitchen, and dining rooms," I said as we walked past and through those rooms. "This is my office."

I turned on the light and stepped aside for her to enter. She walked over to the bookshelves lining the back wall and perused some of the titles then glanced back at me.

"Did you read all these?"

"I did."

"You have quite the variety."

That's a true statement. My collection is a combination of biographies, how-to books, military thrillers, and whatever else catches my attention.

"Things can get pretty boring on the road and I can only watch so much TV before going totally brain dead. My e-reader has at least ten times what's on those shelves."

"Oh my gosh!"

"I know people who have more books than that," I said with a chuckle.

"Not the books," she said, taking a picture off the shelf. "Look at how adorable you guys are. You look so young."

I looked over her shoulder at the picture of Trey, Clay, and me.

"We were young. That's from our freshman year in college"

"What's that you're holding?"

"The trophy from the regional championship our team had just won."

She placed the picture back on the shelf and inspected the others scattered throughout the room.

"This is your family?"

"That's them."

She looked at the photo of my siblings and me from when we were kids and the identical one we got taken to give to our parents as a Christmas present two years ago.

"You and your brothers look exactly alike. In fact, you all look exactly alike." She let out a self-deprecating chuckle. "What a stupid thing to say. Obviously you know that."

"It's not stupid. Most people say something similar when they see us."

"What's the age difference between all of you?"

"My parents had six kids in seven years, so there isn't much of one." I pointed to each of my siblings as I spoke. "Nicky is thirty-five, Eleni thirty-four, I'm thirty-two, Marina is thirty, Chris is twenty-nine, and Angie is twenty-eight."

"Things must have been pretty crazy at your house."

"Still are most of the time."

She studied the rest of the pictures as well as the trophies and awards Angie insisted on putting out, asking about each. We finished off the tour down in the still-unfinished basement before making our way back to the kitchen.

I peeked at the grape leaves.

"Perfect."

While I transferred them to a serving plate and pulled the *moussaka* out of the oven, Anjannette moved the place settings I'd set on the dining room table onto the kitchen island instead. She said since we'd planned a casual evening, it was only right.

Between her lip licking and moans, I was in my own private hell while we ate. But it was worth it. She really enjoyed the food I'd prepared and my mom always says there's no greater compliment than that.

She picked up her glass and drained the last of her wine then looked over at me.

"That is the best meal I've had in a long time."

"Thank you." I stood and distributed the rest of the wine between our glasses. "I also made *milopita* for dessert but we could watch a movie and have that a little later if you're too full right now."

"I'm absolutely stuffed, so watching a movie sounds great." She leaned back and patted her flat stomach. "Plus, I'll admit that I have no idea of what milo-whatchmacallit is."

"*Milopita*," I said, adding an extra accent to the word. "It's Greek apple cake."

"You *baked*?"

I nodded and she looked at me, eyes wide, and shook her head.

"What?"

"I know I said this before but it amazes me that you just seem like a normal guy."

"And again, I *am* just a normal guy."

"Leo, we were just in your office surrounded by base-ball trophies and awards. Pictures of your signing day, championships, and action shots from games. You're a professional baseball player. People collect cards with your picture on it and ask for your autograph. You're *not* just a normal guy."

Her hand gestures had gotten larger as the volume of her voice rose. I'm not sure how the fact that I baked dessert took us back to this point, but I need to nip it in the bud real fast.

I took her hands in mine, to stop them from flailing around.

"Anjannette," I said in as soothing of a voice as I could muster. "You've been spending time with me for a few weeks and I hope by now you realize that I am just a *normal* guy. The fact that I play baseball for a living doesn't change that."

She blinked up at me, seeming to be hanging on my every word, so I kissed the back of her hands then released them and continued.

"Since you don't know any other professional athletes, your perception is based on stereotypes and characters in movies. But I promise you, that isn't me. I haven't lived like a monk, but all my encounters and relationships have been above board. I have three sisters and I treat women with the same respect I'd expect any guy to treat them with. Including you, I hope."

"I'm sorry. I don't mean to treat you like a stereotype. It's just…"

She shook her head and looked down at her lap, dragging her hands through her hair. When she met my gaze again, the uncertainty in her eyes made my heart skip a beat.

"I'm not a good picker." My raised brow prompted her to continue. "Every guy I've dated has had some major issue that should have stopped me from getting involved in the first place. You're the first guy I've dated since three years of therapy made me aware of that, so I keep trying to figure out what your issue is." She gestured helplessly. "But I'm coming up blank."

"I'm not going to sit here and say I'm perfect, but I will tell you that I've never mistreated or cheated on a woman and none of my relationships have ended badly. They've just ended for one reason or another." I leaned forward and placed a soft kiss on her lips then pulled back far enough to look her in the eye. "I really like you, so hopefully you'll keep coming up blank."

ANJANNETTE

"THIS CAKE LITERALLY TASTES LIKE FALL." I shoved a forkful of *milopita* into my mouth and chewed. "It's so good."

"I'm glad you like it."

He picked up the remote and aimed it at the TV. Instead of watching a movie, we decided on *Schitt's Creek*. After our heavy conversation, we needed the comic relief.

I finished my cake then leaned forward and placed my empty dish next to his on the coffee table. As I sat back, Leo held out his arm and I took him up on his invitation. Resting my head against his chest, I wrapped my arm around his waist and enjoyed the show.

My favorite episode came on, the one where Moira Rose is shooting a wine commercial and keeps messing up. I couldn't stop myself from reciting every line. His snickers spurred me on and I sat and put my theatre degree to good use and gave him a real show, using my best Moira voice.

"In the lea of a picturesque ridge, lies a small, unpretentious winery, one that pampers its fruit like its own babies. Hi! I'm Moira Rose, and if you like fruit wine as much as I do, then you'll appreciate the craftsmanship and quality of a local vintner who brings the muskmelon goodness to his oak Chardonnay and the dazzling peach crabapple to his Riesling Rioja. Come taste the difference good fruit can make in your wine. You'll remember the experience, and you'll remember the name: Herb Irvling-ger. Burt Herngeif. Irv Herm-linger. Bing Liveheinger. Live Link. Burt Herkern. Burn...Agh! Bingo Lingfucker!"

By the end of the speech, his chuckles turned into full-blown belly laughs and I couldn't help but join in. Eventually we settled down and caught our breath.

"You're really good. I know you were a theatre major, but do you still act?"

I shook my head, trying not to obsess about the fact that Travis is the reason I stopped being active in local theatre.

"The last role I played was about seven years ago. I was Janet in a local production of *The Rocky Horror Picture Show*."

"I can totally see you in that role. You must have been perfect." He tilted his head and seemed to study me. "Although I think you'd make a great Dr. Frank-N-Furter. Especially with those patent-leather boots you were wearing the first time I saw you."

Sucking in a sharp breath, I pressed my hand against my chest and blinked back the tears that had embarrassingly appeared at his words.

"That is so sweet."

With his brow raised, Leo shifted his eyes left then right before meeting my gaze again.

"Thanks."

He raised his voice slightly, turning that single word into a question. I just smiled and settled back against his chest to watch more of the Rose family's antics.

I'm sure he thinks my reaction is crazy, but no one I've dated ever said anything good about my acting. Which is really bizarre when I think about it. I was a theatre major, for chrissake, but even the guy I was with in college treated it like an annoying pastime. So the fact that Leo not only said that I must have been perfect in the role I played, but also mentioned another one he thought I'd be great at really touched me.

Speaking of touching, I couldn't ignore the rock hard abs beneath my hand. My fingers curled of their own accord and soon I found myself slowly strumming his six-pack. Leo's heartbeat quickened beneath my ear and his chest rose and fell as he took in a deep breath and slowly let it out. His fingers tightened on my shoulder and he pulled me closer.

His respect for the fact that I wanted to take things slow is probably the biggest aphrodisiac I've ever encountered. Since our train ride a couple weeks ago, I've had sex on the brain twenty-four-seven. But jumping into bed with him immediately after that whole third-date conversation wouldn't have been a good idea no matter how much my body craved his.

I know this thing between us has the potential to be something. What that something is I have no idea, but I'll admit I'm interested in finding out. Rushing into a physical relationship before my head was totally straight would have been a sure-fire way to screw it up.

The thing is, my head *is* straight now. As straight as it's gonna get at any rate. When Leo invited me here for dinner, it was in the back of my mind that the night wouldn't end with just a kiss. I got distracted with that amazing meal he cooked, but now that I'm all digested and have my hands on his incredible body, my dirty thoughts are back in full force.

Leo's eyes shifted in my direction as I sat back to look at him. I dragged my hand over his abs and up his chest to cup his jaw. I've never initiated physical contact between us so his surprise was evident when I leaned forward and pressed my mouth against his. At first he remained perfectly still as I nipped and sipped at his lips, then with a low groan, he opened his mouth over mine and slipped his tongue inside.

From there, things escalated fast. I clutched his shoulders as he wrapped his arms around my back, pulled me against his chest, and kissed the ever-loving fuck out of me.

The kiss went on and on, long, hard, and deep. Slow, soft, and sweet. Our tongues tangled, giving and taking, demanding more with each stroke.

Needing to get closer, I shifted my leg and straddled his lap. Without missing a beat, his hands slid down to my hips and pulled me closer until his erection nestled against the apex of my thighs. My low groan vibrated between us as his impressive length pressed against my clit. His fingers tightened on my ass and held me in place as he thrust his hips up, multiplying the sensation by a million.

When I broke the kiss, desperate for a deep breath, Leo didn't miss a beat. He dragged his open mouth down my neck, licking and sucking his way to where my heart pounded at its base. My nipples tingled as he made his way up the other side and nibbled on my earlobe before pulling back to meet my gaze.

"Anjannette." His hoarse voice sounded desperate.

I shifted off his lap and stood, holding onto his shoulder for balance. Leo reached out to steady me, seeming okay with the fact that I'd ended our little encounter. Except I didn't. At least I don't want to.

"Maybe we can take this up to your room?"

His eyes widened then searched mine as he stood.

"Are you sure?"

"Yes."

He took my hand and led me up the stairs and down

the hall to his bedroom. Stepping aside, Leo gestured for me to enter the dark room ahead of him then placed his hand on the small of my back and guided me to the bed. He leaned down and with a soft click, the bedside lamp offered just enough light for me to make out the checked pattern on the dark gray comforter.

Besides the fact this will be our first time, it's been three years since I've had sex, so I should be super nervous. But I'm not. The flutters in my stomach are from anticipation and the unknown, not uncertainty.

I felt Leo behind me. He placed his hands on my hips and moved closer until his erection pressed against my ass. I turned to face him, fighting the urge to wrap my leg around his waist and rub myself against him. Instead I lifted my foot and dragged it up and down along the back of his calf.

Dark brown eyes met mine and I sucked in a startled breath at the raw hunger in his gaze. He placed his hands on either side of my face, then used his thumb and fore-finger to gently tug at my earlobes. With just the right amount of pressure, he rubbed them in a circular motion before slowly working his way around to the backside of my ear and stroking from bottom to top.

I closed my eyes and, with a groan, let my head fall back. His long fingers cradled my neck as his thumbs continued to caress me. I had no idea my ears were an erogenous zone, but when he brushed against my tragus piercing, my clit throbbed as if he'd given it the same attention.

My eyes flew open wide and met his. Leo flashed a sexy smile that promised all kinds of things. Hot things. Dirty things. And if the man could turn me on this much by just touching my ears, I definitely want to experience all the things.

That last thought must have shown on my face because Leo stopped fondling my ears and lightly stroked my cheeks. Even that innocent action sent erotic shivers down my spine.

"Are you sure?"

The fact that he asked me a second time makes me want him even more.

"I'm sure."

"Me too," he said, before crushing his mouth to mine.

Chapter Fourteen

LEO

WE DEVOURED EACH OTHER, finally giving in to the hunger we've tried to ignore for weeks. I opened my mouth wider and deepened the kiss, moving my hands down her body then back up, dragging her T-shirt along with them. I stepped back just far enough to pull it over her head. She watched, panting, as I knelt before her and slipped my fingers into the waistband of her leggings and tugged. I pulled them off one leg then the other, taking her socks off in the process.

Sitting back on my heels, I let my eyes take a lazy tour up her body, pausing at her pale pink bra before continuing up to meet her gaze. I stood and stepped forward, forcing her to back up until the backs of her thighs bumped against the bed. Sliding my hands around and down to her ass, I lifted then set her onto the soft mattress.

"You're so beautiful. Soft. Sexy as hell."

My eyes followed as I traced my fingertips along her

belly, leaving goosebumps in their wake. Resting my knee on the bed next to her, I leaned down to nip at her navel before licking my way up to the edge of her bra. Through the lace, I teased her right nipple with my tongue before drawing it into my mouth, sucking it into a tight peak while pinching and plucking the left between my thumb and forefinger. She tangled her fingers through my hair as I moved back and forth, offering each equal attention as her low moans cheered me on.

I shifted between her thighs and kissed my way across her chest. Our eyes met and held as I ran my tongue down the edge of her bra and over to spiral around her nipple. She tightened her hold on my hair, trying to direct my mouth, but I wouldn't budge. Instead of giving her exactly what she wanted, I ran just the tip of my tongue around her nipple in slow circles, spiraling to its edge before shifting away. Her little mewls were the sexiest thing I've ever heard and I wanted to hear more.

Opening my mouth wider, I lapped then sucked, feasting on her sweet lace-covered flesh. At the same time, I slid my hands down and gripped her ass, pulling her against my hard cock. Her back arched and she let out a long, low moan that ended on my name.

"Leo."

"Hmm?"

She let out another little groan and pressed her pussy against me, dragging my erection against her moist heat. Even with two thin layers between us, it was sweet torture.

I slid my hands up and around her back, fumbling to unhook her bra. I must be really out of practice because I couldn't get the damn thing to budge. Anjannette let out a sound of protest when I released her nipple with an audible pop and backed away.

Kneeling back, I pulled her up and hugged her to me

then reached around with both hands and was finally successful. I laid her back down, sliding her bra off in the process. My mouth watered at the perfect pale pink nipples I'd uncovered and I couldn't wait to taste them without the lace between us. When I went to settle back between her thighs, she put her hand against my chest and pushed me back.

"What's wrong?"

"I'm lying here in my underwear and you're still fully dressed."

I couldn't stop the smile from spreading across my face when I looked down and checked out the amazing, nearly naked woman in front of me.

"I don't see a problem with that."

She reached down and tugged at the hem of my shirt.

"Take it off."

ANJANNETTE

LEO STOOD and reached back with his right hand, grabbed his T-shirt by the neck, and yanked it over his head. He doesn't have bulky, bulging muscles, but he's solid with a six-pack and cuts in all the right places. As I admired his chest, he slipped out of his joggers until he stood in front of me in a pair of black boxer briefs that weren't doing much to contain his erection.

My fingers itched to explore, but as I started to sit to do just that, Leo grabbed my hands and dragged them over my head as he settled back against me.

"You can play next time, I promise." He dragged his

hot mouth down my neck and sucked at its base. "If you touch me right now, this will be over before it starts."

I was about to tell him that it's already started, but he placed his mouth over mine and once again, kissed me senseless. His hips thrust against mine, a scrap of lace and thin layer of cotton the only barriers between us.

Pulling his mouth from mine, he skimmed it down my body, giving each nipple a little nip, before nibbling at my navel, making me squirm. He hooked his fingers into the waistband of my underwear then backed away just enough to pull them slowly down my legs. Leaning forward, he dragged his mouth up my leg, alternately kissing and licking on the way up. When he settled between my thighs and opened his mouth over their juncture, I nearly jumped off the bed. Leo placed a restraining hand on my belly as his hot gaze met mine.

Once again, I twisted my fingers into his hair as he licked and sucked until I whimpered with need. He shifted slightly giving me a reprieve from his sensual torture, but that only lasted a second before he kicked things up a notch. Slipping his middle finger through my slick folds, he started a steady in and out rhythm while the tip of his tongue circled my clit.

I arched toward him, my breath coming in shallow pants. When his tongue slid directly over that tiny nub of nerves and flicked, I tightened my hold on his hair and let out a long, low moan. Leo glanced up and I caught his devilish smirk as he repeated the action, eliciting the same response.

His index finger joined in the action as he increased the tempo. My nipples and clit tingled, sensation zapping between them with his every stroke and suck. Shifting back, Leo kissed his way up my stomach to my breasts, never once losing the rhythm between my thighs. His thumb took over clit duty, circling as his fingers pumped in and out. As if that wasn't enough to push me over the edge, he opened his mouth over my nipple and sucked.

It was all too much.

I dug my fingers into his shoulders as pleasure concentrated in that magic spot between my thighs then burst through my entire body. Leo stayed with me, drawing out each ripple of pleasure with his fingers and mouth.

When the last of the aftershocks subsided, Leo placed a sweet kiss on the swell of my breast then moved back and removed his underwear with a quick swipe.

"Oh wow."

The corner of his mouth kicked up at my words, but the smile looked strained. I can't even imagine how he's feeling. Even after that amazing orgasm, I'm still on edge and want more.

Since I've been rubbing against him for a few weeks now, I was pretty sure Leo's packing in the penis department, but still wasn't prepared for the sight in front of me. The man is truly magnificent. Long and thick, his dick bobbed against his equally impressive abs as he leaned forward to retrieve a foil packet from the bedside table.

My pussy clenched as I watched him rip it open and roll the condom down his spectacular length. I was so mesmerized by the sight, it took me a second to realize Leo was poised at the edge of the bed, seemingly waiting for something. Permission apparently, because when I met his gaze, he raised his brow.

Holding out my arms, I reached for him, pulling him back between my legs. After that, there was no hesitation and he plunged inside.

"Christ."

That growled word was followed by a hiss of breath against my forehead as he held himself perfectly still over me. The man is large and despite the fact that I'm soaking wet, he's a tight fit. I focused on breathing as my body adjusted to the delicious invasion.

Leo pulled back just enough to look into my eyes.

"You okay?" I nodded. "You sure?"

"I'm sure."

I held on to his bulging biceps as he slowly pulled out and pumped back in at the same measured pace.

"You're so tight." Out and in. "It feels incredible." Out and in. "I just don't want to hurt you."

The combination of those sweet words and the feel of him had my inner muscles clenching each time he retreated, trying to hold him inside me.

"You won't," I said.

He flashed a smile that looked equal parts pained and sexy as hell.

"If you knew what I wanted to do right now, you wouldn't sound so confident about that."

I met his gaze.

"Do it. Because I guarantee that I want it as much as you do."

He paused, holding himself perfectly still seeming to consider my words. Then his mouth took mine in a scorching kiss and he pulled out and plunged back in, giving us both what we craved. I lifted my hips to meet his every thrust as he slammed into me over and over again, taking me higher and higher.

Pulling his mouth from mine, his sexy voice rasped against my ear.

"Anjannette."

I groaned in response and dug my fingers into the perfect globes of his ass.

He pistoned his hips even faster, picking up the pace, giving us both more of what we needed and I got sucked into a whirlwind of sensation. Wanting even more, I shifted my arms up to circle his neck and wrapped my legs around his waist, pulling him even closer. The new position had his pelvis pressing against my clit and his chest brushing my nipples with each thrust.

That did it.

"Leo."

His name started as a gasp and ended on a moan as wave after wave of pleasure coursed through my entire body. Some part of my sex-muddled brain registered the fact that Leo had let out his own shout just before he collapsed on top of me.

Chapter Fifteen

I TAPPED my thumb against the steering wheel to the opening beat of *Stone in Love* by Journey as I exited 80E heading toward my New Jersey house. I'd normally be there by this time, but there was no way I was getting out of bed earlier with Anjannette snuggled against me. It was a slow, sexy morning, followed by a big breakfast and an extra-long shared shower.

After what was basically weeks of foreplay, the sex was as incredible as I knew it would be. From the first moment I laid eyes on Anjannette, there was a chemistry between us that I've never felt with anyone. She was a little slower to realize it, but the more time we spend together, and especially after last night, I'm convinced she does.

She's definitely more relaxed than when we first met and it's so much fun watching her personality come to life. When she recited *Schitt's Creek* lines, then sat back and acted out the scene, I saw a side of her she hadn't shared with

"

me before. And after that, we shared something even more amazing.

I'm not normally so sappy when it comes to women, but this is different. *She's* different. And as I pulled into my driveway next to three familiar cars, I tried to focus on anything but her so I can get rid of the goofy smile that's been on my face since I woke up this morning.

As I walked through the back door, rapid-fire conversation assaulted my ears that I knew could only mean one thing. I made my way to the living room and my suspicions were confirmed when I spotted my three sisters each talking over each other.

I stood in the doorway and listened to them bitch about my mother pressuring them to get married and have babies. The six of us are regularly reminded that by the time she was our ages, she was already married with whatever number of children, but I'll admit the "girls" definitely get the brunt of it. They have a biological clock to consider, after all. Those are my mother's words, not mine.

"What's that smile for?" Eleni asked.

Before I could answer, Angie chimed in.

"More like *who* is it for?" She smirked. "I'm guessing things are progressing with Anjannette."

I walked across the room and settled into the oversized chair and put my feet up on the ottoman.

"What happened to call for this coven?" I asked.

"You're not going to answer?" Marina chimed in.

Looking pointedly at each of my sisters, I said, "When have I ever talked to you three about my love life?"

"Never," Eleni said. "But Angie said this one is different."

I rolled my eyes and looked over at Angie.

"*This one?* You make it sound like I'm some kind of gigolo."

"Please, you're a single professional athlete. I'm not that stupid," she said. "But Anjannette does seem different, and I'm sure that's not something you want us mentioning to mom."

"Are you blackmailing me?"

Angie shrugged. "That's a strong word. We're just curious."

"Whatever you call it, it's not gonna work. Mom already knows about Anjannette, remember?"

As if we summoned her by saying her name too many times, my mother walked through the back door like a maternal Greek Beetlejuice. She stopped at the edge of the family room, her gaze scanning my sisters before landing on me.

"I was worried," she said.

"I called and told you I'd be here later than usual."

"Leonidas, I knew when you bought that house this would happen."

"Mom, I'm here."

"It's Saturday evening. The first few weeks, you were here Friday afternoon. Then it was Saturday morning. And now this."

Her accent thickens when she's tired or upset. She's probably both right now.

I stood and walked over to give her a hug, throwing her a bone in the process. Even if it is a bit of a white lie.

"Sorry, mom. I had a breakfast date this morning."

I heard my sisters snicker and glared at them as I released my mother and led her to the chair I'd just vacated. She sat then looked up at me with manic hope in her eyes.

"That same girl?" I nodded. "Anjannette, right?"

As if there's any doubt in my mind she knows her

name. I'm just glad my mom doesn't go on the internet or she'd know Anjannette's entire history.

"Right. Anjannette."

"Is she coming for Thanksgiving dinner to meet the family?"

"Oh uh, I don't know."

"You didn't invite her? Of course she'd be welcome. There's always room for one more." She narrowed her eyes. "Does she eat?"

"Yes, she eats."

I told her about the dinner I made last night and she smiled.

"See, you were angry with me for making you help in the kitchen, but a girl likes a man who can cook." Before I could comment, she shifted her eyes to my sisters. "What are you all doing here?"

Eleni made up some bullshit excuse about discussing a job opportunity with Angie. Which was enough to distract my mother from asking why Marina is here, too. Not that it's unusual for my sisters to be together, but as far as my mother knows, this isn't usually the place they gather. They use my house as a safe haven when they want to bitch about something, and they do it in secret so no one bothers them.

My phone buzzed as Angie was explaining that she's still exploring her career options. I pulled it out of my pocket and glanced at the caller ID then held it up for my mom to see.

"I'm gonna grab this, it's Trey."

She nodded and turned her attention back to my sisters.

"Hey, what's up?"

I stood and walked toward the kitchen to get away from the chattering.

"Uh oh, are you already hanging at Chez Marakis?"

"No, my mom and sisters are here at my house."

I explained how that happened and heard the expected chuckle.

"You know you're a lucky son of a bitch to have them, right?"

"I'm well aware."

Trey's blueblood family looks great on paper, but they're totally messed up. He couldn't count on them to give him anything but a hard time. No one in my family would hesitate to give me a limb. Having them constantly up in my business is a small price to pay for that kind of loyalty and support.

"I won't keep you," he said.

"Oh please, feel free to keep me."

"Are you doing anything the first weekend in December?"

"I don't think so. Why?"

"Remember that golf tournament fundraiser Jack and Hannah's foundation is hosting?"

"Yeah."

Hannah mentioned it to me, but since I didn't plan on being in Myrtle Beach and they had enough interest, I didn't plan on attending.

"I need a fourth." I groaned. "Don't act like you totally hate the idea of coming down here."

"What I hate is golf."

"If you really don't want to, I'll find somebody else. I just figured it might give you a reason to whisk your new lady love away for a few days and hang out with your friends. Plus, even though you complain about the game, you're really good at it."

As much as I hate golf, I do like the idea of getting

away with Anjannette. If she'll go. She does have a business to run after all.

"Count me in," I said.

"I'll tell Hannah. You know she always likes to have a shit-ton of swag for us at these things."

"I'll let you know my plans after I speak to Anjannette," I said. "Speaking of plans. Are you and Nori coming to Thanksgiving dinner?"

"I think we're going to hang here. Nori is looking forward to cooking. Don't mention it to your mom yet though. I'll call and let her know."

"I won't say a word."

I shook my head as I hung up. In the last ten minutes, I was handed two opportunities to spend a weekend with Anjannette. As thrilled as I am about the prospect, I'm just not sure how she'll feel about it. After all, we've only spent the one night together.

All I can do is ask and see what she says. Hopefully it doesn't freak her out too much, because I really want her to say yes.

ANJANNETTE

THE LAST CLASS of the day ended and I was left alone in the studio. Not for long though. I have a bachelorette party coming in a couple hours and Keera should be here soon to help decorate.

After slipping into a pair of leggings and a cropped sweatshirt, I finished up some computer work then grabbed the tote of decorations from the closet. I stepped out of the office just as Keera walked into the studio.

"Hey," I said.

Without answering, she closed the door behind her, never taking her eyes off me.

"Everything okay?" I asked.

"I don't know." She narrowed her eyes. "You tell me."

"Yeah, everything's okay. Why?"

I bent down to place the tote on the floor, wincing as I stood. I'm in pretty decent shape, but what Leo and I did last night and again twice this morning has muscles I didn't know I had protesting. Not that I'm complaining. What happened between us is worth every single ache. Scenes flashed through my mind, memories of Leo's hands, mouth, and body on mine but I was ripped from my trip down memory lane by Keera's shriek.

"I knew it! You and Leo…" She finished the sentence by thrusting her hips forward a few times.

"What makes you say that?"

"At first it was just a hunch, but that twinge when you stood gave it away."

"Maybe I'm just sore from class."

"That is a possibility, but class wouldn't explain the sappy smile."

I looked at myself in the mirror, taking in my flush cheeks and the smile I haven't been able to get rid of since last night.

"Maybe I'm just happy today."

She slowly walked toward me until we were nearly nose to nose.

"Or maybe it's because Leo Marakis knocked your bottom off last night."

"Keera!" I half-screeched, half-laughed. "You're awful."

"That may be true, but I'm also right." She bobbed her eyebrows. "Right?"

I shrugged then nodded. "Right."

She pulled me into her arms and squeezed, rocking us back and forth.

"I'm so happy for you." The rocking abruptly stopped and she stepped back, still holding my shoulders. "Oh my God! You had sex with Leo Marakis." She wrinkled her nose. "And you're not going to tell me one detail, are you?"

Chuckling, I pulled away from her.

"Nope."

I squatted and dug through the tote, pulling out the decorations for tonight. The maid of honor requested the "Miss to Mrs. with all my bitches" banner and also asked if she could bring champagne, so I'm guessing it's going to be a fun night here at the studio. And after the party breaks up, Keera and I are going out for tacos and Margaritas.

"If you want to see him again tonight, we can go out some other night. After your three-year dry spell, I'd totally understand if you want another night with him."

She followed me to the wall and we each took an end of the banner and taped it up. I shook my head.

"He visits his family on the weekends, so he's in New Jersey. Remember?"

"When's he coming back?

"Tomorrow or Monday, I guess. He usually has yoga Monday afternoon, so I assume he'll be back by then."

I stepped back and checked our handiwork, making sure the banner was hanging straight.

"Don't you have plans for when he gets back?"

"Nothing specific. Should we?"

"I don't know if you should or not, but I'd think you *would*. With the way he looks at you, I doubt Leo is going to be satisfied with just one night. And I *know* you're not a one-night kind of girl."

I grabbed some more decorations from the tote and looked over at her.

"This is the new me, remember? I'm not obsessing over or expecting anything from Leo."

"It's just hard to believe that the first man you've had sex with in three years is just another guy. Throw in that it's Leo Marakis and I believe it even less. I imagine a night with him would bear repeating."

"I didn't say he's just another guy. We've been dating for a few weeks now and I have no reason to think that won't continue. I'm just not packing up my stuff to move in with him like I would have been before."

"I like how you ignored my last comment."

"Keera, we're not college freshmen anymore. I'm not gonna kiss and tell."

"Can't you make an exception?" When I shook my head, she placed her hands together like she's praying. "Just please tell me if his ass is as spectacular as it looks."

I couldn't stop my mouth from curling into a knowing smile at the thought of Leo's naked ass. It's like a perfect peach and more than once, I had the overwhelming urge to bite it. But I restrained myself and just squeezed it instead.

"It's pretty great," I said, figuring I wasn't telling her something that isn't obvious.

We finished decorating and sat on the floor facing each other, talking about our plan of attack for the party. When we first started offering bachelorette parties, we figured we'd just show the women some moves, and they'd hang out and twirl around the pole a little bit. But after doing a couple, we realized we needed something more structured.

"I think they'll like the new dance you choreographed. It's fun and everyone should be able to do it," Keera said.

With my legs straight out in front of me, I reached

forward and wrapped my hands around my feet, giving my hamstrings and lower back a good stretch.

"They should all be good with it. I had my beginner's class do it and no one had a problem, even the first timers." Spreading my legs, I walked my hands forward and rested my elbows against the floor. "They're bringing champagne, so we need to make sure they don't try to climb the poles after they start drinking."

"If they try to climb at all, we'll stop them just in case they primed the pump on the way."

"Good idea." I sat back and smiled. "If they want to climb, they can sign up for a class."

"You're turning into such a boss bitch."

Keera held up her hand for a high five and I didn't leave her hanging.

"Boss bitch, bitchy boss. Po-ta-to, po-tah-to."

Resting back on my hands, I looked around the studio. This has been my dream for years and sometimes I still can't believe it's a reality. The road to get here has been long and bumpy and uphill, but I finally made it to a place where I'm happy and comfortable in my own skin.

"Hey, where'd you go?" I shook my head in answer to Keera's question. "Your whole vibe just changed. Why?"

I looked up at the ceiling and shook my head then met her gaze.

"Leo is really great."

"Yeah." She raised her voice slightly, turning the word into a question.

"I just need to make sure I don't get totally sucked into his vortex and lose myself again."

"You won't."

"I wish I felt that positive."

She crawled over to sit next to me and wrapped her arm around my shoulders, pulling me in for a side hug.

"Aside from the fact that Leo *is* a good guy, you're not the same person you were three years ago."

"I can't help but feel like a recovering addict and getting really involved with anyone will make me slide back to where I was before."

"You're too strong now and if we're talking about Leo, he wouldn't want that to happen."

I nodded at her words, hoping like hell she's right because no matter what I keep saying, I don't do casual and where Leo is concerned, I'm already in pretty deep.

Chapter Sixteen

LEO

I SHIFTED the pizza and six-pack into one hand and rang the doorbell. The door opened and Anjannette stood in front of me, looking adorable in a pair of gray joggers and a white sweatshirt with the Peaches & Pole logo on the chest.

"Let me help you with that." She reached for the beer and moved back, standing in front of the door to hold it open. "Come on in."

I stepped over the threshold and heard the door close. Anjannette stepped around me and I followed her through the living room and into the kitchen. I've never been inside her apartment. We've always gone out and I dropped her at the door. And of course, last week, we were at my house.

"This is it," she said, holding her arms out wide. "I told you it could fit inside your bedroom."

I looked around the space. We're basically in one big

room, with the kitchen separated from the living/dining room combo by a breakfast bar. Stairs along the side wall lead up to a loft bedroom that looks over the living room area.

"It's not *that* small. I think that's an exaggeration."

"Not much of one." She reached into an upper cabinet and pulled out two dishes then set them on the table. "But honestly, it's perfect for me."

"I like the open concept, especially the loft."

"Yeah, I really like it, too. It's one of the things that sold me on the place."

She gestured for me to sit and added two slices to a plate and handed it to me. After adding one to the other dish, she sat across from me.

"Beer?" I asked.

"Sure."

I pulled two bottles from the six pack.

"Do you have a bottle opener?"

She shifted her chair sideways and grabbed one that doubled as a magnet from the refrigerator and handed it to me. I popped the top off two bottles and held one out to her.

Her mouth curled into a smile as she checked out the label.

"Eat a Peach?"

"I like the beer from Susquehanna Brewing and when I saw this one, I couldn't resist." I ended the sentence with a wink and smiled as her cheeks turned pink. "Considering your last name and all."

She rolled her eyes, but the smile she tried to conceal spoke volumes. Instead of commenting, she lifted the bottle to her nose and sniffed then took a small sip.

"Mmm, pretty good."

She took a longer drink then set the bottle down and

picked up her pizza and took a big bite. I did the same and looked around the space as I chewed.

"How long have you lived here?" I asked, before taking another bite.

"Three years." She hesitated for a few seconds then added, "I've been looking at houses for the last year or so, but haven't made any offers. This is the first place I've ever lived by myself and I'm kind of emotionally attached, as silly as that sounds."

I finished my first slice and moved onto the second.

"It doesn't sound silly."

She rolled her eyes.

"Says the man who owns a gazillion houses."

"Four," I said, punctuating the word with my beer bottle before taking a drink.

"And here I am hesitating about buying one."

"It took me a while to buy my first place, too. It's definitely a big commitment."

"Where was the first house you bought?"

"In Jersey, and I didn't buy that until six years ago. I used to stay with my parents during the off season before that. Then once I signed with the Waves, I bought a house in Myrtle Beach and a condo in St. Pete."

"So why'd you buy the house here instead of staying down South when you're not playing?"

"My family. Despite the fact that I decided to live in Scranton off season, I do like spending time with them. Living within driving distance is a good balance." I chuckled. "Besides, my mother would never forgive me if I stayed away year round. She likes all her children within a certain radius. I'm not sure what she'd do if one of us moved away permanently."

"That's actually very sweet," she said. "And it's even sweeter that you care so much."

"I wouldn't be where I am without my parents. They always encouraged me and made a lot of sacrifices so I could play travel ball and take lessons. They won't let me send them on fancy vacations or buy them anything, so I spend time with them and help out at the store when I'm around, which is what they really want." Anjannette stared at me, eyes wide. "What?"

She shook her head.

"I've never met anyone like you."

"Is that a good thing?"

Instead of answering, she stood and walked over to sit on my lap. Looping her arms around my neck, she pressed her soft lips against mine, then pulled back just far enough to look into my eyes.

"It's a very good thing."

She rested her hand on my cheek and leaned in for a lingering kiss. I wrapped my arms around her waist and pulled her closer, nibbling at her bottom lip before fully opening my mouth over hers and tasting her for the first time in nearly a week. Our tongues tangled and soon the lingering taste of peach beer disappeared and was replaced with her even sweeter essence.

Moving my hand up to twist into her hair, I pulled her closer and feasted. No teasing. No playful nips. Just our mouths pressed together, wet, hot, and demanding.

With our mouths still joined, she shifted back then returned, fully facing me, straddling my lap. I slid my hands down and cupped her ass, pulling her flush against me. Anjannette curled her fingers into my hair and held tight as she pressed her hips forward, grinding against the erection that was doing its best to bust through the zipper of my jeans.

We continued to devour each other as she rode me, the pleasure so sweet, I didn't want to stop. But it just feels too good. Much more of this and I'll really embarrass myself. I dug my fingers into her ass to slow down her movements. She got in a couple more good thrusts before breaking the kiss and dragging in a deep breath.

"Upstairs."

I didn't need her to tell me twice.

"Hold on."

She shrieked and wrapped her legs around my waist as I stood and practically sprinted toward the stairs. Navigating them as quickly as possible, I reached the top and took the few steps to put us next to her bed, loosened my hold, and let her slide down my body. She slapped my hands away when I went to remove her shirt.

"Last time, you promised I could play."

My heart skidded to a halt then pounded uncontrollably when she dropped to her knees in front of me. Her fingers brushed against the tip of my erection as she unbuttoned my jeans and I closed my eyes while she carefully eased the zipper down. Shifting her hands around, she squeezed my ass and lowered them, taking my jeans along for the ride.

"I know what I promised, but—"

That sentence ended on a long groan when my dick bobbed forward and she caught it in her tight grip and stroked.

"Nope. A promise is a promise."

I watched, fascinated, as she licked her lips then shifted closer, taking me into the warmth of her mouth in one slow, torturous slide. The heat and the drag of her tongue were enough to push me over the edge, but her little moans vibrated right through my balls, kicking the sensation up a million notches.

"*Shit.*"

Dragging my fingers through her hair, I held on tight,

because it was pretty obvious she had no intention of stopping any time soon. She licked and sucked, her hand stroking my cock while her lips and tongue drove me crazy.

I mentally conjugated Greek verbs, trying to distract myself from the goddess in front of me, but eventually gave up. What she was doing just felt too damn good.

Her fingers tightened around the base of my shaft and she slowly pulled her mouth back. But instead of releasing me, she alternately sucked at and twirled her tongue around the head over and over again. My fingers tightened against her skull as my hips jerked forward.

"Anjannette."

"Hmm?" she asked, without losing rhythm.

That little sound resonated right through my overly-sensitive dick. I managed to hold on, but know I won't last much longer.

"*Anjannette.*"

Her eyes shifted up, and the sight of her big blue eyes looking up at me with her pink lips wrapped around my cock literally weakened my knees. She released me with an audible pop and backed me up until my legs hit the bed.

"Sit."

I did as she ordered and leaned back on my elbows, taking advantage of the break in action to gain some control. She removed my jeans and tossed them aside then crawled forward and settled between my legs.

"Your body is amazing." Her fingertips trailed up my thighs to my abs before splaying out over my chest and moving back down again. "And *this* is truly spectacular."

She grabbed hold of my shaft with both hands and slowly stroked.

I closed my eyes and groaned, then opened them again when I felt her warm breath brush against me.

"Anjannette. I'm so close to the edge. If you put your mouth on me again, I'm gonna burst."

Her smile was temptation itself.

"Just lie back, relax, and enjoy."

She wrapped her mouth around me and slowly slid down until I hit the back of her throat, then reversed the process. Swirling her tongue around the head, she sucked before moving back down again and settling into a rhythm intent on pushing me over the edge. Her head bobbed up and down, faster and faster, and I fell back against the bed, dug my fingers into her hair, and did what the lady said.

I *enjoyed* until she dragged her tongue over the sensitive spot on the underside of my head and flicked.

"I'm gonna…"

My words trailed off as she slid her mouth down over me and sucked. Hard. I couldn't hold back anymore. I came with a loud groan, my hips bucking forward. Anjannette stayed with me until I settled back against the bed, eyes closed, totally spent.

The mattress dipped as she crawled onto the bed next to me. I wrapped my arm around her shoulders and she rested her head against my chest. Her fingers traced a lazy pattern on my abs as my heartbeat slowly returned to normal. Pulling her closer, I kissed the top of her head and shifted slightly sideways to wrap my other arm around her waist.

"When I recover from that, it's payback time."

She settled into the nook between my shoulder and neck, letting out a long sigh before I felt her mouth curl into a smile.

"Can't wait."

ANJANNETTE

LIGHT FILTERED through the window and I opened my eyes and groaned, cursing the fact that I didn't pull the room-darkening shade before going to sleep last night. My mouth curled into a smile at that thought. I didn't fall asleep so much as I passed out after going three rounds with Leo. The man promised payback and he absolutely delivered. And then some.

I rolled onto my side and studied him asleep beside me. His thick, dark hair is a glorious mess after being clenched in my fingers most of the night. I resisted the urge to lean over and kiss his slightly swollen lips. He looks so peaceful, I don't want to disturb him. We had quite a workout last night.

My stomach let out a loud growl at that thought. I only had one slice of pizza for dinner and we burned a lot of calories. Between the acrobatics and all the orgasms, I'm pretty sure I lost a few pounds.

I got out of bed and closed the shade then grabbed Leo's discarded T-shirt from the floor. Holding it up to my nose, I inhaled his clean, sexy scent before slipping it over my head. After donning my fuzzy unicorn slippers, I headed downstairs to use the bathroom. If I use the one upstairs, I'll definitely wake him. The toilet makes an obnoxious banging noise when it flushes. I'm used to it at this point, but I know it's startling to people who aren't.

After taking care of business, I washed my hands and examined myself in the mirror. I'm not as pretty as Leo this morning. Just-fucked hair doesn't suit me. I dried my hands and retrieved a brush from the drawer then dragged it through my hair in an attempt to bring order to the chaos. It wasn't much of an improvement but at least I cleared the knots enough so I could put it up into a messy bun without getting my fingers stuck.

I made my way to the kitchen and opened the refrigerator to see what I could scrounge up for breakfast. The shelves are pretty empty, but there is a half a loaf of cinnamon swirl bread and a pound of bacon. Thankfully I also have a few eggs and the milk is still fresh. I make a pretty decent French toast and since Keera's mom showed me how to cook bacon in the oven, it comes out perfect every time.

After starting a pot of coffee and preheating the oven, I turned on some music and got to work. David Bowie sang about changes as I beat eggs and milk together in a large bowl then added the bread and set it aside to soak.

I pulled a baking sheet from the cupboard and placed the bacon on top, thinking about how my life has changed in the past month. The pole studio celebrated its year anniversary, our first recital was a resounding success, and despite my initial reluctance, I started dating Leo.

When I said yes to that first date, I thought it would be one and done. I had no idea I'd like him so much. But seriously, what's not to like? He's sweet, thoughtful, and the sex is extraordinary. I could definitely get used to having him around. Which makes me equal parts thrilled and terrified.

After popping the bacon into the oven, I quickly washed my hands then set the timer and got to work on the French toast. I just set the platter full of golden slices in the microwave to keep warm when I heard Leo behind me.

"It smells delicious in here." He wrapped his arms around my waist and dragged his nose along the curve of my neck then placed a kiss behind my ear. "And you smell even better."

I turned in the circle of his arms and kissed his jaw.

"Better than bacon?" I raised my right brow.

"MmmHmm. Better than anything."

He pulled me against his chest and opened his mouth over mine, applying a wonderful suction that nearly brought me to my knees. I wrapped my arms around his neck, melting into his hard body as our tongues met. Things were just getting good when we jumped apart as the timer went off.

"Bacon's done," I said, pressing my hand against my chest, as if it would slow my pounding heart.

"I'll get it."

I watched him pick up the hot pads and open the oven door. He pulled out a pan of perfectly-cooked bacon and set it on the trivet I'd set out earlier. Bare-chested and bare-foot, the man looks like a wet dream come to life in his well-worn jeans. The fact that he's so comfortable in the kitchen just makes him more attractive.

Shaking my head to knock me out of my Leo-induced trance, I walked over to the cupboard and pulled out three plates. Leo reached over and took one then ripped a couple paper towels on the roll and placed them on top. I handed him a fork and he used it to transfer the bacon to the plate. When he was done, he picked up a piece and took a bite.

"Mmm, perfect."

Leo held out the half that was left and I opened my mouth. He pushed it inside with his forefinger and before he could retreat, I wrapped my lips around it and sucked, twirling my tongue over the tip for good measure before letting go.

I chewed the bacon, my mouth curled into a smile.

"You're right, it is perfect."

Before he could respond or push me onto the table and fuck me senseless, I gestured toward a chair.

"Have a seat."

He grabbed the plate of bacon and placed it on the

table as he sat. I retrieved the French toast and grabbed the syrup and set them down, then filled two mugs with coffee before joining him.

"This looks delicious."

We filled our plates and he made appreciative sounds as he quickly cleared half of his. He paused to take a drink.

"And it's even better than it looks," he said.

"I'm glad you like it. I figured I owed you a decent meal after the feast you made for me last week."

"You don't *owe* me anything, but feel free to make this for me anytime you like," he said with a wink.

"I'll be sure to keep the ingredients on hand."

"Does that mean I'm welcome to spend more time here?"

"You're definitely welcome, but I have no idea why you'd rather spend time here instead of at your amazing house."

"I'll spend time wherever you are."

I nibbled at my bottom lip, turning his words over in my head. He'd said them so casually, as if he didn't just utter the sweetest thing any man has ever said to me. Instead of spiraling into memories of every shitty guy I've ever dated, I just smiled.

"We'll have to mix it up so we don't get bored hanging out in the same place."

"Sounds like a plan." He popped a piece of bacon into his mouth and rested his forearms on the table as he chewed. "Speaking of mixing up locations, I know it's late notice, but do you have any plans for Thanksgiving?"

"I'm going to Keera's. Why?"

"I was going to ask if you wanted to come spend it with me and my family."

"Oh." I blinked, processing his words. "I appreciate the invite, but I already made plans to go to Keera's."

"That will probably be a good time."

"Yeah, her family is great, especially her grandmother. I always have fun with them."

"Do you have plans the following weekend?"

"Just work. Why?"

"Trey asked me to be a fourth in a charity golf tournament and I was wondering if you'd like to be my date."

"To a *golf tournament*?"

"There's the tournament, then a reception later that night, and a brunch on Sunday. So you wouldn't just be bored stiff watching golf."

"Where is it?"

"In Myrtle Beach."

"Oh wow. Um…" I looked at him and shook my head. "I don't think I can get away for a whole weekend."

"I kind of figured that, especially with the late notice but wanted to ask just in case." His mouth twisted into an adorable frown. "It just sucks that I won't see you for two whole weekends. Think you can squeeze me in during the week?"

"Definitely."

I forced a smile, but it felt wobbly so I picked up my mug and took a sip of coffee before Leo could see it. I'm not sure how I feel about meeting his whole family right now, but a long weekend in Myrtle Beach sounds amazing. But I have a business to run and I don't want to fall into past behaviors and drop everything for a man, even if he seems different from all the others.

Chapter Seventeen

LEO

MY PARENTS WALKED out the back door of the store just as I just turned into the parking lot. I pulled into the spot next to their car, then quickly got out and took the big box my dad was carrying off his hands. After placing it into their trunk, I leaned down to give my mom a kiss on the cheek. She didn't waste a second bringing up Anjannette.

"I'm so disappointed your girl couldn't make it. I was looking forward to meeting her," she said.

"Annita, he just got here. Give him a minute before you harass him," my dad said.

"Leo knows I'm not harassing him, just stating facts."

I'm sure this won't be the last time this weekend I'll hear her *just stating facts*.

"She already had plans for the holiday."

I'm sure that won't be the last time I'll be saying that either.

I was going to say I'd bring her some other time, but if I do, my mother won't let me rest until I deliver Anjannette to her front door. So I kept the thought to myself.

"Maybe she'll be here for Christmas if you make it a point to ask her before she makes other plans."

"I'll mention it when I talk to her." Then in an attempt to change the subject, I nudged my head toward the store and said, "Anything special you need done?"

"There are a couple of orders being picked up late, but that's it. Nicky is in there and already started cleaning."

That last sentence just left my dad's mouth when my brother walked out the back door of the store carrying two garbage bags, which he tossed into the dumpster.

"I appreciate you helping out," my mom said.

"Anytime."

"You're a good boy, Leonidas Marakis." She smiled and patted my cheek.

I smiled.

"Okay, I'll see you guys later."

My siblings and I have been trying to get our parents to cut back on their hours, but it's not easy getting them to leave. They're used to working at least twelve hours a day, but now that they're financially-independent empty nesters, they should be able to relax and enjoy themselves more. Of course when we say that, my mother tells us if she had grandchildren to spend time with, she wouldn't work all the time.

We waved as they drove off and I followed my brother inside.

"What still needs to be done?"

"Nothing really. Angie was here earlier helping out so I was able to get the paperwork done. After these orders are picked up, you can mop out there, but everything else is good," he said. "I was gonna tell you not to come, but you know they wouldn't have left if you weren't here."

I hooked my foot around the rung of the stool, pulled it toward me, and sat.

"I planned on being here anyway, so it's not a big deal."

Nicky leaned against the counter.

"You know she's already planning the wedding."

"She's been planning all of our weddings since we were born."

"Yeah, but now you have an actual person she thinks you're going to marry."

"If you were a good big brother, you'd get married to take the pressure off the rest of us."

He crossed his arms over his chest and scowled.

"Not me. I'm not crazy enough to get that involved again," he said. "Once bitten, twice shy."

"So what do you do?" He raised his right brow. "Don't act like you don't know what I'm asking. Mom might think you're celibate, but I'm not buying it."

"I get by."

"You just don't get involved."

"Exactly," he said. "And I make it a point to *not get involved* past a certain radius from here so she doesn't find out."

While this conversation might make my brother seem like a total douche, he's not. If you've ever seen the movie *The Wedding Singer*, his story is the same as Adam Sandler's character, Robbie Hart.

Nicky dated a girl through high school and college, and they got engaged. Everything seemed great, but when she left him standing at the altar, it was pretty obvious Daphne didn't agree with that.

"She had such high hopes when you, Eleni, and

Marina all had long-term relationships in high school and college."

"I know we joke about it, but sometimes I do feel bad." He held out his hand and shook his head. "Not bad enough to try to walk down the aisle again, mind you."

"It is kind of funny that out of six kids, none of us are married."

"You say funny, Mom calls it a tragedy."

"Which is why none of us tell her when we're dating someone."

"Except for you."

"*I* didn't tell her anything. Angie did."

"But you didn't deny it." He rubbed his chin then tapped it. "And why is that?"

"Because she already knew."

"Still, you're in Scranton. She'd have no way of knowing."

"Yeah she would. She'd know as soon as the denial left my mouth," I said. "Omitting the truth is one thing, but totally lying is a whole other story. She sees right through all of us."

He opened his mouth to say something, but the bell over the front door rang as Joe Gatto walked through.

"I appreciate you staying late," he said. "I was supposed to be off today but ended up going into the office and of course got stuck there."

"No problem," Nicky said.

I stood and grabbed two boxes off the rack and set them on the counter.

When he reached for his wallet, I ripped off the order slip and pushed the boxes toward him.

"It says the order is paid for, so you're good."

We chatted for a minute before the bell was dinging again as he left.

I looked over at the lone box on the rack.

"You can go if you want," I said. "No reason for both of us to stay here for one order."

"You just don't want me asking questions about *Anjannette*."

He said her name in a sing-song voice then added some kissing noises.

"Real mature."

"But you're not denying what I said."

"What do you want to know?"

"Angie said you really like this girl."

"That's not a question."

"Is it true?"

"Yeah, it's true."

"So it's serious?"

"I think it is. If not, it's getting there."

"Okay." He drew out the word, letting me know he had no clue what I meant.

"I was immediately interested the first time I saw Anjannette, but she wasn't as eager to date me," I said. "She hasn't shared specifics with me, but from what I understand, her last relationship wasn't great and it left her gun-shy." I thought about the difference in her the past few weeks and added, "But she seems to be getting over that and we're moving forward. She's really opening up and things are going well. I'm just making sure to take it slow so I don't scare her off."

"Just make sure you find out about what happened in her past so you know what you're dealing with before you get in too deep. There are some things people can't get over no matter how much time goes by."

I know he's speaking from personal experience so I didn't ask him to elaborate. It's been over a decade since Daphne failed to show up at the church, but Nicky still doesn't talk about it or her. I just hope whatever happened between Anjannette and her ex didn't leave as deep a scar.

ANJANNETTE

I RINSED soap suds off a platter then handed it to Keera to dry. Her mom and grandma did most of the prep work and cooking, so cleaning up is the least we can do. The dishwasher is already full and running. We're just finishing up the last of the big items before setting out dessert.

"What are you up to this weekend?" Keera asked.

"Not much. Since the studio is closed, I think I'll just curl up on the couch under a comfy blanket and find something good to binge watch. Maybe do some online shopping." I cleaned the last serving bowl and set it on the drying rack for her to grab when she's ready. "As boring as it sounds, you're welcome to join me."

"Granny Vi and I decided to have a *Gilmore Girls* marathon tomorrow, complete with tons of food, just like Lorelai and Rory do when they have movie nights. Why don't you come?"

I rinsed out the sink and turned off the water, then grabbed a towel and dried my hands.

"I don't want to intrude."

"For chrissake, you're not intruding," Granny Vi said as she entered the kitchen. "You're family and we'd love to have you with us."

"Thanks. What time does the marathon start?"

"Eleven."

"Great. I'll bring the candy."

"Excellent."

Violet Jordan is one of my favorite people in the world. She's seventy-six and more energetic than me most days. Of course that could be due to the fact that she always has a fresh pot of coffee available and drinks copious amounts daily. As if she heard my thoughts, she grabbed a mug from the cupboard and filled it with coffee then sat at the kitchen table. Keera and I finished putting the platters and bowls away then joined her.

We heard cheers and shouts from the living room where the rest of Keera's family had gathered after dinner to watch football.

"Must be a good game," I said.

"Our marathon tomorrow will be better," Granny Vi said and took a sip of coffee. "I'm actually surprised you're not with your young man for the holiday. Keera said you two have been getting close."

I shifted my eyes toward Keera then looked down at my fingers as I twisted them together. Since I'd turned down Leo's invitation, there wasn't a reason to mention it.

"Something you want to tell us?" Keera asked.

"Not really."

"Anjannette, did Leo ask you to spend Thanksgiving with him?"

"Yes he did."

"Then why are you *here*?"

"Because he just asked me Saturday morning and I already had plans to come here." She raised her brow. "What?"

"That's a cop-out and you know it."

"How is it a cop-out?"

"Because we all would have understood if you went there instead of coming here."

"I'm sure you would have, but I didn't want to change my plans."

"Why?"

Granny Vi cut in before I could answer.

"I'm still in awe of the fact that you're dating Leo Marakis. He's such a cutie," she said. "And Keera said he's really sweet."

"He's definitely both of those things."

"So you like him?"

"I do."

Her mouth curled into a cat-that-ate-the-canary smile.

"Then I'll repeat Keera's question. Why are you here?"

I took in a deep breath and let it out on a sigh.

"I already had plans to come here." When Keera started to argue, I held up my hand to stop her. "You know that I have a history of changing my whole life to fit into the life of whoever I'm dating. I'm breaking that cycle."

Granny Vi put her hand over mine and squeezed.

"Anjannette, at some point you're going to have to trust your instincts."

I shook my head.

"I don't have good instincts where men are concerned."

"Sure you do. They just got muddled for a bit," she said. "My Marty and I fell in love in high school and I know how fortunate I was that we found each other so young. He was a good man and I loved him until the day he died. You and Keera weren't that lucky, so now you have to forget about all the things every shitty guy you dated put you through so when you meet a good one, you don't make him pay for them."

"I don't think I'm making Leo pay."

Keera rolled her eyes.

"Until recently, you kept that poor man at arm's length when it's obvious he's crazy about you," she said. "Plus he's such a sweetheart and even better, I love the way he treats you."

I love the way he treats me too, but then when I'm not with him, I second guess things. But Keera has been rooting for this relationship from the start and that's something she *never* did with the other guys I dated. Most times she begged me not to get involved.

"Just don't be a Miranda," Granny Vi said.

"I don't know what that means."

"Like Miranda from *Sex and the City.* She was horrible to that poor Steve at the beginning. He was a sweet guy and treated her well, but she kept expecting the worst and sometimes wasn't so nice to him."

I chuckled, not even surprised she watched that show.

"I definitely don't want to be a Miranda."

"He's visiting his family for the whole weekend, right?" Keera asked.

"Yes."

She pushed my phone toward me.

"Then call him right now and tell him you're driving there tomorrow to spend the rest of the weekend with him."

I shifted my gaze between her and Granny Vi then picked up my cell and stood.

"Okay." I turned to walk away then stopped. "I also didn't tell you that he's playing in a charity golf tournament and asked me to go to Myrtle Beach next weekend."

"You told him yes, right?" Keera asked, although judging from the look on her face, she knows the answer to that isn't what she wants it to be.

"I said I didn't think I could get away for the weekend because of the studio."

"I'll cover the studio. Call him right now and tell him you can get away."

"Are you sure?"

"Positive."

I leaned down and hugged her and kissed her cheek, then did the same to Granny Vi.

"You two are seriously the best. I'm going to go upstairs and call him."

Chapter Eighteen

LEO

AFTER A QUICK SHOWER, I got dressed and double-checked that the house looks decent. I usually keep things pretty neat, but Angie is another story. She's not a total slob, but she has a tendency to leave things all over the place. There are usually glasses and plates on the end tables and now that the weather is cooler, socks can be found scattered wherever she took them off.

If I told her Anjannette was coming she'd clean up, but I didn't tell anyone. I figured I'd surprise them, especially my mother. If I gave her advance notice, she'd make a huge fuss.

Hell, I still can't believe Anjannette will be here any minute. When she turned down the invitation to Thanksgiving dinner, I never even thought to ask her if she'd want to come and spend the weekend. So when she called me last night and asked if she could join me, I was thrilled. The fact that she's also accompanying me to Myrtle Beach is just the icing on the cake. Things with us are definitely moving forward.

I'd just washed the last of Angie's dirty dishes when I heard a car pull into the driveway. After drying my hands, I walked out the back door just as Anjannette pulled her bag from the back seat and slammed her car door shut. She looked over and smiled at me as I stepped off the deck.

"Let me help you with that." I took the bag from her then leaned down and gave her a quick kiss. "How was the drive?"

"Pretty good. I didn't hit any traffic so I just cranked up the tunes, set the cruise control, and cruised along."

I opened the screen door and stepped aside for her to enter the kitchen ahead of me.

"Oh wow." She looked over her shoulder. "This is such a great kitchen. I love the mix of old and new."

"Thanks, but I can't take credit for any of it. Angie managed the whole remodel."

She trailed her fingers along the butcher block top of the island.

"Is this original?"

"Yeah, it was sanded down and stained. The base is original too and so are the subway tiles. They just had to be cleaned and regrouted." I pointed toward the wall and backsplash across the room. "The cabinets are new. The original ones were avocado green and made out of particle board."

"Sounds attractive."

"Oh it was. Add in the matching appliances and dark brown linoleum flooring and it was

like being transported through a time warp." We walked into the next room with its cream walls and warm Earth tones. "This used to be a dining and living room with a big arch between them but I knocked that down and made one big room."

"Angie decorated your house in Scranton too, right?"

"Everything except the basement."

"She's really good. She should be an interior decorator."

I gestured toward the stairs and followed her up.

"I actually told her that but she just wrinkled her nose and said she'd think about it. So I'm guessing that's a no."

We reached the top and I pointed toward my room, which was right in front of us. Anjannette turned to face me after we entered and looped her arms around my neck. I dropped her bag and placed my hands on her waist.

"This is so cozy. I love it."

"The room isn't as large as the one in Scranton, but the bed is the same."

I bobbed my eyebrows then leaned down and pressed a kiss to the corner of her mouth. When I moved to pull back, she held me in place and nibbled at my bottom lip. I was happy to follow her lead when she opened her mouth and brushed her tongue against mine.

Sliding my hands down, I squeezed her ass then held her tight as I backed up and sat on the edge of the mattress. She rested her knees on either side of my legs and straddled my lap. Our collective groans echoed through the room when I grabbed her ass again and pulled her flush against me.

"I'm so glad you're here," I muttered against her lips when I pulled back just long enough to change the angle of the kiss.

She curled her fingers into my scalp and thrust her hips forward.

"Mmm, I can tell."

I was about to flip around and splay her in the middle of the bed when I heard the front door slam shut.

"Leo, who's parked in the driveway?" Angie shouted.

I'm surprised she's home so early. She went shopping with Eleni, Marina, and whoever else and they're usually out all day.

Anjannette hopped off my lap and looked at me with wide eyes. I stood and gave her a last lingering kiss then took her hand and led her back downstairs.

We found Angie sitting cross-legged on the couch surrounded by shopping bags.

"Who's parked in the driveway?" she asked again. When I didn't comment, she glanced over her shoulder. "Anjannette," she screamed and jumped off the couch. She pulled her into a hug then released her and slapped me on the shoulder. "Why didn't you tell me Anjannette was coming?"

"I figured we'd surprise you."

She twisted her mouth.

"You didn't want mom to know and thought I'd tell her."

I placed my hand on the small of Anjanette's back and led her to the oversized chair and settled in next to her.

"No, I knew you'd tell Eleni and Marina and one of them would tell mom. Then she would have driven me crazy all last night and this morning."

"I don't tell Eleni and Marina *everything*." I raised my brow. "What? I don't!"

"I'm not going to argue with you about it," I said with a chuckle.

She flashed her pouty lip, but her mouth quickly curled into a smile as her eyes shifted between Anjannette and me.

"So what's the plan for the weekend?" she asked.

"We'll go to mom and dad's tonight and since the weather is supposed to be so nice, I thought we'd go for a hike tomorrow." I shifted and looked down at Anjannette. "Nothing crazy, but there's somewhere I think you'll like."

"That sounds like fun," she said with a smile.

"And I figured we'd play tomorrow night and Sunday by ear. I'm sure that even if mom doesn't plan something, someone in the family will."

"That's if they like me," Anjannette said.

"What's not to like?"

I kissed her forehead and wrapped my arm around her.

"He's right, Anjannette. They're going to love you." Angie stood and collected her bags. "You might want to watch *My Big Fat Greek Wedding* to prepare her for what to expect."

ANJANNETTE

I'D CHUCKLED when Angie mentioned *My Big Fat Greek Wedding*, but that movie isn't far off from what I'm experiencing. I'm doing my best to remember everyone's name, but there are so many people it's not easy.

I'm in a sea of tall, dark, beautiful people who all look alike. Name tags would be helpful, but since there are none handy, I've focused my attention on Leo's parents and siblings. They're easy enough to remember, and thankfully he hasn't left my side much.

In between trying to keep up with the different conversations surrounding me and answering his family's questions, I managed to clear my plate for the second time, wishing I wore stretchier pants. Resisting the urge to pop the button on my jeans, I sat back in the chair and rested my hand against my stomach. I noticed Leo's mom watching me and I smiled.

"Everything is delicious, Mrs. Marakis."

Every available surface in the kitchen and dining room is covered with platters of food, each dish better than the last. According to Leo, this is similar to the spread his mother makes every Sunday. The only difference is the traditional Thanksgiving fare that's leftover from yesterday. I can't even imagine.

"Please call me Annita."

She'd told me that twice before, but I keep forgetting.

"Annita," I said with a smile.

"Would you like something else?"

"Oh no, thank you. I'm stuffed."

"There's baklava. Leo said you like that." She smiled at my answering groan and patted my hand. "Take a break. You can have some in a little bit." Turning her attention to Leo, she said, "Go get some more wine. Your girl's glass is almost empty."

"Just water, please," I told him as he stood.

Aside from the fact I'm so full I'm ready to bust, I've already had at least two glasses of wine. I can't give an exact amount because people kept topping me off through dinner. The last thing I want to do is get fall-down drunk in front of Leo's family. I don't even want to get buzzy enough that I say or do something embarrassing.

Leo returned carrying two bottles of wine and a glass of water.

"Thank you."

He handed me the water and I took a big sip. That drink totally topped me off and I immediately had to pee. I set down the glass and leaned closer to Leo.

"I need to use the bathroom. I'll be right back."

I stood and as I walked out of the dining room and made my way toward the half bath in the hall. My hand was on the knob, but before I could turn it, Angie approached and hooked her arm through mine.

"Uncle Markos just used that so you definitely don't want to go in." She wrinkled her nose and steered me toward the stairs. "You can use the one upstairs."

As we walked up the stairs, I was torn between looking at the pictures hanging on the wall and getting to my destination as quickly as possible. My full bladder won and I followed Angie to the top of the stairs and down the hallway. She stepped aside and gestured for me to enter the bathroom.

"Thanks so much."

I stepped inside and closed the door, then looked around the large room while I did my business. The room is large and bright with a double vanity and huge clawfoot tub. Similar to the rest of the house, it's neat and tidy, with a style that's more traditional than modern. I like it. In fact, I like his whole family. They've been welcoming and friendly, and even when they were shooting questions at me left and right, it felt more like a conversation than an interrogation.

After washing my hands, I opened the door and barely stifled a screech when I nearly crashed into Angie.

"Sorry, I didn't mean to scare you," she said. "But I wanted to speak to you alone."

"What's up?"

"Is Clay seeing anyone?"

"I don't think so." I smiled. "Are you interested in him?"

"I've *always* been interested in him. But I was only fourteen when we met and he still treats me like I'm a kid."

"We're not all that close, but I'd be happy to put in a good word for you."

"That'd be great, but I was hoping maybe you could kind of play matchmaker. You know, I'll come to visit and the four of us could go out. No pressure. No expectations." She shrugged. "I'm hoping if he spends time with me, he'll see me as something other than Leo's little sister."

"I can do that," I said. "Leo and I are going to Myrtle Beach next weekend, but maybe the weekend after that?"

Her eyes widened.

"You guys are going away together?" I nodded. She squealed and squeezed my hands. "That's so awesome."

"He's in a golf tournament and asked me to go along."

"You know he really likes you, right?"

I half-shrugged, half-nodded.

"I don't understand it, but he seems to."

"What do you mean? You're awesome."

"Thanks." I looked over her shoulder at the wall full of pictures and zeroed in on the large one in the center. "Oh mygosh, look at all of you. So cute."

Angie chuckled.

"Not a very subtle change of subject, but I'll let it go for now."

"I appreciate that. And while I'll admit I am trying to change the subject, I really am interested in the pictures."

I turned my attention back to the picture that had caught my attention. Angie is a baby in her mother's arms so Leo would be around three. I looked at the boys and pointed at the one I figured was him.

"I'm guessing that's Leo." She nodded. "I'm basing that totally by age because the three of them could be triplets."

She named her other siblings and then we moved onto

the other pictures. Most are posed portraits, but there are a few candid shots. Once I looked at every last photo, Angie nudged her head toward the stairs.

"There are more downstairs."

Leo looked over as we descended the steps and joined us in the hallway.

"Everything okay?" he asked.

"Yeah, I was just checking out the pictures upstairs."

"And I was about to show her the rest," Angie said with a smirk.

"Just be quiet about it." He groaned when his mother approached. "Too late."

Annita put her arm around my shoulders and pointed at the pictures, describing any events taking place in the candid shots in colorful detail.

"If I'd known you were coming, I would have gotten the photo albums out," she said after we looked at the last photo.

"That's okay," Leo said. "I think Anjannette has been bored enough for one weekend."

"Oh I'm not bored at all. I love looking at family photos."

"Then I'll tell you what," Annita said. "You come over tomorrow night and we'll make a baklava for you to take home and look through some photo albums."

"I'd love that, but I think Leo mentioned that we're going hiking."

I looked over at him and raised my brow. Out of the corner of my eye, I saw Annita and Angie doing the same.

"We'll only be gone a few hours so we can come over if you'd like."

"I would definitely like."

"Wonderful," Annita said. "Oh! I'll pull out the family movies, too."

Leo groaned behind me and I glanced over my shoulder and smiled.

"I can't wait."

Chapter Nineteen

LEO

I FOLLOWED Anjannette to the top of the rock steps and directed her to the left, then to the left again as we approached a fork in the trail. The Palisades Interstate Park is one of my favorite places to hike. The trails range from easy to challenging, and I've explored them all, sometimes alone and other times with my brothers or Trey.

Today, we decided to take Carpenter's Loop, which is considered moderate. Anjannette is in great shape, but since this isn't something she's used to, it seemed like a good compromise. Plus, the view from up here is amazing.

We reached a panoramic viewpoint overlooking the river and I stopped walking and gestured toward the bench and removed my backpack.

"Let's take a break here. We can have a snack and enjoy the view."

She placed her right foot on the bench seat and stretched, then did the same with the left before folding at the waist and touching her toes. I pulled out two bottles of water then sat, placing the backpack on the ground at my feet.

"You doing okay?" I asked as Anjannette joined me on the bench.

"Yeah, I feel good."

She took in the view as she twisted the cap off the bottle I handed her then took a drink.

"Is that the George Washington Bridge?"

"It is."

"Leo, this is incredible." She looked over at me. "Thank you for bringing me here."

I took her hand in mine, lifted it to my lips, and placed a kiss on her knuckles before entwining our fingers together.

"Thank you for coming. And not just on this hike, but to visit in general. I wasn't lying when I said I was thrilled when you called."

She looked down at her hands then out at the water.

"I'll admit, I was a little nervous, but I'm glad I'm here. I'm having a good time."

When I didn't comment, she shifted her gaze to me.

"Why were you nervous?"

"Oh, I don't know. Calling you up and inviting myself to stay with you? Meeting your family for the first time?"

I shifted closer and smiled.

"First of all, you had an invitation. So you weren't inviting yourself to stay. And as far as my family goes, I know they can be a lot, but they mean well."

"Meeting them was a little overwhelming at first. In case you didn't notice, there are a lot of people in your family."

She didn't even meet all of them, but she'll find that out eventually.

"You know, we don't have to go to my mom's tonight if you don't want to. I know yesterday was probably a lot. We can just have a quiet night at my house."

"I definitely want to go. I'm not sure if I'm more excited about learning how to make baklava or looking through the photo albums."

I groaned.

"I'm sure my mom will find the most embarrassing pictures to show you."

"I doubt an embarrassing picture of you exists. You looked perfect in every one I looked at last night."

"I'll refrain from commenting. I don't want to tip my hand before I see what she brings out."

I let go of her hand and reached into my backpack and pulled out a thermos and set it on the bench between us.

"Are you trying to distract me with food?"

"Would I do that?"

"I think you would," she said. "But I won't complain because I know what's in that thermos and my mouth is already watering."

"Not a traditional hiking snack, but it works," I said as I pulled a container of pita chips out of my backpack.

"No, it's a hundred times better." She picked up the thermos and removed the top then inhaled deeply. "This is salty, garlicky goodness."

Reaching for a pita, she scooped up some Greek layered dip and popped it into her mouth. Her groan vibrated straight through my balls. She's made some sexy sounds in bed, but nothing like that. Now I have a goal.

"I brought some *pasteli* too."

"If I lived with your mom, I wouldn't do anything but eat."

I finished chewing and swallowed, then took a quick drink.

"That's pretty much what we do," I said with a chuckle. "But enough about my gang. Tell me about your family."

"They were quiet. Especially compared to yours."

"Most are."

"My parents were older when they had me and they were both only children, so I didn't have any aunts, uncles, or cousins hanging around. For the most part, it was just us. Once I met Keera in college, we started spending holidays with her family."

I grew up surrounded by so many people, I can't imagine what she's describing. It sounds lonely. Before I had to comment, Anjannette continued.

"I watched a lot of TV and used to amuse myself by doing little skits. It's probably how I ended up being a theatre major."

"That makes sense."

"My parents really were great though. Even though I was so different from them, they loved me and were always supportive. I still miss them."

"Of course you do. I imagine you always will. I'm so sorry you lost them."

"Me too." She looked over at me and blinked away tears then gave me a wobbly smile. "It was bad when my dad died, but at least I still had my mom. When she died, I felt so alone. Sometimes I still do."

The last words were said in a hoarse, anguished voice. I moved the empty containers to the other side and shifted closer, pulling her into my arms. She rested her head against my shoulder and I rubbed her back in long, soothing strokes until she totally relaxed. Then I wrapped my arm around her shoulders and just held her close.

We sat like that for a long time, until the moment was interrupted by other hikers. I kissed the top of her head.

"I guess we were lucky we were alone this long."

She pulled back and nodded then looked me in the eye. My stomach twisted at her serious expression.

"Thank you."

"What for?"

"Being so understanding."

"Who wouldn't be understanding about losing your parents?"

She shook her head and snorted.

"You'd be surprised."

I'm guessing she's referring to her ex, so I didn't push for more details. We're having too nice a day, and even though things just got a little heavy talking about her parents, throwing him into the mix would totally ruin the mood.

I pulled the sunblock out of the side pocket of my backpack and handed it to her.

"Your face is getting red."

While she applied more sunblock, I put the empty containers and garbage into the backpack.

"Is it all rubbed in?"

I reached over and rubbed at her cheek until the white streaks were gone then leaned over to give her a quick kiss.

"Ready to head back down?"

Anjannette took in a deep breath and let it out as her eyes scanned the view, then she looked at me and smiled, the melancholy seemingly over.

"We probably should. I want to shower before we head to your parents'."

"I need a shower too." I bobbed my eyebrows. "Maybe we should take one together to conserve water."

She kissed me on the cheek and stood.

"*That* sounds like a great plan."

"Let's go."

After I shrugged into my backpack, we made our way back to the trail and walked double-time back to the parking lot.

ANJANNETTE

THE RIDE from the park to Leo's house seemed to take forever. We didn't hit traffic, so I'm sure it didn't take any longer than the drive there, anticipation is just making it seem that way. Leo must have felt the same way because every once in a while, he'd glance in my direction and his hand would tighten on the steering wheel.

After what seemed like an eternity, we pulled into his driveway. We both jumped out of the car and he came around to my side, took my hand, and led me across the deck and through the back door. He paused just long enough to drop his backpack on the kitchen table, then we continued up the stairs and into his room. My heart pounded as he closed the door behind us.

He slowly walked toward me, placed his hands on my hips, and backed me against the wall next to the bathroom door. Lowering his head, he nibbled at my bottom lip before pressing his mouth against mine. Slow and sweet, our mouths melded together and I wrapped my arms around his neck and melted into his hard body as our tongues met.

I matched his tongue stroke for stroke and twisted my fingers into his hair, pulling him closer. He groaned against my mouth and pushed his hips forward, pressing me into the wall. I'd expected him to thrust against me, but he just held me in place and feasted on my mouth.

The man should write a book on how to kiss, or maybe teach a class. He's truly a master. And those oral skills definitely work well in other places. My pussy clenched at that thought.

He slid his hands beneath my shirt and stroked up along my waist, breaking the kiss just long enough to pull my shirt over my head and toss it on the floor then did the same with my sports bra. Taking a step back, he looked down, his gaze devouring me. My boobs might not win the size prize, but they're perky as hell and to quote Teri Hatcher in that old *Seinfeld* episode, "They're spectacular." Not to mention super sensitive.

Sensation zinged down to my clit when he cupped each breast and flicked his thumbs against my nipples. My head banged against the wall as I arched my back and let out a long, low moan.

His warm breath brushed my skin and a second later I felt the flat of his tongue drag along the underside of my right breast before he latched on. My knees turned to jelly as his tongue swirled, drawing my nipple further into the moist heat of his mouth. His hand teased the left, pinching, rolling, and tugging and I pressed my hips against him, seeking relief for my throbbing clit.

Shifting his hands to my ass, he pulled me closer and thrust forward over and over as his mouth moved back and forth, giving my breasts equal attention. His erection rubbed against me, but wasn't hitting the right spot. I wrapped my leg around his thigh and tilted my hips.

"Leo."

My desperate voice echoed through the room and he shifted, pressing me closer to the wall as he lifted me. I wrapped my legs around his waist and he moved between my thighs, putting his hard cock exactly where I needed it.

His mouth took mine again, his tongue teasing, hot,

wet, and demanding as his hips pulsed, pushing me closer to the edge. It wouldn't take much more for me to come, but I didn't want to do that without him inside me.

I dragged my mouth from his, panting to catch my breath.

"Condom."

That single word was all I could manage, but he didn't need to be told twice. He set my

feet back on the floor and after making sure I was steady, walked across the room and pulled a condom from the top drawer of his bedside table. He paused just long enough to remove his T-shirt and toss it on the floor.

My gaze locked on his tented shorts as he walked back toward me and I enjoyed the view as he removed them and his boxer briefs with one swipe. My hand reached out of its own volition to touch his erection as it bobbed forward. He wrapped his fingers around my wrist, halting my movement.

"Uh-uh," he said. "You do *not* want to do that right now."

I kept my gaze focused on his magnificent cock and bit my lower lip then slowly dragged it between my teeth before looking him in the eye.

"That's debatable," I said with a smirk and wrapped my hand around his shaft and stroked.

His sexy chuckle vibrated through every erogenous zone in my body.

"When did you become such a brat?"

"She's always been there. She was just hiding for a while."

Before I could think about why I hid any part of myself, he stepped back, pulling himself from my grasp. I was about to protest when he hooked his thumbs into the waistband of my leggings and pulled them down, then did the same with my thong. He stepped back and ripped open the foil packet and I watched, fascinated, as he slowly rolled the condom down his long, thick length. Stepping forward, he pressed his chest against my aching nipples.

"Well it seems she's back."

"Is that a problem?"

He kissed his way along my jaw and nibbled at my earlobe before whispering against my ear.

"I told you before, I'll take you anyway I can get you."

I don't understand why that is, but I'm certainly not going to complain. Especially when he lifted me up again and pushed forward, this time filling me with his hot, hard cock. Wrapping my arms around his neck, I held on tight as he moved in and out, each thrust harder and shorter.

"You feel so good."

Leo shifted me higher against the wall, the movement causing my nipples to brush against his chest. They tightened and tingled as my inner muscles clenched. He let out a low groan and pushed into me and stilled, the base of his shaft pressing against my throbbing clit.

"Hold on."

His words barely registered when I felt myself spinning. I did what he told me and held on as he lowered us both to the floor while still buried inside me. I looked up at him and smiled.

"That's pretty impressive."

"Glad you think so." He slowly pulled out. "Let me see if I can impress you some more."

He plunged back inside me with one hard stroke. I braced my feet against the floor as he moved in and out, picking up the pace with each thrust, giving us both what we needed.

I dug my fingers into his ass and arched my back as his every stroke sent zings of pleasure through my entire body.

It was too much. Way too much.

My orgasm slammed through my body and I let out a long, hoarse moan. Some part of my brain registered the fact that Leo had let out his own shout just before he collapsed on top of me.

Chapter Twenty

LEO

KEERA OPENED the front door of Anjannette's apartment as I walked up the sidewalk.

"Hey." She stepped aside for me to enter. "Anjannette is upstairs grabbing some last-minute items. Come on in."

I walked into the living room and settled into the over-sized chair.

"I'll be right down," Anjannette yelled.

I glanced up and spotted her looking over the railing.

"Take your time. I expected traffic, but there wasn't any so I'm a little early. " She disappeared and I turned my attention to Keera. "I owe you a big thank you."

"Why's that?"

"For taking care of the studio so Anjannette can get away for the weekend."

"You don't have to thank me for that. Just keep making her happy."

"I'm trying my best."

"Well, whatever you're doing is working because she's getting back to herself again."

I was going to ask what she meant by that but heard Anjannette walking down the stairs.

"I'm sure I'm forgetting something," she said.

"If you are, we can always grab whatever you need down there."

"True." She looked around the room. "I guess I'm ready to go then." Turning her attention to Keera, she added, "Enjoy the quiet here and call me if you have any questions or need anything."

"You enjoy your trip, I've got it all under control." She gave Anjannette a big hug then pulled back and looked at me. "She's all yours."

I walked over and picked up the suitcase from the corner then grabbed the small duffle bag she'd set on the couch.

"Is this it?"

"Yeah." She grabbed her purse from the kitchen island. "I'm ready."

I followed her to the door and we both stepped outside.

"Seriously," Keera said from the doorway. "Forget about everything here and go have fun."

We walked to the truck and I opened the passenger door for her and she settled into the seat.

"You okay?"

She nodded. "I will be. Right now, I feel like I'm leaving my child behind."

I leaned forward and kissed her.

"Don't worry. Keera will be fine."

As I'd hoped, she laughed, seeming a bit lighter because of my pathetic joke. She reached out for her seatbelt and once she clicked it into place, I closed the door. After tossing her bags in the back seat, I climbed behind the wheel and started the truck. Keera waved from the doorway as we pulled onto the street.

"Why don't you put on some good vacation music?" I said as I made my way through her neighborhood.

She leaned forward and poked her finger against the touchscreen, scrolling through my playlists. Out of the corner of my eye, I saw her smile a second before the opening chords of *I Only Want to Be With You* by Hootie and the Blowfish started to play.

"Hootie seems appropriate since we're going to South Carolina and that's where the band is from."

"I like the way you think."

"I love having a theme."

I stopped at a red light and clicked on my left blinker.

"Are we taking the turnpike?"

"Yeah. Sorry we have to drive to Allentown, but there aren't direct flights to Myrtle Beach from Avoca."

"No worries there, but I know an easier way to get there. Turn right instead."

I turned right and followed her directions and before long, we merged onto the turnpike.

"That was definitely a more straightforward route than I was going to take. Thanks for pointing it out."

"You're welcome."

She opened her mouth to speak then hesitated.

"What?"

"Hmm?"

"What were you going to say?"

"You're way too observant."

"Don't try to distract me from the question."

She let out a sigh.

"I was just going to say that I wasn't sure I should tell you to go the other way."

"Why not?"

"In my experience, some guys don't like that."

At some point, I'm going to have to ask her about her ex just so I have a reference of what she dealt with. From the little I know, it seems like the guy's a real asshole. I shifted my gaze in her direction.

"That's ridiculous. Don't ever be afraid to offer suggestions, or whatever." I turned my attention back to the road. "In fact, don't censor yourself at all. Okay?"

I loosened my grip on the wheel when I heard her chuckle.

"Okay, but you might be sorry you said that."

"I'll take my chances." Deciding it's time to change the subject, I asked, "Keera's staying at your place while you're gone?"

"Yeah, for the past couple years she's been bouncing between her parents' and her grandmother's, so she jumped at the chance to stay by herself for a few days."

"I get that," I said.

"Considering she's manning the studio by herself for four days, the least I can do is let her crash at my place."

"I'm really glad you're coming. It will be much more fun with you there."

"I wasn't sure what we'll be doing exactly, but I think I packed something for every occasion."

"Tonight we'll just hang out with Trey, Nori, Crispin, and his boyfriend, Ben. The tournament starts at ten tomorrow morning and I'm guessing that will last until two-ish. Then there's a reception-type thing at seven tomorrow night. And Sunday, Jack and Hannah are hosting a brunch."

"They're the people who run the foundation hosting this fundraiser, right?"

"Yeah, Jack is the shortstop for the Waves and his wife Hannah works in the PR Department. At least she did.

They had twins last month so I don't know what her plans are."

"She had twins and they're hosting this whole weekend?" I nodded. "Holy shit. I can't even imagine."

"Hannah is a force of nature. She's the most organized person I've ever met."

"I envy people like that."

"You seem to keep things together pretty good."

"For the most part, but it takes all my effort. And honestly, I live by my calendar." She held her phone up. "If it's not in there, chances are, I'll forget about it. That's how I missed my last hair appointment. I forgot to put it in the calendar, so as far as my brain was concerned, it didn't exist."

"Oh, I forgot to mention that I'm getting my hair cut later," I said. "You're welcome to come and see Crispin's salon or if you'd rather hang out at the house or with Trey and Nori, that's fine, too."

"Crispin cuts your hair?"

"Yeah."

"So you just fly to Myrtle Beach when you need a haircut."

"Considering the fact that I live there part of the year, it's not as ridiculous as the tone of your voice makes it sound. Besides, the first time he met me, he begged me to let him cut my hair and to give the guy credit, he does a great job."

She shifted in her seat and leaned her elbow against the console.

"You know, it's not easy having a boyfriend with such pretty hair."

Even though we've been seeing each other for over a month now, that's the first time she's referred to me as that.

Instead of making a big deal out of it, I just chuckled. But I wanted to shout for joy. It seems things are moving forward with Ms. Peach and I couldn't be happier about that.

ANJANNETTE

AFTER WE LANDED, we headed to Leo's house to drop off my stuff. It seemed bizarre to me that he got on the plane without even a small bag, but I suppose it makes sense that he keeps enough things at each house so he can travel light.

His place here is as amazing as the other two and I have serious house envy. It still boggles my mind that he can afford three houses...well, I guess it's four with the place in St. Pete. I mean, I know what he does for a living, so it stands to reason he makes good money. But he's so down-to-Earth and modest, it's easy to forget that.

We took a walk on the beach and relaxed for a while before heading to Trey and Nori's. She convinced me to stay behind instead of going with the guys while they got haircuts. I was looking at the pictures scattered around the living room when Nori returned carrying a bottle of wine and two glasses.

"I'm so glad you decided to hang out instead of going to Haven with Leo and Trey. It'll give us time to get to know each other better," she said, gesturing for me to join her on the couch.

After taking one last glance of a candid shot of her and Trey, I took the glass she held out to me and sat directly across from her.

"I have to say, I kind of love the pink hair you used to have."

She snort-laughed.

"Yeah, you and Trey."

"Trey liked it?"

"From what I understand, he hated both the color and pixie style when we first met. But I guess it grew on him. He's told me more than once that I should do it like that again."

That's really sweet. I used to do all kinds of crazy things with my hair. In fact, it was purple and shaved on the sides when I first met Travis and he supposedly loved it. Of course, as the years went on, what he initially called my "cute quirks" were just more cause for criticism.

Before I could fall down that rabbit hole, I took a sip of wine and refocused my attention on our conversation.

"It looked cute on you, especially with that shorter style."

She tucked her chin-length hair behind her ear.

"I'm not the same person I was when I cut and dyed it like that." I raised my brow as I sipped my wine. "Bad breakup."

"I totally understand that."

"But I'm not opposed to the idea of doing my hair like that again after the wedding. I wanted to grow it out a little so I have more options."

"When are you getting married?"

"The last Saturday in January. That gives us just enough time to sneak in a honeymoon before spring training starts in mid-February."

"Are you having a big wedding?"

"No, it'll only be about fifty people, and eight of those are the Marakis family."

"Leo said Trey is tight with his family."

"He's like their seventh child. Which is great considering his real family sucks as much as mine does." She took a drink then shook her head. "But enough about Trey and me. Tell me about you and Leo."

"Oh, uh, we've been dating. I guess it's going well."

That last sentence came out more like a question.

"Sorry, I didn't mean to put you on the spot like that. I'll stop being nosy."

"No, it's fine. I'm just never sure how to answer that." I shrugged. "I met his family last weekend and now I'll be meeting his teammates, so I guess we're doing well."

"His family is really great and I'm sure his parents loved you."

"Yeah, I think it went well, but I'll admit it was really overwhelming at first. But everyone made me feel welcome, especially his mom. She was really sweet. It was just his immediate family Saturday night and Annita showed me how to make baklava. Not that I'm fooling myself into thinking I could replicate what we made."

Nori groaned.

"Her baklava is so good. All the food is. We're supposed to go there for Christmas and I'm not bringing any pants with a button. It will be leggings all the way. Hopefully you'll be there too so we can stuff ourselves together."

"Um, maybe." Before that answer got super awkward, I said, "First I have to focus on meeting his teammates and their wives tomorrow."

"Don't lose sleep about that. The guys and their wives are all great."

"I'm picturing a *Real Housewives of Baseball* scene."

"Oh God no. That's not what they're like at all. I've been in their presence a lot,

especially the wives, and really like them. From what I

understand, the Waves are a unicorn team in that aspect. The owner doesn't tolerate egos or nasty behavior. In fact, everyone was surprised when he traded for Trey since he had a reputation for being a conceited hothead."

"That surprises me since he and Leo are so tight."

"It was all a front that Leo saw through shortly after they met." She smiled. "Leo really is

a great guy."

I nodded. I'm getting more convinced that Leo really is as perfect as he seems. For the past couple weeks, instead of waiting for the other shoe to drop with him, I've just relaxed and enjoyed myself. Keera keeps telling me I'm more like "my old self" and I'll admit I'm feeling that way.

I'm still worried about getting too comfortable in this relationship. Or worse, getting so immersed in Leo's world, I lose myself again. After all, his career has him traveling half the time and since I have the studio, I wouldn't just be able to run off and follow him.

"Can I ask you something?" I asked.

"Sure."

"How do you handle it when Trey travels?"

She set her empty wine glass on the coffee table then settled against the back of the couch, tucking her legs beneath her.

"It's a little easier since I live here so when he plays at home, it's no different than if he had a regular job. When he's away, we FaceTime. If I had a break in my schedule, I'd meet him on the road." She shrugged. "This is a topic the wives and girlfriends talk about all the time. They all have their own way of dealing with the crazy schedule."

"I don't even know if Leo and I will be together by the time the season starts, but I was curious."

"If Leo has anything to say about it, I'm sure you will be."

Chapter Twenty-One

LEO

I GRABBED a bottle of Gatorade and headed out to the deck to relax while Anjannette finished getting ready. After playing golf in the sun all afternoon, I'm dehydrated as hell. The alcohol that was flowing all day probably didn't help. Thankfully I'm older and wiser when it comes to drinking so I didn't imbibe too much. Still, I probably had more than I should have.

Leaning against the railing, I opened the bottle and drank half its contents in one long gulp, careful not to spill any on my crisp white shirt. The weather might be warmer down here but the sun sets just as early, and since it's a new moon, I'm standing here looking out into the darkness. Still, there's something relaxing about being near the ocean, even if I can't see it.

After finishing the rest of the Gatorade, I tossed the empty bottle into the recycling bin then turned to head back inside, and froze in place. Anjannette stood on the other side of the threshold, looking like a fantasy come to life in a midnight blue lace dress, its hemline ending just below mid-thigh, making her legs look impossibly long. Especially in the strappy silver sandals that have her standing at least five inches taller.

Without taking my gaze off her, I stepped inside and placed my hands on her waist. I'd expected the lace of her dress to be scratchy, but it's silky and I moved my hands around to the small of her back, enjoying the feel of it against her curves. With her high heels, the top of her head is at my nose instead of my chin, putting her luscious lips closer to mine. Her mouth is normally kissable, but coated with a dark berry color, it looks even more full and lush. Every fiber of my being is screaming at me to kiss her, but I don't want to ruin her perfectly-applied lipstick. That will have to wait until later.

"You look beautiful."

"Thank you." She looked up at me through impossibly-long eyelashes. "You look pretty handsome yourself. I've never seen you in a suit."

I stepped back and flashed a smile before grabbing my jacket.

"You haven't seen the full effect yet." I shrugged into it and put my hands on my hips in a cheesy catalogue pose. "What do you think?"

"Gorgeous."

She stepped toward me and dragged her fingertip along my tie then tugged when she reached the bottom. Even though it's not physically possible, I'd swear on a stack of bibles I felt that pull in my dick.

"I like the tie."

I looked down at my navy blue tie with Waves logos embroidered all over it.

"Chances are, most of the other guys will be wearing something similar, if not this exact tie."

Her mouth curled up into a smile.

"But none of them will wear it as well, I'm sure."

I closed my eyes and let out a pained chuckle before opening them.

"I'm trying to be good so I don't mess you up, but you're not making it easy."

"Hmmm, sorry. I didn't mean to make it...*hard*."

I reached out and wrapped my finger around her wrist and pulled her to me. After kissing the top of her head then her forehead, I placed my mouth softly against hers for just a second before pulling back.

"You always make it *hard*." I bobbed my eyebrows. "I'll be on my best behavior for this event, but be forewarned that once we get home later, I plan on messing you up good."

"Mmm, can't wait."

TREY HAD PURCHASED a table for this evening's event and we'll be sitting there with him and Nori, Crispin and his boyfriend Ben, and our teammate Phillip Riddle and his date. So it should be a fun night.

"There's the hustler," Jack Reagan said as we entered the reception hall. He turned to Anjannette and said, "He's talked for years about how much he hates golf and he never wants to play, then he goes to the tournament today and looks like Tiger Woods."

She looked up at me with a raised brow.

"*Are* you a hustler?"

"Just because I don't *like* golf doesn't mean I can't play it. My brother Nicky loves the game and you know I'm not going to let him beat me."

"I stand by my accusation," Jack said.

"Stop picking on Leo." Hannah gave her husband a playful pat on the chest then turned her attention to me. "Thank you again for your donation. The whole team has been so supportive. It's heartwarming." Her voice wobbled on that last word and she blinked her glistening eyes rapidly. "I'm sorry." She chuckled. "Please excuse my post-partum hormones. One minute I'm fine and the next I'm a sappy mess."

"I'm so impressed with this whole event," Anjannette said. "Especially considering the fact you planned it with month-old twins at home."

Jack wrapped his arm around Hannah's waist and kissed the top of her head.

"My wife is a rock star."

I glanced over my shoulder as a group of people entered the room then turned back to Jack and Hannah.

"We don't want to hog the two of you so we'll head to our table."

"Trey and Nori are already over there." Hannah pointed to the left. "We'll catch up later."

I placed my hand on the small of Anjannette's back and led her in the direction Hannah had indicated. We're sitting up toward the front of the room and I made a point of not making eye contact with people we passed as we made our way to the table. This isn't a meet-and-greet, but chatting with fans goes with the territory. But I did that at the tournament earlier. I'd like to just relax and enjoy myself for a while.

We just sat when Crispin and Ben arrived. I'd met his boyfriend before but Anjannette hasn't, so I introduced them as the two men sat.

"You're the one who owns the pole dance studio, right?" he said.

"Yep, that's me."

"Crispin showed me some video of your recital and I was impressed. Some of what I saw seemed to defy gravity, but it looked like so much fun."

"It is fun. I absolutely love it."

That led to a whole pole discussion and I sat back and enjoyed watching Anjannette's face shine as she talked. Her love for the sport is obvious and I'm so happy she's able to run the studio full-time.

Hannah had just stepped up to the podium and asked everyone to take their seats when Phillip Riddle and his date arrived. I'm no relationship expert, but in my opinion, they're fighting. They both look tense and if looks could kill, he'd be dead at least ten times now with the side glances she's throwing at him.

After Hannah and Jack thanked everyone for coming, they gave a short summary of their foundation's purpose then dinner was served. Riddle chatted a little bit but Haley responded to any attempts to pull her into the conversation with one-word answers and pushed food around her plate instead of eating.

The band had been playing dinner music but as the main course was cleared, a singer stepped up to the microphone as the first strains of *The Way You Look Tonight* by Frank Sinatra filled the room. I'm not surprised this is the song that will kick off the dancing portion of the night. It's Jack and Hannah's wedding song and from what I understand, it's the first song they danced to at an event similar to this one.

Our hosts took to the dance floor and some other couples joined them. I stood and held my hand out to Anjannette.

"Would you like to dance?"

She smiled and placed her hand in mine.

"I'd love to."

We made our way through the tables and I pulled her into my arms as we reached the dance floor. I rested my hand against the small of her back and tucked our joined hands against my chest.

"You were right," she said as we moved around the floor.

"About what?"

"The ties. They're all around the room." She shifted closer and said, "I was also right about the fact that none of them wear it as well as you."

"I don't think it's the tie making me look good so much as the woman on my arm."

"You're pretty smooth."

"Just stating the facts, ma'am."

The song ended but another slow one began so we kept dancing.

"You're good for my ego, Leo Marakis."

"Why's that?"

"You make me feel…" She trailed off and seemed to search for a word then finally shrugged and said, "Special."

Even in the dim lighting, the vulnerability in her eyes was obvious.

"You're not special. You're extraordinary," I said, knowing she'd appreciate the Buffy quote but also because the words are one hundred percent true.

She took her hand from mine and wrapped her arms around my neck. After leaning forward and giving me a quick kiss, she rested her head on my shoulder.

"So are you."

ANJANNETTE

. . .

SO MANY GOOD-LOOKING men in one place should be illegal. I'd met everyone here last night at the reception, but concentrated into this smaller space, their presence is magnified.

"Is it part of the Waves' contract that all the players have to look like models?"

The women sitting with me chuckled.

"Seems like it might be," Nori said.

Karen Montgomery glanced across the yard where some of the guys were playing corn hole while the others watched and heckled.

"They're a lot to take in all at once, aren't they?"

"That's for sure."

"You'll get used to them," Sabrina McMullen said.

I probably won't be around enough for that to happen but before I had to respond, Hannah returned from answering a phone call.

"Does anyone need anything?"

"Sit and relax," Sabrina said. "Enjoy the quiet while the babies are sleeping."

She settled into the chair next to me and set her phone on the table.

"I wish I had that when Jeremy was a baby," Karen said. "I had an audio monitor and carried it with me everywhere, but every time he made a noise, I ran to check on him, especially the first couple months."

I was totally lost until I looked at Hannah's phone and realized that what I thought was a picture of the babies in a crib was actually a live stream of them sleeping.

"I have video and I do that," Hannah said with a chuckle. "But enough baby talk. I don't want to be one of those women who can't talk about anything else after they give birth." She turned to me. "Anjannette, how did you and Leo meet?"

"He's taking yoga in a studio upstairs from my pole dance studio and we ran into each

other there."

"Pole dance?" I nodded at Sabrina's question. "Is it as good a workout as they say?"

"It really is and it's a lot of fun. It's the first exercise that I immediately loved and have managed to stick with long-term."

"Are you in New Jersey?" Barbara Chase asked.

"No, Scranton."

"Oh that's right. I forgot Leo bought a house there."

"Don't mention that to Dale," Karen said. "He's obsessed with *The Office*."

"You should come up for a visit. There's a huge Dwight Schrute mural you can take his picture in front of. There's also a smaller mural of all the characters at Coopers."

"How far are you from New York?"

"A couple hours."

"I'll have to take a look at the schedule and see if we can take a detour when the Waves play New York. Unless we can squeeze in a trip before the spring training starts. Jeremy and I have never experienced winter in the north. That could be interesting." She picked up her phone. "Do you mind giving me your number so I can reach out if we do decide to come?"

"Not at all."

She handed me her phone and I entered my number. A second later, my phone buzzed.

"Now you have my number so you don't think I'm a spammer."

A cry sounded from Hannah's phone.

"Guess my break is over."

"Looks like they're both awake," Jack said as he approached, followed by Leo.

Jack and Hannah excused themselves and went inside.

"How's everything going over here?" Leo asked.

"We're taking good care of Anjannette," Karen said. "In fact, we're discussing the possibility of Dale, Jeremy, and me coming up to Scranton to visit."

"That's right, he's a huge *Office* fan. Has he ever been?"

"I don't think so."

Jack came back outside.

"Barbara, Michael just woke up, too. He's not crying, just kicking his legs and looking around."

"Guess my break is over, too," she said as she stood.

Sabrina also stood. "I better go check on Gavin. I'm surprised Lexi hasn't brought him back outside."

"Since you're heading back in, would you mind showing me where the bathroom is?" I asked Jack.

"Follow me," he said with a smile. "In fact, why don't you all come inside and you can come see Nori's master-piece in the nursery. Once we decided on a design, she worked double-time to get it finished."

Jack showed me to the powder room in the hallway then told me how to get to the nursery.

"Although I'm sure you'll be able to find your way there just by following the noise."

After doing my business, I washed my hands and checked my hair and makeup in the mirror then headed back into the living room. Jack was holding open the front door with a garbage bag in his hand as an older woman stepped inside.

"Mrs. Button, I'm glad you made it." He leaned down and kissed her. "Let me put this outside. It's amazing how much crap comes out of two tiny bodies." After introducing us, he said, "I'll be right back."

She nodded at him then turned her attention to me.

"It's nice to meet you Anjannette," she said. "How do you know Jack and Hannah?"

"We actually just met yesterday. I'm here with Leo Marakis."

"Lucky girl," she said. "That man has the best backside I've ever seen."

"Behave Mrs. Button," Jack said when he returned and gestured for us to follow him to the nursery. "You're dating Walter, remember?"

"Only because you went and got married."

"Are you flirting with my husband again?" Hannah asked as we stepped into the nursery.

She was standing at a changing table snapping a onesie closed on the baby girl. At least I assume it's the girl since the onesie has pink butterflies all over it.

"Did she poop again?" Jack asked.

"No, she spit up all over herself."

"You're a messy girl," Jack said in a sing-song voice as he picked up his daughter.

"I just saw them last week and they look so much bigger now," Mrs. Button said.

"I know, they're growing fast." Hannah said.

"That's because all they do is eat and sleep," Jack said then turned his attention to his daughter. "And poop, right?"

The baby's eyes widened as he spoke to her.

"Be happy they sleep," Barbara said as she entered the room carrying a little boy, with his father's dark, curly hair and her light blue eyes. "This one didn't sleep more than two hours at a time until last month."

"I have Mrs. Button to thank for that. She helped us set up their sleeping routine and so far it's working."

I walked toward Leo and Nori on the other side of the room and looked around, admiring the mural that spans all four walls.

"Nori, this is amazing."

"Didn't she do a great job?" Hannah asked. "Plus she was so patient. It took us forever to decide on a theme."

"It's perfect." I said.

"I love how the bottom of their feet and the inside of their ears are either blue or pink. It really adds something to the design." Hannah shifted her baby boy onto her shoulder and patted his back.

The babies' names are written in puffy letters on opposite walls, looking like they're being spewed out of an elephant's trunk.

"Aaron and Holly," I said. "Great names."

"Thanks. We named them after my dad and Jack's mom."

"That's so nice."

Voices sounded from down the hallway.

"We don't have to hold this party in the nursery," Jack said with a chuckle. "We have a whole house out there to mingle in. And it sounds like the corn hole match is done so the guys are ready for round two."

"Which is good because I ordered way too much food," Hannah said.

Leo and I were the last to file out of the room and I took one last look around, admiring the mural. My gaze skimmed over a picture on the dresser and I figured I must be seeing things so I went over to investigate, and blinked. The man holding a twin in each arm looked awfully familiar.

"Is this Aaron Diskin?"

Leo stopped and turned around.

"Yeah, he's Hannah's father."

"Aaron Diskin is Hannah's father?" He nodded. "That baby is named after Aaron Diskin?" He nodded again. "Oh my God! Aaron Diskin."

I know I'm sounding like a deranged fangirl, but *Aaron Diskin*. The man is a legend.

"He's a really nice guy."

"You've met him?"

"He comes to visit and attends games sometimes now that word is out that he's her father," he said. "It was a big story about three years ago. Before that, no one knew they were related. I'm surprised you didn't see it."

Three years ago. That's when I was at my lowest so I wouldn't have paid attention to anything beyond my own misery.

"No, I guess I missed it."

"You okay?"

"Yeah, why?"

"You looked upset for a second."

I refuse to let bad memories of Travis invade my thoughts while I'm making good memories with Leo.

"No, I'm good."

Chapter Twenty-Two

LEO

"I TOLD your mother Nori and I will be up for Christmas,"
Trey said.

"Yeah? For the whole week?"

"That's the plan."

"What about you?" I asked Crispin. "You know you're
both welcome and I have room if you want to stay at my
house."

"We're spending Christmas with Ben's family." He
looked at his boyfriend. "Do we have plans for New Year's
Eve?"

"No, nothing yet," Ben said. "I'm off until the second
week of January so I'm up for whatever you want to do."

"We'll talk about it and I'll let you know when we'll be
up. You'll be there?" he asked Anjannette.

"Yes, I'll be there. The studio is closed for the week so
I'm free."

Like I told my mother I would, I'd asked Anjannette if

she could come for Christmas early. In fact, I did it while she was visiting Thanksgiving weekend.

"What's on the list for the New Year's Day movie marathon?" Trey asked.

"I didn't ask. It's not like I have a say anyway."

The movie marathon started twenty-some years ago when there was a massive storm and we were snowed in. We ate leftovers and my mom made copious amounts of popcorn and it was so much fun, we decided to make it an annual tradition.

Back then, we voted on the movies but as the years went on, the girls pretty much dictated the lineup. Mostly because the movies Nicky, Chris, and I wanted to watch had either too much violence, bad language, or sex and my mother vetoed them all.

"What's this about a movie marathon?" Anjannette asked. "You didn't tell me about that."

"Sorry, I didn't even think about it." I looked at her then over to Nori. "Bring something comfy to wear because you'll be vegged out in my parents' family room for hours eating, drinking, and watching movies."

"I love that," Nori said.

"It honestly sounds like a perfect day," Anjannette said. "Especially with Annita making the food."

I'm glad she's looking forward to hanging out with my family again. Myra, aka "the one who didn't eat" said she'd be reluctant to go back after that first time. She didn't like all the people or the loud family dynamic. Not to mention the food. I don't know if she thought I'd choose her over my family or what, but if that was the case, she was obviously wrong.

"All this talk of food has my stomach grumbling," Crispin said. "Should we go somewhere to eat or order in?"

After going for a low-key hike earlier, we grabbed sushi and settled onto the deck to enjoy the perfect day. Other than getting up to grab a drink or go to the bathroom, we've pretty much been planted in our seats.

"If you want to go somewhere, we could walk to Ike's. The food is good and it's close."

"Define close," Crispin said.

"Five blocks."

"Okay, because after that hike today, I'm not looking to take many more steps."

"Oh my God, you looked and sounded exactly like David Rose when you said that. Do you practice that in a mirror?"

When I first met Crispin, I thought I knew him from somewhere, then I realized he reminded me of Dan Levy's character David from *Schitt'$ Creek*. And once I saw it, it's hard to unsee and I notice it ninety percent of the time he speaks. I usually don't say anything, but every once in a while I toss in a comment.

"Look, I can't help it if Dan Levy borrowed my persona for his character."

I could have added fuel to the fire but my stomach growled, reminding me to get back on topic.

"Will five blocks put you over the edge or will you be okay?"

"It will technically be ten blocks walking there and back, but I think I'll manage."

Trey said, "Actually I was just thinking we could grab a rideshare home from Ike's and I'll come back tomorrow for my truck. That way I don't have to worry about having another drink and I can give you two a ride to the airport in the morning." He looked down at Nori. "Plus I can relive the memory of meeting this beautiful lady."

"You met in a rideshare?" Anjannette asked.

"We did." Nori smiled at Trey then looked over at Anjannette. "Trey had gotten called up to the Waves and needed a ride from Fayetteville. I finished up a commission in Fayetteville and had allowed myself plenty of time to get back to Myrtle Beach for a meeting with a potential client, but my car broke down. I called the same company he'd used and they reached out to his driver since he was going to the same place and Trey agreed to share his ride."

"That is so sweet. It's seriously like a meet cute in a movie," Anjannette said. "Was it love at first sight?"

They both laughed.

"Not quite," Nori said. "I thought he was a snob and he thought I was a freak."

"But they had good friends who made them realize how much they loved each other," Crispin said, drawing out the word love.

"How did you do that?"

Before Crispin could launch into a detailed explanation, I cut in.

"Why don't we continue this story over dinner?" I suggested. "I'm starving and I have a feeling this conversation isn't going to end anytime soon."

"That sounds like a good plan." Trey stood and reached out for Nori's hand and pulled her out of her seat. "Then we can talk about how Anjannette slammed the door in your face the first time she laid eyes on you."

Anjannette bit her lip and glanced up at me, holding back her laughter. I don't know why because no one else is. She finally let go and I enjoyed watching her lose herself.

Both Clay and Keera have commented on how she's getting back to normal. While I haven't known her as long as they have, I see a difference in her behavior since we met. She's more free and relaxed.

We filed off the deck and walked out the side gate then

made our way to the street. I took Anjannette's hand and entwined our fingers together as we headed toward Ike's.

"I'm so glad we decided to stay the extra day," she said.

"Yeah?"

"MmmHmm. It's nice to have time to just relax."

We initially planned on flying back today, but Keera offered to cover the studio for another day and Anjannette took her up on it. I'm hoping that's a good sign that she'll be willing to do the same thing once the season starts. But that's a conversation to have with her another day.

ANJANNETTE

"I CAN'T BELIEVE I woke up in Myrtle Beach this morning and now I'm here in Scranton, freezing my ass off, having tacos and margaritas like any other Tuesday."

"You know you're basically living my dream life, surrounded by all those sexy baseball players," Keera said.

"Most of them are happily married so they wouldn't be of use to you anyway."

"I can still look." She picked up her glass and after licking some salt from the rim, took a drink. "Tell me again who you met. The players only, please."

"Phillip Riddle sat at our table Saturday night, but other than being introduced, I didn't really interact with him. Then there was Dale, Cal, Dan, and a guy with red hair, but I forget his name."

"Chris Russell," she said. "They call him Rusty."

"Oskar, Jimmy, and Sam."

"Marquez, Chavez, and Cherry." Keera filled a chip with salsa and popped it into her mouth. "And of course

Jack Reagan. That man is so hot. Does he smell as good as he looks?"

"I didn't stand there sniffing him." I thought about it as I took a drink. "But I guess he smelled spicy."

"Spicy?"

"Yeah, spicy. Kind of like walking into one of those all-natural stores that sell essential oils."

"In that tell-all book his ex wrote, she said he's obsessed with his skin and makes his own lotions and stuff. I saw him in an interview and he said he has severe eczema, so maybe that's why."

I shrugged.

"He's really nice though. All the guys are and so are the wives I met. They're not at all what I expected."

"Are you glad you went?"

"I am. It was a lot of fun and everyone was so friendly."

"That's so great. As jealous as I am, I'm happy for you."

The waitress arrived with our tacos and we both dug in.

"And did I mention it was in the seventies down there?" I asked after I finished my second taco.

"Only a million times."

"We walked on the beach and hung out on the deck. Maybe I had such a good time because it was so different from what I would have been doing here."

"Or maybe it was the company?" She bobbed her eyebrows.

Her words were meant to be playful and they're definitely true, but instead of making me smile, I felt an overwhelming sense of melancholy. I don't know, maybe the second margarita hit at that moment, but all of my insecurities floated to the surface, making me feel unsure about the future of our relationship.

"Yeah, Leo is really great."

"Woah! Wait, what happened between your sentence and my question? Anjannette from three years ago just took over your face. Why?"

I dragged my fingers through my hair trying to figure out how to put what I'm thinking into words.

"You know, I went on my first date with Leo figuring it would be a one-time thing. I didn't think he could be as nice as he seemed." I rested my elbows on the table and held out my hands. "But he is. He's amazing. I honestly can't find anything wrong with him, and you know I've looked."

"I agree. Leo is great. Why is that a problem?"

"Once that first date turned into a second and the second into a third, I figured I'd just keep taking it one day at a time and enjoy myself. But now, it's going beyond that. We're making *plans*. I'm spending Christmas and New Year's with him and his family *and* he asked me to be his plus one for Trey and Nori's wedding in January."

"So your relationship is moving forward. That's a good thing."

"Not really."

"Why not?"

"Because." I gestured wildly and shook my head. "Where could it possibly go? He's on the road half the year. Actually, it's more than half the year and I have a business to run. I can't just take off and meet him wherever he is."

"You met some of the wives. What do they do?"

"Sabrina is a partner at a physical therapy facility a couple hours away from Myrtle Beach. She gave up meeting patients there and just holds the financial interest. Now she works through the sports academy Cal and Dan own. Same thing with Karen Montgomery. She was living in St. Pete working as a realtor but when things got serious with her and Dale, she and her son moved to Myrtle Beach. Nori lives there already but she does work her schedule around Trey's."

"See? They all make it work."

"Yeah, because the women make concessions."

"Honey, you're spiraling. Leo is kind, thoughtful, and sweet and he's obviously crazy about you. So you're starting off at a better point than with any other guy you've been with. Don't ruin things between you because of what ifs." She reached out and squeezed my hand. "I know my own relationship history is less than stellar but if a guy looked at me the way Leo looks at you, I'd hold onto him with both hands."

She has some valid points. I do have a tendency to worry about things I've fabricated in my brain. But the long-term issue I'm talking about isn't totally imagined. Still, I don't have to worry about it right now. If we stay together that long, we'll figure something out.

"You're right," I said.

"Of course I am."

I took a deep breath in through my nose and let it out the same way.

"I'll just keep going with the flow and see where it leads. Thanks for talking me down."

"What are friends for?"

She finished her margarita in one gulp and set the glass on the table with a triumphant thump, looking very satisfied with herself.

"Now that my love life is solved for now, I have to point out the fact that you do have someone who looks at you like you're the best thing since sliced bread."

"Who?"

"Simon Parker."

She snort-laughed.

"You're insane. Simon and I are just friends."

"That's just because you keep throwing him do-not-touch signals."

"Because we're just friends." She looked at a spot over my shoulder and dragged her fingers through her hair three times before meeting my gaze again. "Besides, Simon isn't my type at all."

"Did you ever think that maybe that's a good thing?"

Chapter Twenty-Three

LEO

"ANYONE ELSE HAVE ANY QUESTIONS?" Benji asked his players.

Clay and I are at Lackawanna College, visiting our old coach and talking to the team. We each gave a short speech—I talked about my journey from college to the Minor to Major Leagues and Clay told them about his path and how it changed after his car accident. After that, we asked what they wanted to know. Some of them had serious questions and others were more interested in asking about big-name ballplayers I've played with and against.

"How did you decide to go into the draft instead of continuing your education?"

The kid who asked that question had a couple other well-thought out ones so it's obvious he wants to make a career out of the game.

"That's something you can talk to your coaches about. They'll tell you where you're at compared to where you need to be for both the draft and getting into a good four-year school," Clay said. I nodded when he looked to me for confirmation of what he'd said.

"And don't wait to talk to them until a month before you graduate, do it now," I said. "If you're a Freshman, you can start to work on strengthening any weaknesses, whether that's your swing or Math class. Even if what you do here doesn't result in a baseball contract, it can offer you a full ride to a D1 school, and that's not too shabby."

"You talked about how you made your decision to quit baseball," a tall, lanky kid in the back said to Clay. "Did you get to keep your signing bonus even though you weren't going to be playing anymore?"

"Yeah, I did," Clay said with a chuckle. "At the time it was cold comfort after losing the career I always wanted, but once I licked my wounds and stopped pouting, it was great having it to help set up my business."

No one else raised a hand so we wrapped things up, and both Benji and the team thanked us for coming in. As the guys filed out of the gym, Benji ushered us to his office.

"Seems like a good bunch of kids," I said and I lowered into the chair in front of his desk.

Clay settled into the one next to me as Benji sat in his big leather swivel chair.

"Most of them are. Like always, there are a few that like to disrupt things, but we deal with that before it gets out of hand. We had a couple scholarship kids quit in the fall because they didn't want to do the work and disrupted everyone who did." He waved his hand. "But enough about the team. What's going on with the two of you?"

We gave him the Cliff Notes version of what we've been doing since we last saw him. And I'm ashamed to say, it's been a couple years since I've seen Benji in person.

"So now that I'm in Scranton during the off-season, I'd

like to be more involved here," I said. "I owe my career to you and this school."

"You're giving me too much credit," he said. "You both had the talent and the drive to get where you wanted to go."

"Yeah, but you showed us how to get there," Clay said.

It was obvious Benji was uncomfortable with the praise, so I changed the subject.

"After the holidays, Clay has graciously agreed to pitch to me and I was hoping we could do it here."

"Oh yeah, sure. Whatever you need."

"Let us know the team's schedule and we'll try to overlap a little bit so we can give some pointers if they're interested."

"They definitely would be. You know you would have loved it when you went here if guys with your experience came in to show you how it's done."

"That's for sure."

"You know, in my career, I've had players go to D1 schools and even enter the draft, but none have had the success that you two and Trey have." He looked at Clay. "And before you say you didn't reach the same levels as Leo and Trey, I'm gonna stop you. If it wasn't for that car accident, you would have been right there with them. Your Minor League numbers were pretty impressive."

Before Clay could comment, Benji's phone buzzed.

"Christ," he said. "I have a meeting with the athletic director."

"We'll leave you to it," I said as Clay and I stood.

"I'll send you the practice schedule when I have it. They'll be back from break the second week of January, which will give you more than a month to work out before you have to report to spring training. If you want to get in here between now and then, just let me know. You know I'm always around."

"Thanks," I said. "I may take you up on that."

"Like I said, just let me know."

We said our goodbyes and left the building. Clay and I had already decided to grab dinner at the diner when we finished at Lackawanna so we got into his car and drove there.

"Trey said you kicked ass at the golf tournament," he said after we ordered.

"I did all right."

The waitress walked over with two glasses of water and set them in front of us.

"How was the rest of the trip?"

"It was good. The weather was perfect and Anjannette seemed to enjoy herself. She got along well with my teammates and their wives, which is good. I'm hoping to convince her to come down to St. Pete for a few days or however long she can get away. *If* she can get away. At least if she does, now she'll have someone to sit in the stands with that she already knows if Nori isn't there."

"Planning events a couple months out. Impressive."

"Yeah, she's spending Christmas week with my family and agreed to be my date for Trey and Nori's wedding, so that takes us into January. So I figure spring training isn't too much of a stretch from there."

I'll be honest, I've never made advance plans like that with a woman. I've never wanted to. But Anjannette is different. I'd spend all day, every day with her if that was possible.

"So things are going well?"

I took a drink and nodded.

"More so the past couple weeks."

"Why do you say that?"

"She just seems more comfortable with the relationship and more relaxed in general."

The waitress brought our burgers and while we ate, I debated whether or not to ask the question that's been running through my head. I was more than halfway through my burger when I figured I have nothing to lose. I'm not looking for gossip, just an answer.

"Can I ask you something?"

"Sure."

"Keera said something to me and I'm curious about it."

"What's that?"

He popped a fry into his mouth and looked at me as he chewed.

"She said Anjannette has been more like herself since we got together. I'll admit that I've noticed a difference in her, but I figured that was just with me, that she's opening up more as we get to know each other."

Clay shoved the last of his burger into his mouth and wiped his hands as he chewed. After taking a drink, he rested his elbows on the table and leaned forward.

"I've known Anjannette for about six years now, but for a good portion of that, our relationship was strictly professional. I only spoke to her whenever I needed my website updated. But even though that's the case, I can honestly say, she's not the same person today that she was then."

"In what way?"

He shrugged.

"When I first met her, she was very toned down. Not to be too woo-woo, but it was like she didn't have an inner light."

"I can't even imagine that."

"She was still with her ex-boyfriend and from what I understand, it wasn't a healthy relationship. I met the guy once and thought he was a tool, so it seemed like a good thing when I heard she left him about three years ago. And since then, she has changed. She's more confident and that missing inner light I mentioned slowly started to glow. Once she opened her studio, she came to life even more." He smiled at me. "Then you came along."

"Hopefully I've been a force for good."

"You seem to be. She smiles more, seems more relaxed."

"Thanks Clay. I appreciate the conversation."

"Anytime."

The waitress cleared the table and brought our check and we headed back to the studio. Anjannette will be finishing up a class soon, then she's done for the night so I'll stop in and see her.

I thought about what Clay said and decided to give Anjannette some more time before bringing up her ex. Despite what Nicky said, I don't need to know the details if she's totally moved on. It stands to reason that if she spent five years with that guy and he's the last person she was with, it would take a little time to expel any bad memories. I just hope that with time, I can do just that.

ANJANNETTE

"LET'S do it one more time all the way through. If you want to video, now's the time," I said.

I had a small beginner's class tonight, just six people, so we not only managed to get through the whole dance I choreographed, we also got to practice it from beginning to end twice so they're pretty comfortable with the steps.

After the flurry of activity as the women set up their phones, they stood at their poles ready to start.

"Okay, here we go," I said and pressed play. The unmistakable first notes of *Toxic* by Britney Spears sounded through the studio.

They stood poised, hands high on their poles and when Britney sang the first line, they went into a step around then held onto the pole with their right hand and leaned out, raising the left in a ta-da gesture. Then they repeated that on the other side before going into a fireman spin down to the floor.

I stood in the corner, doing my dance-mom routine, miming the next move instead of yelling it out like I did every other time. I'd shortened the song so they're dancing for less than two minutes instead of the full three and half, but it's still a longer routine than we've done at one time.

They're coming up on the last moves and everyone is doing really well. Even though they're not totally in sync, they're close enough, especially considering they just learned this dance tonight.

I watched as they did one last step around and flowed right into a back spin that they took all the way down to the floor. After landing on their knees, they let their upper bodies fall forward, resting on their palms with their heads down, then did a quick hair flip and shifted into a kneeling position before falling forward again.

With arched backs and high asses, they sexy crawled forward three times and on the fourth, extended their arms in front of them until boobs hit the floor. Rolling onto their backs, they slowly sat up with their arms behind them. With their left legs straight, they bent the right and leaned back on their palms, sticking their chests out, into a mudflap girl pose.

My loud clapping filled the silence as the music ended.

"Oh my God! You guys were so amazing!"

I know my shouting will be on everyone's video, but I didn't care. They all looked so amazing. I love it when students let go and really feel what they're doing. And it's so obvious when it happens because they look empowered and sexy and comfortable in their bodies.

Waving my hand in front of my face, I said, "You guys were perfect. You're seriously going to make me cry."

I turned on a playlist, lowering the volume so it just acted as background noise then pulled on my joggers.

"Anjannette." I turned toward Sophie Baxter. "Could you get into your elbow stand from your stomach again so I can videotape it?"

"Oh sure." I said goodbye to some of my students as we walked over to the pole she'd been working on and I got onto the floor then shifted to my stomach with my arms extended, hands wrapped around the base of the pole. "Ready?"

"Yep. Go ahead."

I slowly pulled my ass up until my toes brushed the floor and my back bumped the pole. From there, I lifted my legs and straightened them, pointing my toes toward the ceiling. I stayed upside down for a couple seconds before reversing the process with my muscles still fully engaged.

"You make that look so easy," she said.

"You're doing a good job pulling yourself up from your knees. With practice, you'll be doing this in no time."

"Thanks. I'm definitely going to practice at home," Sophie said as she moved over to the corner and put jeans and a sweater on over her pole shorts and top.

Everyone else had cleared out and I spotted Leo in the open doorway and walked toward him.

"I'm surprised you're still here," I said.

"After my session, Clay and I went to see our old coach at Lackawanna then grabbed a bite to eat at the diner. We took his car so he dropped me off to get my truck. I figured your class would be ending, so I thought I'd stop in."

Sophie walked toward us and said hi to Leo.

"I'll see you tomorrow," she said and left us alone.

"I saw your handstand," he said and leaned down to give me a quick kiss. "It was pretty impressive."

"It was actually an elbow stand." I wrapped my arms around his neck and kissed him. "But I won't hold your error against you."

"No?" He placed his hands on my waist. "What will you hold against me?"

I'd put on joggers but was still only wearing my pole top so his hands rested against my bare skin. I dragged my fingertips across his chest and shrugged.

"I'm open for suggestions."

He closed his eyes and took in a deep breath and after giving me another quick kiss, stepped back.

"I'll make a list and we can discuss it in detail when we're not standing in your studio."

Since I was on a sexual hiatus when I opened the studio, the thought of fooling around here never crossed my mind. But right now, alone here with Leo, I can't think of anything else.

"Do you want to try the elbow stand? I'll spot you."

"The thought of going upside down doesn't thrill me," he said. "But I'll show you what I can do."

He laid down on his stomach and extended his arms out to the side and his legs shoulder-width apart. I watched, fascinated, as he slowly lifted into a plank without using his elbows or knees to push. It looked like he had a string attached to his back, pulling him up. He lowered back to the floor, rolled to his side, and propped his head in his hand.

"That was very impressive," I said as I sat next to him.

Shifting onto his back, he said, "Come here, I'll show you what else I can do."

"I'm aware of what you can do and I am extremely impressed."

"I'm not talking about *that*, but I thank you for the compliment." Holding out his hand, he said, "Straddle my lap." I raised my brows and smirked. "Just trust the process."

I stood and placed my feet on either side of his hips before lowering down. He reached out and laced our fingers together.

"Okay now, shift forward and put your feet either on top of mine or on my ankles. Wherever they reach."

Stretching my legs back, I rested my toes on his ankles. With his arms holding my chest up, it was an awkward position, but I'll trust the process like he said. Even though I have no idea what either the process or the end result may be.

"Engage your muscles and hold my hands tight."

I did as he said and held on as he proceeded to press me slowly up and down, like a push

up. It was wobbly at first, but once I felt more comfortable, my body was solid. He must have felt the change because he got more daring with his actions, pushing me higher then lowering me down far enough to kiss me before sending me back up.

"I'm not even going to ask how you got so good at this," I said.

"It was kind of a party trick back in college."

"Is that so?"

He chuckled at my sarcastic tone and lowered me down onto his chest.

"That's so," he said as he wrapped his arms around my back. "It's been a while since I did it, but since you're in such good shape, I figured it'd be easy. And I was right."

He lifted his head and pressed his lips against mine. I think he meant for it to be a quick peck, but I opened my mouth over his and turned it into something hotter. Shifting his hand up to cup the back of my head, he thrust his tongue inside to tease and tangle against mine and I met him stroke for stroke.

Letting my legs slide down until I straddled his lap again, I pressed against his erection. That kicked things up a few notches and soon I was riding him as our mouths continued to feast on each other.

I needed to breathe, but didn't want to release his mouth so I took in quick, shallow breaths through my nose but it wasn't enough. Ending the kiss, I sat back and sucked in big gulps of air and watched him do the same.

"Don't move."

"I'm not going anywhere," he said.

I stood and crossed the room to lock the door. We're the only ones in the building, but with my luck one of my students or Clay would come back and get quite a show.

As I walked back toward the sexy man sprawled on my floor, I pulled off my bra and tossed it behind me. Once I reached his side, I slowly pulled down my joggers, adding an extra little wiggle to my hips before stepping out of them. My pole shorts and thong quickly followed.

"You are absolutely gorgeous."

I smiled at the compliment and lowered to my knees next to him. I'm getting more comfortable with him telling me that because honestly, he makes me feel beautiful.

Tucking my fingers into the waistband of his sweatpants, I pulled them and his boxer briefs down and watched his cock bob up against his stomach. *Way* up.

I reached out and dragged the tip of my index finger from the base all the way up to circle around the plump head.

"Oh fuck!"

I snatched my hand back and shifted my gaze to his face.

"Did I hurt you?"

"No. God no. I just realized that I don't have a condom," he said. "Do you by any chance have one on you?"

"I don't."

I looked around the studio. For what, I don't know. It's not like there's a secret stash here.

Nibbling on my lip, I considered my next words, then figured I have nothing to lose by speaking them.

"Before you, I hadn't had sex in more than three years, but I never stopped my birth control shot. I'm comfortable with skipping the condom if you are."

The intensity of his dark eyes as they bore into mine reiterated what a monumental step this is. If I'd really considered that before I spoke, I never would have gotten the words out.

"I get regular blood tests for the Waves. The last one was at the beginning of September and everything was good. I haven't been with anyone but you since then. So if you're sure, so am I."

Instead of answering with words, I straddled his lap again. Leo placed his hands on the outside of my thighs as I positioned myself over him, then let out a long, low groan as I slowly slid down.

"Shit that feels good."

I would have teased him about both his words and his

strained voice, but the feel of Leo inside me, hot and hard with nothing between us has left me speechless.

I'd love to go slow and make this last, but I'm already so wet and achy it won't take much to push me over the edge. I moved my hips in tiny circles, slowly at first then faster as I lost myself in the feeling.

He skimmed his hands up my sides then cupped my breasts before pinching my nipples between his thumbs and forefingers, twisting and pulling, using my own rhythm to drive me wild. I moved faster and faster, my inner muscles clenching him tighter every time my clit brushed against his pelvis.

"Leo." His name came out as a strangled moan.

I'm close, so close but I want to make it last as long as possible. Leo apparently has other plans.

Releasing my nipples, he gripped my ass, pressing me tighter against him as he lifted his hips to meet my every thrust. I rested my hands against his chest and continued to ride him, my movements shorter and more focused with every pass.

Leo tilted my hips forward, the slight adjustment pressing his dick against *that spot*. "Right there." I thrust harder, rubbing him against me over and over. "Oh God, Leo.

Right *there*."

That last word was said on a long, low moan as my inner walls spasmed over and over again, my orgasm crashing through my entire body. I heard Leo shout my name just before I collapsed against his chest.

Chapter Twenty-Four

AS I WATCHED Anjannette charm a customer, I couldn't keep the sappy smile from spreading across my face. The woman gives me "all the feels" as she would say. And I've finally admitted to myself that I am totally and completely in love with her.

The feeling has been brewing for a while—if I'm being honest, it was an insta-love kind of thing when I first saw her hanging off that pole. But I've never been in love before, not *real* love anyway, so it took me a bit to assign that particular word to my feelings. Now that I have, I'm dying to tell her. I'm just waiting for the right time and place. Hopefully this week will provide both of those things.

She said my name and from her tone, it's obvious it wasn't the first time.

"Hmm?"

"Was that okay?" she asked.

"Oh yeah, you were perfect."

"You were staring at me so I thought maybe I did something wrong."

Since we were teenagers, one of the Christmas gifts my siblings and I give our parents is a week off from the store. Sometimes they come in anyway to "see how it's going," but this year, they're not responsible for opening, closing, or anything in between from December 23rd through January 3rd. The store is closed for the holidays themselves, but we work it out between the six of us for the rest of the days.

I figured Anjannette would hang with my sisters or relax at the house while I put in my shifts, but she insisted on coming with me today. And once she got here, she jumped in with both feet.

"No, I'm just amazed that you're here serving up moussaka and scooping olives like a pro."

"It's so sweet that you and your siblings do this for your parents."

"It's the only way they take time off. We keep hoping that if they see how nice it is they'll at least partially retire and enjoy themselves more."

"Will Nicky take over when they retire?"

"That's the plan." I grabbed a broom and dustpan from the corner and walked around the counter to sweep. "We'll see if it ever happens."

"I guess as long as they're happy, it's all good."

"Yeah, I guess it is. I just hate to see them work so hard."

I moved everything I'd collected into a pile then swept it into a dustpan and emptied it into the garbage. Anjannette's arms wrapped around me from behind and I felt her kiss my back. Setting the broom and dustpan aside, I turned around to face her.

"You really are one of a kind, you know that?"

"So are you." I leaned down and pressed my mouth against hers then rested my forehead

against hers. "You really did a great job here today. You're a natural."

She pulled back and scrunched her nose.

"I didn't feel like I was much help most of the time, but I'll take an A for effort."

"Seriously, you did great. And I appreciate you being here at all. It's definitely above and beyond."

"Your family has been so welcoming, it's the least I could do. Besides, I like spending time with you."

"Yeah?" She nodded. "That's a good thing because I like spending time with you too."

Anjannette pulled away as the bell over the door jingled and she walked over to the counter to wait on the two women who came in. I didn't recognize them so I went back to cleaning up instead of chatting like I'd do with the regulars.

One of the women told Anjannette she heard about the store on Facebook so I guess Nicky's advertising is working. In fact, I didn't personally know a good portion of the customers today, so the clientele is definitely expanding.

By the time the women were finished picking what they wanted, a stack of boxes and two bags sat on the counter. When Anjannette finished ringing them up, they took me up on my offer to help them carry everything out to the car. I grabbed the boxes then followed them out to their car and set them on the floor of the back seat. They tried to hand me a tip but I waved them off and wished them a Merry Christmas.

"They cleared out a lot of stuff, especially the cookies," Anjannette said when I came back inside.

She picked up a broken sugar cookie and popped it into her mouth.

"That's a good thing since we're closed for the next two days."

I grabbed the empty trays she'd stacked on the counter behind her and put them in the sink.

"What do you do with stuff that's leftover?"

"It depends." I squeezed detergent onto the pans then turned on the hot water. "My mom makes extra food to drop off at the local police stations and hospital for the staff working the holiday, so sometimes we just add it to that. If there's only a small amount, one of us will just take it home or give it to a neighbor."

"I love your parents even more now," she said. "And after meeting your family, the way you are makes a lot of sense."

I rinsed off a pan and placed it on the rack to dry.

"The way I am?"

"Nice, sweet, kind. When we first met, I thought you were too good to be true and kept waiting for you to drop the facade and show your true colors." She shrugged. "But I've since learned that what you see is what you get and that's really refreshing."

After placing the last pan on the rack, I rinsed out the sink, turned off the water, and dried my hands, not sure what to say. Thankfully she changed the subject before I had to think of something.

"So what's the plan for the week?"

"Trey and Nori are flying in tomorrow, I'm working here again on the 28th, and Crispin and Ben will be here on the 30th, later in the day. The movie marathon is New Year's Day. There will be people hanging out at my parents' house all week but we don't have to be there all the time."

We'll be going into the city on the 29th, but she doesn't know that yet.

"What about New Year's Eve?"

"I don't usually go out, but we can if you want to."

"No, I'm good with staying in." She wrinkled her nose. "I always find New Year's Eve a little depressing. Add in a bunch of drunk obnoxious people and it's even worse."

"We can see what everyone else wants to do. And if there's anything you want to do during the week, just let me know."

"I just want to hang out with you and get to know your family better."

"Sounds perfect."

ANJANNETTE

I THOUGHT there were a lot of people at Leo's parents' house Thanksgiving weekend, but that was nothing compared to Christmas. Earlier there were people everywhere, including in the three-season room and on the deck where Leo and his brothers had set up propane heaters earlier.

I'm much more comfortable than I was at Thanksgiving and Leo must have sensed that because he didn't seem to feel the need to stick next to me the way he did the last time. In fact, he and Trey went out to the driveway with Nicky and Chris to play basketball a couple hours ago and it turned into a whole tournament-type thing with his cousins joining in. They're still out there playing with the spotlight on. Nori and I watched for a little bit, but came inside when the sun started to set and we got too cold. We settled into the family room with some of his aunts and cousins, but people had come and gone over the past hour and now it's just the two of us and Leo's sisters

It's so much fun being around this family dynamic. All the smack talk and teasing is balanced with the love and affection that's obvious between them. And spending this holiday here gives me all the feels, like those Christmas movies I binge watch every year.

"I can't even imagine how magical Christmas must have been growing up in this house," I said, looking around the family room.

When I was younger, I remember my mom fussing for the holiday, but once I stopped believing in Santa Claus, that pretty much stopped. But even though Leo and his siblings are grown, his mom still goes all out. Case in point, the tree in this room that we'd decorated last night before heading to midnight mass is what Annita refers to as "the family tree." It's covered with all the ornaments Leo and his siblings made through the years and silly or personal ones they'd gifted each other. The tree in the formal living room sits in front of the big bay window for the neighborhood to see and looks like something in a showroom.

"Yeah, it was," Marina said. "Hell, it still is. You see this place."

Every corner of the house is decorated and she even filled their stockings with little gifts.

"I never really thought about how much time and energy goes into doing all this," Eleni said. "But I put up a tiny tree in my apartment and hang a wreath on the door, and that's pretty much all I have energy for after working all week. Mom worked at the store a million hours a week, had the six of us, and still did all this."

"And I still don't know where she used to hide our

presents. Once we got to a certain age, we snooped all over the house, including up in the attic and never found anything," Marina said.

Angie's head snapped in my direction.

"Speaking of presents. What did you think of your gift from Leo?"

"I totally freaked out. I'm so excited, I can't even tell you. I've wanted to see that forever," I said, drawing out that last word. "Nori's ears are probably still ringing from my screech. Unfortunately for her, she was sitting next to me when I opened it."

Leo and I had exchanged gifts with each other earlier at his house and I'm still in shock. The man bought me tickets to *Hamilton*. Freaking *Hamilton!* And not just any seats—orchestra center, row J. Seriously. I can't even.

As if the tickets weren't enough, we're taking a limo into the city and having dinner before the show. How is this my life?

"My gifts to him paled in comparison, but seriously, how could anything I give him be as good as tickets to *Hamilton?*"

"You can't compare what we mere mortals give to Leo with what he bestows on us." Angie looked at her sisters for confirmation. Once they nodded, she continued. "But seriously, Leo appreciates personal or well-thought out gifts more than something that costs a lot of money."

"That's a true statement," Marina said.

It had taken me forever to think of something to give Leo. He has contracts for clothing, underwear, shoe, and sunglass brands so he's flush with those things. I've seen three of his houses and they're all well-decorated and well-stocked.

After agonizing over it, I decided on a few little things I

thought he'd like. Keera had suggested a Peaches & Pole shirt, shorts, sweatpants, and sweatshirt and I'm glad I listened to her, because he seemed to love them. A little gift shop near the studio had two coffee mugs I couldn't resist. One says *I Hate Being Sexy, but I'm a Baseball Player So I Can't Help It* and the other one *Dibs on the Baseball Player*, the latter being more for me than him, but I figured he'd get a kick out of it, and he did. But what he spent the most time oohing and aahing over was the afghan and crocheted peach I made for him.

I don't have very many real skills, but I do know how to crochet. My mom taught me and as much as I hated sitting still when I was younger to learn how to do it, I'm so glad I did. More so now after seeing Leo's reaction to my hand-made gift.

Loud voices sounded outside the room which I assume meant the guys were done with their games. Leo walked into the family room a second later. Sweaty with his button-down shirt pulled out of now-dirty khakis and messy hair, he should have looked vile, but that just isn't the case. He looks as hot as ever and my lady parts clenched in response. As if he sensed that, he flashed a sexy smile, which made it happen again.

Trey appeared beside him looking just as rumpled, but much less sexy. In my opinion anyway. Based on the change in Nori's breathing, I'd say she feels differently.

"We're gonna head back to the house to shower. If you want to stay here, we can come back for you," Leo said.

I looked over at Nori and we shared a smile.

"No, we'll just go with you now."

I stood and heard Angie chuckle then whisper to her sisters, "Maybe I should sleep here tonight."

She's probably not wrong. Because I don't plan on

letting her brother up for air tonight, and I'm pretty sure Nori has the same plans for Trey. Thank God the room they're staying in is all the way on the other side of the hall.

Chapter Twenty-Five

LEO

I'M NOT A MATERIALISTIC PERSON, but sometimes it's nice to have the resources to give people things and experiences that require money. Like prime *Hamilton* tickets, a limo into Manhattan, and dinner at a five-star restaurant.

We left my house early and once we got to the city, enjoyed some touristy things like going to see the tree in Rockefeller Center and a carriage ride through Central Park.

Anjannette lived in Manhattan for a few years so we had the driver cruise past her old haunts—the building that housed the two-bedroom apartment she shared with five other women, the corner diner where she used to wait tables, and some of the places she and her friends hung out. After checking out a few boutiques and consignment shops, we tossed our purchases into the trunk and headed to dinner, then the show.

The luxury of having a driver navigate the congested

streets makes getting around much more pleasurable. All we had to do was sit back, relax, and enjoy the ride. Watching Anjannette enjoy the experience made me appreciate it that much more.

She'd vibrated with anticipation all day and that excitement lasted all the way through the play. But when the curtain dropped, it seemed inevitable that high energy would too. Now that we're headed home, she's curled up against my chest, exhausted.

While I hired the limo to give her a full first-class experience, being able to hold her like this all the way home is more of a gift for me.

"I can't thank you enough for today, Leo. It was so perfect."

"You don't have to thank me anymore. It was my pleasure. I'm just glad you enjoyed the day."

Anjannette sat back to look me in the eye.

"Enjoyed? *Enjoyed?* Seriously Leo, that's too tame a word. This limo ride, the day in the city, that dinner and the show. I swear at one point, I was having an out-of-body experience."

She was in full theatrical mode and went on to describe the show in detail, as if I hadn't been sitting right next to her watching the entire thing. But I love seeing her so animated. Hell, I love *her* and as she took a breath, I decided I couldn't wait another second to tell her.

"I love you, Anjannette."

Cue the dramatic pause.

"What?"

I smiled at her expression. It's a combination of shock, wonder, and is-he-seriously-saying-this-now-when-I'm-talking-about-*Hamilton?*

"I love you," I repeated more slowly, enunciating each word.

"You love me?"

"I do."

She blinked, then nibbled on her lower lip, seeming to process my words before a smile slowly spread across her face.

"I'm glad I'm not the only one," she said before launching herself at me and pressing her mouth to mine. Before I could deepen the kiss, she pulled back. "I love you too."

"Thank God."

I pulled her onto my lap and those were the last words either of us uttered the rest of the way home.

"ARE you ever going to wipe that stupid smile off your face?" Trey asked.

"What are you talking about?"

"You look all sappy," he said.

We entered the supermarket and I grabbed a basket before leading the way to the seafood department. None of us want to go out for dinner tomorrow night, so we decided to celebrate New Year's Eve at the house. Trey and I are grabbing steak, lobster tail, and whatever else catches our eye before heading to the airport to pick up Crispin and Ben.

"You're busting my ass about looking sappy? With the way you and Nori are always making googly-eyes at each other," I said, using one of my father's favorite expressions.

I found the freezer with the lobster tail and, one at a time, tossed six into the basket. Then just for the hell of it, added a bag of shrimp.

"I'm not busting your ass exactly, just letting you know what you look like," he said, ignoring my last sentence.

"Thanks, I appreciate it."

We made our way to the butcher counter and asked him to cut six thick filet mignons.

"I'm just glad things are going well for the two of you."

"Yeah, they are." I chuckled. "I'm starting to think there may be something to the theory that there's something in the water at First Allegiant Bank Park."

My relationship with Anjannette has had a few major turning points. Our third-date conversation on the train and the first time we had sex being two of them. Not to mention the first time we had sex without a condom. I know she took that as seriously as I did and it brought things to a whole new level.

But exchanging those three little words in the limo last night changed things even more. I've only told one other woman that I loved her and that was my high school girlfriend. But that was a young love. This thing with Anjannette is more serious and much deeper, and hopefully it will only grow stronger from here.

ANJANNETTE

THIS WEEK HAS FLOWN by but I've really had a great time. Spending the holidays with Leo's family, working with him at the store, and of course, our trip into Manhattan were so much fun. Last night, we enjoyed a quiet New Year's Eve at the house with Trey, Nori, Crispin, and Ben. Everyone pitched in to cook the amazing surf-and-turf dinner then we just hung out and talked. It was fun getting to know them all a little better.

We're heading back to Scranton tomorrow afternoon, and as good as I know it will be to get home, I'm going to miss this. But, I still have today's movie marathon to enjoy.

Leo and I are curled up together on the oversized chair in his parents' family room surrounded by his siblings, Trey, Nori, Crispin, and Ben. This room is perfect for this kind of thing, not only because it's huge and has super comfy furniture, but also because instead of a TV, it has a home theater system, so we're watching the 90's-themed movies projected against the far wall. It's like we're sitting in a cozy cinema.

We started our marathon with *My Cousin Vinny* then took a short break before switching to *Clueless*, which is one of my favorites. I shifted closer to Leo and rested my head against his chest.

Leo had told me to bring something comfortable to wear for today and I'd listened. My once-black leggings are gray from years of washings that have left them so thin and soft, it feels like I'm not wearing pants. I'd brought a sweatshirt, but snagged a Waves hoodie from Leo's closet. It hangs down to my knees and is keeping my legs warm in the aforementioned thin leggings, but best of all, it smells like him. And of course, my feet are snug in my fuzzy unicorn slippers.

His version of comfortable is gray sweatpants and a well-worn Carolina Waves T-shirt. And while my old clothes and messy bun make me look destitute, he looks good enough to eat. Because you know, hot man in gray sweatpants.

"Seriously, this movie came out in 1995," Crispin said when the camera panned in for a close up of the actor's face. "How does Paul Rudd look exactly the same?"

"I think he's a vampire," Marina said.

"Ooh, next time you're all here, we'll have to plan a *Twilight* marathon."

Other than Crispin and Ben, the guys told Angie to count them out. Those aren't my favorite movies, but I'm game. Leo's sisters, in fact his whole family, are so welcoming, I'd love to spend more time with them.

As much as I hate it, my mind drifted back to my relationship with Travis. We were together for five years, and I never felt this comfortable with his friends or family. His mother hated me, his brother hit on me, and his sister acted like she was better than everyone, especially me. So needless to say, spending time with them wasn't on the top of my list. And his friends were misogynistic jerks who constantly made snide comments and cracked inside jokes trying to make me feel like an outsider.

Of course, Travis totally gaslighted me into thinking all that was in my head. He liked to compartmentalize his life anyway. He had friends, family, and a girlfriend and never the twain shall meet. So often I would stay home while he spent time with his friends and family without me because by that time, he'd isolated me from all *my* friends. Or should I say, I isolated myself without even realizing it. It's funny how I didn't think that was strange back then. Looking back now, it seems bizarre, not to mention pathetic, that I allowed all that to happen.

"You okay?" Leo whispered. I nodded, not trusting myself to speak.

He kissed the top of my head, pulled me closer against his chest, and rubbed my back in long, soothing strokes. The man really is too good to be true. But as he's proven to me time and time again, he is as real as real could be. And by some miracle, he loves me.

Pushing thoughts of Travis from my mind, I focused on the movie again. And thankfully I did, my favorite line is coming up.

I waited, and when Brittany Murphy's character Tai

says, "You're a virgin who can't drive" to Alicia Silverstone's character Cher, I recited each word right along with her. Leo's laughter rumbled beneath my ear and I pushed back to look around the room, with a shocked smile on my face. His sisters and Crispin had done the same thing.

How much more obvious could it be that these are my people?

I settled back against Leo and watched the rest of the movie.

His parents came home just as the credits rolled and his mom insisted on making us sandwiches so we took a break to eat.

"What are we watching next?" I asked.

"*10 Things I Hate About You.*"

"Ohhhh, that's one of my favorites." Crispin pressed a hand against his chest. "Heath Ledger was a full snack. It's a shame he died so young."

"You're not going to cry during the movie, are you?" Nori asked.

"No, but I might start belting out *Can't Take My Eyes Off You.* Sometimes I can't help myself when that marching band starts to play."

"Please try to refrain yourself," Nori said with a big smile.

He looked at Ben and blinked dramatically.

"I think she just insulted me."

"She just doesn't want you to put poor Heath to shame with your perfect voice."

"That man must love you a lot," Trey said. "Because I've heard you sing."

"The happy truth of that first sentence is all I heard," Crispin said.

"Before you two start throwing down, let's just go watch the movie," Marina said.

We shuffled back into the family room and I relaxed against Leo again, full and content and watched as Heath Ledger made Julia Stiles fall in love with him. Unfortunately there's always a black moment before the happy ending in Hollywood so he also broke her heart before winning it in the end.

With Leo, I feel like I'm living out my own Hollywood romance. Hopefully we'll skip over the broken heart, and move right to the happily ever after.

Chapter Twenty-Six

LEO

I WOKE and smiled before even opening my eyes and that had everything to do with the warm woman still asleep in my arms. Kissing the back of Anjannette's head, I pulled her tighter against my chest and buried my nose in her hair, inhaling her unique scent, which I now know is a custom blend of cinnamon, tea tree, and vanilla she gets made at a local perfume shop. She told me she switches to a citrus scent for the spring and summer and I'm looking forward to experiencing that.

We drove back to Scranton yesterday afternoon and during dinner, I convinced her to spend the night at my house. After waking up with her next to me all week, I dreaded the thought of the other side of my bed being cold this morning. She must have felt the same way, because after stopping at her apartment to pick up clothes and her Jeep, she followed me here and we climbed right into bed.

"Did you bring one of your bats to bed?"

Her sleep-sexy voice made the morning wood she was rubbing her ass against even harder.

"You're good for my ego, you know that?"

"I'm just calling it like I see it." Another wiggle. "Or rather, *feel* it."

I skimmed my hand up her belly to cup her breast. She pressed back against me as I squeezed and molded her plump flesh and let out a long, low moan when I plucked her nipple between my thumb and forefinger.

"I like waking up next to you," I whispered before latching on to her earlobe then tugging it between my teeth.

She wiggled against me.

"It does have its advantages."

"Yes it does."

Especially when I wake up spooning her naked body from behind. It gives me all kinds of sexy ideas. Deciding to act on one of them, I gave her nipple one last tug then moved my hand back down over her stomach and slid my middle finger between her slick folds.

"Leo."

The way she says my name when she's turned on is all husky and moany and sexy as hell. She moved her foot back to rest on my knee, opening herself to me, and I took full advantage.

I stroked, flicked, and pinched that tiny nub until her breath sawed in and out in throaty gasps. Knowing she's close, I pulled her tighter against me and slipped two fingers inside to stroke while my thumb alternately pressed against and circled her clit. I want her to come at least once before I slide into her, because once I feel her tight pussy squeezing me, it's not going to last long.

Her hips moved with my rhythm and I felt the telltale

flutters against my fingers a second before her body stiffened. Anjannette chanted my name over and over and I stayed with her until the spasms subsided.

I removed my fingers and kissed her shoulder, holding her until her breathing returned to normal. She shifted her leg over my thigh and rubbed her ass against my throbbing erection.

"Are you gonna keep that all to yourself?"

"Why?" I nibbled at her shoulder. "Do you want it?"

She glanced over her shoulder at me, those big blue eyes peeking through her lashes.

"More than anything."

"Anything to make the lady happy," I said.

Placing my hand on her hip, I shifted her ass back and filled her with one hard thrust.

"Oh hell, this isn't gonna take long."

She tightened her leg around mine, holding me close as I thrust into her over and over again. I wasn't kidding when I said it wasn't going to take long, but I don't want to come alone. I slid my hand down and circled her clit with my index finger as I kept up a steady in and out rhythm.

Her breathing became more erratic and soon I felt her tightening around me. I fought against my own release, wanting to wring every last second of pleasure before letting go. When her inner walls clamped down on me then spasmed, I couldn't hold on any longer. I thrust once, twice, three times then growled her name before collapsing against her back.

AFTER SHOWERING TOGETHER, we lingered over a late breakfast and all too soon, it was time for Anjannette to leave for the studio. Our Christmas vacation is officially over.

She kissed me goodbye and walked out the door as I cleared the table.

When I was done, I headed toward the stairs but stopped when I saw Anjannette through the window. The hood of her Jeep was up and she was looking at the engine. I slipped on my shoes and went out to see what's wrong.

"It won't start," she said as I approached.

I looked at the engine then checked wires and connections, but everything seemed tight.

"Is it trying to start or not doing anything?"

"It's making a grinding noise but nothing else happens."

"Let me listen."

She slid behind the wheel and turned the key, eliciting a horrible noise.

"Okay," I said before she tried again.

She got out of the Jeep and slammed the door.

"Any ideas?"

"I think it's the starter. Let's go inside and call a tow truck."

After the tow arrived, we hopped into my truck and followed it to the garage. She filled the mechanic in on the issue and he agreed that it's probably the starter. But he said he'd let her know for sure when he gets a chance to check it out.

We got back in the truck and headed for the studio.

"You're done at seven-fifteen?"

"That's when my class ends but I'll stick around for Keera's and catch a ride home with

her."

"I have yoga then Clay and I are heading to Lackawanna College and he's going to throw to me. I'll catch a ride with him and leave my truck at the studio. Come pick me up when you're done."

"I can't take your truck."

"Why not?"

"Because."

I glanced over at her, my brow raised.

"That's not a reason. Besides, it's not like I'm trying to give you the pink slip. You're driving it less than a mile."

"The thought of driving your shiny new truck makes my stomach twist," she said,

placing her hand on her abdomen. Then sighing, she added, "But you're right. I'm not going that far. Thank you."

ANJANNETTE

WE ENTERED the building and Leo kissed me goodbye then handed me his fob. I appreciated the site of his ass as he walked up the stairs before unlocking the door and stepping into my studio. Since it's been closed up for a week, it's a little musty, so I turned on the air purifier in the corner.

My broken Jeep put me a little behind schedule but I still have time to work on the choreography that's been running through my head for a few days. After warming up, I stripped down to my pole shorts and top and put *Love on the Brain* by Rhianna on repeat and the pole on spin.

At first I just freestyled, but then I found myself repeating moves that worked best with the sultry beat. I got lost in the music and the movement and jumped when the song ended and I heard clapping before it started again.

I looked over and spotted Keera sitting in the corner.

"Sorry, I didn't mean to scare you, but that was fucking amazing."

"Thanks."

"I'm guessing you hitched a ride with your sexy ball player?"

"I did, but only because my Jeep wouldn't start. It's at the garage right now waiting to be diagnosed."

"That sucks."

"Yeah. Hopefully it's not anything super expensive."

She held up both hands with her index and middle fingers crossed.

After switching to a playlist and lowering the volume, I grabbed a rag and sprayed it then tucked it into my bra and climbed to the top of the pole. Keera stayed quiet but I felt her watching me as I slowly made my way down to the floor, cleaning the pole on my descent.

"*Love on the Brain*, huh? Did you pick that song for any particular reason?"

"I like it?"

"Sure, it's a great song, but I'm thinking something big happened last week." She tapped her index finger against her chin. "Is it possible that words were exchanged?"

My face heated at her question and Keera knew the answer before I even nodded. She pulled me into a bear hug and squeezed.

"Oh my God. This is so awesome."

"I have so much to tell you," I said as she released me.

"Sounds like it."

"Tomorrow at taco Tuesday," I said.

"It's a date."

AFTER NOT EXERCISING FOR A WEEK, I struggled through flexibility class, but it felt good to move. Plus everyone seemed happy to be back and the class had a great energy. Still, when my muscles protested as I changed back into street clothes, I know I'll be sore as hell tomorrow. Maybe I'll have Leo rub me with Arnica cream later. That'll be fun.

Speaking of Leo, I better get out of here and go pick him up. After saying goodbye to Keera and her intermediate class, I headed out to his truck, tossed my bag in the back seat, and climbed behind the wheel. This is so much bigger than my Jeep and I'm thankful I don't have far to drive.

After finding the button on the side of the seat to move it forward, I pressed it until my foot reached the pedals. Shifting into drive, I stepped lightly on the gas and pulled forward, looking left and right three times before turning out of the parking lot. I slowly headed toward the gym at Lackawanna College holding the wheel with a white-knuckled grip.

It was only a short distance but through the winding city streets, the ride seemed to take forever. I let out a breath I didn't realize I'd been holding when I turned into the parking lot and spotted Clay's car. I parked and walked into the building, following the sounds down the hall.

"Can I help you?"

I backtracked when I heard a man's voice emerge from the office I'd just passed.

"Yeah, hi," I said, standing in the doorway. "I'm here to pick up Leo."

The man's face transformed with his smile.

"You must be the famous Anjannette." I raised my brow. "I'm Benji Alvarez. I was Leo and Clay's coach when they went to school here. He's told me a lot about you."

"It's nice to meet you, Benji. I've heard a lot about you, too. Leo says you're one of the best coaches he ever had."

He blushed at my praise then cleared his throat and hitched his thumb toward the end of the hall.

"As you can hear, Leo and Clay are in the gym. They've been throwing for a while now so I'm guessing they're almost done."

His words were proven true when we stepped through the double doors just as the ball landed in Leo's mitt with a resounding smack. He stood and removed his helmet.

"Thanks Clay."

"Thank you. I miss this."

Leo dropped his glove to the ground and pulled his chest protector over his head, giving it the same fate. Bending down, he released the straps of his shin guards and kicked them aside. Slicking his sweaty hair off his forehead, he stood and twisted from side to side.

"You still got it. My hand is stinging."

"Yeah, I'm an All-Star until my arm unexpectedly dies."

"Let me know if this gets to be too much for you," Leo said as he straightened.

"As long as I don't push it too much, I should be fine."

My eyes widened as I took in Leo all hot and sweaty in his baseball pants with a Waves T-shirt tucked into the waistband. Keera showed me pictures of him in his uniform and sure, he looks super-hot, but that was a two-dimensional image on the computer screen. Live and in person, he's a freaking god.

He spotted me and smiled and I'm sure he walked toward me at a normal pace, but my lust-induced brain had him moving in sexy slo-mo. My mouth went dry and other parts of me went well, not so dry.

It's ironic that the first time I saw Leo, his resemblance to John Stamos made me think about all my Uncle Jesse fantasies. Because right now, the only thing running through my head is *have mercy*.

Chapter Twenty-Seven

LEO

"I CAN'T BELIEVE you're here and your wedding is in two weeks," Keera said to Nori.

"The wedding is so low-key. Once we found a venue, the rest just kind of took care of itself. I have to pick up my dress when we get back, but that's pretty much it."

I'll admit I was shocked when Trey called and said they were coming up to visit so close to the wedding. I figured they'd be running around taking care of last-minute details. Besides, it's freaking freezing and the snow that got dumped on us by the storm that blew through a few days ago is not going away because of the frigid temperatures.

Of course, once my sister found out Trey and Nori would be here, she decided to come too. I told Anjannette to invite Keera because I want to get to know her better. Our short conversations coming and going at the studio aren't cutting it. Supposedly for that same reason, Anjannette also invited Clay, who should be here any minute. I think there might be some matchmaking going on, but I won't complain about that. There are worse people Angie could date.

"You're seriously the calmest bride I've ever seen," Angie said. "I was in two weddings last year and I swear I was ready to throat punch the brides by the time the big day arrived, and they were my best friends."

Nori shrugged and looked at Trey, her eyes full of love.

"As long as Trey and I are pronounced man and wife, nothing else about the day really matters."

"See how lucky I am?" Trey said in a sappy voice I wouldn't have thought him capable of a year ago.

"Awww, that's so sweet," Keera said.

"I'll tell you what's really sweet, my parents are shutting the store down for four whole days to attend. That should be written in the history books," I said.

"They've never closed like that before?" Anjannette asked.

"Random days here and there, but I could count those on one hand. Usually it's for family weddings. But since all our family lives closeby, they usually manage to work at least part of the day."

"But Trey is special." Angie added attitude to that last word.

"You know your mom loves me best, especially now that I'm getting married." Trey rebutted. "She keeps saying if one of you got married, they'd close the store." He chuckled. "Hell, at this point, they'd probably declare it a holiday."

Angie threw her napkin and hit him square in the face.

"Jerk."

Trey stuck his tongue out and Angie opened her mouth to say something but just started laughing instead.

"I want to know about the most important part," Keera said. "Where are you going on your honeymoon?"

"We're touring England, Ireland, and Scotland." Nori squeezed Trey's arm. "Thankfully this guy is a pro at navigating on the left side of the road from the right side of the car. We're getting a rental in each country and we'll just roam around. There are a couple major spots we want to see, but other than that, we're going wherever the roads take us."

"That sounds like heaven."

"We talked about going to Iceland, but January is the coldest and darkest month there and the weather is really unpredictable. So we'll go there some other time."

"How long will you have after you get back before you have to report to spring training?" Angie asked.

"Four days," Trey said.

"Are you going?" Angie asked Nori.

"Not immediately. I have some commissions booked that I want to get done."

"So business is still going well?"

"It's going better than well," Trey answered. "My soon-to-be-wife is in demand."

"I've been really busy," Nori said. "I'm trying to figure out a schedule that will work once Trey is on the road so we're never apart too long. Being based out of Myrtle Beach makes it easier when he's home, for sure. But this is still relatively new for us, both my business booming and the logistics of keeping our time apart to a minimum." She shrugged. "We'll figure it out. All the other couples do."

"Let me know when you'll be in St. Pete," Angie said. "I'd like to go and it would be fun if I had someone to hang with." She looked at Anjannette. "Do you plan on going to spring training at all?"

"Oh uh, I don't know."

She looked unsure of what to say, so I interjected.

"We haven't talked about it yet. I'm hoping she'll be able to come down, but with the studio, I know it's difficult for her to get away. So we'll play it by ear."

"Thankfully I have a great friend and awesome teacher who's running things for me when I go to your wedding," she said to Nori, then looked at Keera and smiled. "But I don't want to abuse that or she'll get angry."

"Hell, maybe we'll just let Clay run things and we'll both take off for paradise in the middle of winter." Keera laughed, but I'm not totally sure she's joking.

Angie brought the conversation back to Nori's business and I listened with half an ear as she discussed something new she's been working on. I heard the words book covers, teasers, and graphics, but wasn't paying enough attention to make sense of it. She stopped speaking when the doorbell rang and she hopped out of her chair to answer it. Definitely some matchmaking going on tonight.

I looked over at Anjannette who'd gotten quiet and was giving her wine glass more attention than it deserved. She looked like a deer in the headlights during the discussion about spring training. And I'll admit, I'm feeling the same way at the moment. I've always looked forward to the start of the season, but this year, I realize I'm not exactly dreading it, but I'm not chomping at the bit for pitchers and catchers to report either.

This is the first time I'll be leaving a girlfriend behind while I'm traveling around the country playing baseball. It makes me have a lot more empathy for the guys who have wives and/or families and have done it for years.

I love Anjannette and I'm willing to do whatever it takes to keep our relationship intact during the time apart. I just hope she feels the same way.

ANJANNETTE

"OKAY, spill. What's wrong? You've been quiet and distracted since Saturday."

I'm not ready to discuss what's on my mind, but I know Keera won't stop pushing until I tell her.

"I don't know if Leo and I are going to work out."

"What?" she screeched, then in a more moderate tone repeated the one-word question.

"After the spring training discussion Friday night, I really started thinking about it. How are we going to make this work? This is his career we're talking about. It's not like it's only for this year."

"If you love each other, you just will."

The waitress set our plates down in front of us and topped off our water. Surprisingly, my margarita is still full. I don't even know if I've had a sip yet, so I took one before Keera commented about it.

"That's a pretty idealistic vision, don't you think?" I asked.

"I don't think so."

"Keera, I looked up the schedule. There are a hundred and sixty-two games during the regular season and another thirty in spring training. Plus pitchers and catchers report early, so Leo will be down in St. Pete fifteen days before it starts. If they make it to the post-season, that adds a few weeks, depending on how far they go."

"Anjannette, you're spiraling."

"I'm not spiraling, I'm facing the facts. After Leo leaves for spring training in a few weeks, I may not see him again until October." I rubbed my forehead. "If I lived in Myrtle

Beach, it would be a little easier, but I don't. Even if I lived in a city with a team he plays against, there'd be more of an opportunity to see each other. But the closest teams the Waves play are in New York and Baltimore, which aren't exactly in our back yard.

"Stop focusing on all the scary numbers and try to figure out when you can take small increments of time and go see him. You know I'll take care of the studio for you. Plus you've been thinking about hiring another teacher."

"What am I going to do, hire someone then be like, 'here are the keys, I'm off, see you later?'" She rolled her eyes instead of answering. "And I can't expect you to fill in all the time. You have a full-time job."

"Maybe not for long," she mumbled under her breath but I heard it anyway.

"Why? What's happening with your job?"

"There are rumors of cutbacks and since I'm middle management, my job will be one of the first to go."

"What are you going to do?"

"I'll wait and see what happens. If they do let me go, I'll get a severance package, plus I'll be able to collect for a few months. It will only be a fraction of what I'm making, but I'll be fine. I have some savings and I don't have any living expenses right now." She picked up a taco and gestured with it. "And that's all I'm saying about myself. We're talking about you."

She took a bite of her taco and I figured I should at least pretend to eat mine. Normally I have one gone by now, but my stomach has been in knots for a few days now and I'm just not hungry.

"What's the real issue here?"

"I told you the real issue."

"No, there has to be something else because there's no way in hell any sane person would even think about giving up on a relationship with a great guy like Leo because of what's basically a scheduling conflict."

"It's more than a scheduling conflict."

"Not really."

I set the taco back on my plate and pushed it to the side. And you know it's a sad day when I don't want to eat a taco.

"Leo will basically be gone for the next seven months. If our relationship was further along, I might feel more confident that we could make it work."

Keera popped the last bite of taco into her mouth and watched me while she chewed, like she was trying to figure out some big mystery. But I can't let her do that. It's too embarrassing. I don't even want to think about the big fear lingering in the back of my mind. Unfortunately, all this talk has brought it front and center. Namely, how am I supposed to make things work with Leo when he's away for more than half the year when I couldn't keep it together with a man I lived with for five years?

To distract her from reading my mind, I threw her a bone.

"I'm not making any decisions right now, just thinking of all the possible scenarios. We still have a few weeks to spend together, plus Trey and Nori's wedding."

"While you're *thinking of all the possible scenarios*, just remember what Granny Vi said, 'Don't be a Miranda.'"

Chapter Twenty-Eight

LEO

TIME IS FLYING and Anjannette and I still don't have a plan for the spring training or the season. We've talked about it in general terms, like "Oh, you'll be in St. Pete then," but that's as far as it's gone. Part of me wants to nut up and sit her down for a frank discussion, but the other part doesn't want to ruin the time we have left before I have to leave.

I finished slicing marinated mozzarella and arranged it on the cutting board next to the bowl I plan to fill with an assortment of olives. My phone alarm beeped, signaling that it was time to put the Greek flatbread into the oven. Once that was done, I finished assembling my charcuterie board.

Anjannette had a bachelorette party after class tonight so I'm cooking. French onion soup and a charcuterie board seem like a perfect late-ish dinner. She loves both of those things as well as my mom's flatbread, which I had in my freezer leftover from Christmas.

Trey and Nori's wedding is tomorrow, so we're leaving for Myrtle Beach in the morning. Since the ceremony and reception are at the venue, there's no formal rehearsal the night before. There's really nothing to rehearse. Crispin and I will stand there next to the bride and groom as they recite their vows, I'll hand them the rings when prompted, and they'll be pronounced man and wife. Seems easy enough.

I heard the front door open and a second later, Anjannette walked into the kitchen.

"What smells so good?"

"French onion soup."

"One of my favorites." She picked up a Kalamata olive and popped it into her mouth. "Mmm, this too."

The oven timer dinged and I walked over, pulled out the flatbread, and set it on the counter. Still wearing my oven mitts, I grabbed a knife and cut it in quarters then placed it on the only empty spot on the cutting board.

"Leo, this looks amazing," Anjannette said. "I thought we'd order a pizza or something, but this is a feast."

"I know you like both of these things and I had all the ingredients on hand. It didn't take much to throw it together."

I opened the cabinet next to the stove and pulled two crocks from the top shelf. Anjannette leaned against the island and picked at the charcuterie board while I divided the soup between the crocks and topped it with toasted French bread and provolone cheese. After popping them in the oven, I joined her.

"How'd your party go?"

"Good. They were all really nice and seemed to have a fun time." She dipped flatbread into the hummus and took a bite. "Mmm, is this the bread your mom sent home with us from Christmas?"

"It is."

"It's still so good."

"Yeah, it freezes well."

While we picked at meat, cheese, and olives, she told me about her party and how she and Keera tweaked the format again and it seemed to work well.

"But after work I got some bad news."

"What's that?"

"I realized I forgot to pack my curling iron so I stopped by my apartment to grab it and found a letter in the entry-way. Apparently someone had slipped under my door."

"What was it?"

"Stand down big guy, it wasn't anything ominous" She patted my arm. "My building was sold and the new land-lord isn't renewing any of the leases. So I have to find a new apartment before March."

"That stinks," I said. "But at least they gave some notice."

I walked over to the oven and checked on the soup. The cheese is melted and brown on top, just the way I like it. Grabbing my trusty oven mitts again, I grabbed one of the crocks and placed it on a plate, then did the same with the other. I carried them over to the island and set them down.

"This looks so good." She picked up one of the spoons I'd set out earlier and pushed the cheese away from the side to let some of the heat escape. "Yeah, it would have definitely been worse if they said I had to be out by next week. It's still a huge inconvenience. I like my apartment and I *hate* moving. It's such a pain in the ass."

I toyed with my soup as I sorted through my thoughts. Anjannette has been staying here since we got back from

Christmas. There's no reason she can't put her stuff in storage and continue to live here. Or I could make room for her stuff if she wants, some of it anyway.

"Why don't you just live here?"

The timing of my question wasn't ideal. She'd just placed a spoonful of soup into her mouth and she started to cough. I watched to make sure she wasn't truly choking, but it seemed like a wrong-pipe situation and eventually she was okay.

She took a drink of water then cleared her throat and took another sip as she blinked to clear the tears from her eyes. After taking one more drink, she set her glass down then took in a deep breath and blew it out.

"Leo, I can't live here."

"Why not? You've been staying here the past couple weeks."

"Yeah, but staying here and moving in are two totally different things. I mean—" She shook her head and gestured wildly with her hands. "I love you, but we've only been dating a couple months."

I took her hands in mine and kissed the back of the right one and the inner wrist of the left. Lacing my fingers through hers, I rested our joined hands on the island between us.

"I'll be leaving in a couple weeks so you'll have the place all to yourself."

"But Leo, this is your house. I can't live here and creep around when you're away."

I laughed at both her words and the look on her face when she said them.

"What exactly would you do? Wear all black and sneak around like a burglar."

"Don't try to make me laugh, this is serious."

"It is serious, but at the same time, it's not a big deal." I rested my elbows on the island and leaned closer to her. "I love you Anjannette, and if I can help you out in any way, I want to. And I hope you'll let me. Why should this house sit empty when you need a place to live?"

I probably shouldn't bring up my sister in this discussion but I'm going to anyway.

"That's how Angie ended up living in my other house. She moved into a townhouse with a couple friends and within a year, one got engaged and she and her fiancé moved in together and the other decided to move to Colorado. While she could have moved back home, she didn't want to do that, and she was having trouble finding an apartment she could afford on her own. My house was sitting empty and I told her to just move in there."

Anjannette nibbled at her bottom lip and looked down at our joined hands. After what seemed like forever, she looked up and met my gaze.

"I'll take you up on your generous offer on two conditions." I raised my brow, prompting her to name them. "It's temporary and you have to let me pay rent."

I don't want to agree to either of those things, but I know if I don't, she'll say no.

"Okay, I accept your terms," I said, not planning on doing any such thing.

ANJANNETTE

NORI SAID she fell in love with this venue as soon as she saw it and I could see why. It's a fun combination of formal and funky that makes for a very welcoming space.

When we first arrived, Angie and I went upstairs to visit Nori, who was getting her hair and makeup done in what's normally a boudoir studio but today is serving as the bride's room. With its purple walls, ornate fireplace, and glamorous furniture, I see how it would speak to her artist's soul.

The room I'm in right now where the ceremony will be held is more traditional with its dark wood floors, cream walls, and crystal chandeliers. A harpist is sitting next to the makeshift altar, surprising me with the songs she was plucking out. She finished playing *Adventure of a Lifetime* by Coldplay and segued right into *Best Day of My Life* by American Authors.

"This is the kind of wedding I want," Angie said. "Small and comfortable."

I nodded toward Annita sitting in the row in front of us with the rest of the Marakis clan.

"I think your mother might have a different idea," I said with a chuckle. "With your family, small seems impossible. There were more people than this at Christmas dinner."

"I know." She sighed. "Maybe I'll elope and let her throw me a happily-ever-after party. That way, I can avoid all the wedding drama and just show up and have fun. What about you?"

"What?"

"Do you want a big or small wedding?"

Before I had to answer that, the officiant, Trey, and Leo walked through a door at the front of the room. They stepped onto the decorated platform serving as the altar. Leo looks so sexy in his tuxedo and my face heated when he glanced in my direction and caught me eye fucking him. He winked and I couldn't help the smile that spread across my face.

"It's kind of strange seeing Leo in a relationship," Angie said when she witnessed the exchange.

"Why's that?"

"It's just been a while. He had a girlfriend in high school, but they broke up after he went away to college. Then there was the one he brought home a couple years ago. And honestly, I don't know what he was thinking. She was awful." She nudged me with her shoulder. "But you're awesome and you two are so cute together it's a little sickening sometimes."

"You're awesome, too. Your whole family is."

The first notes of *A Thousand Years* by Christina Perri filled the room and, prompted by the officiant, everyone stood. I turned to look down the makeshift aisle, my gaze skimming the guests on the other side and behind me. Other than the Marakis family, the guest list consists of Trey and Leo's teammates, Clay, and a few people I don't know.

Crispin walked into the room through a door in the back with Nori on his arm. She looks absolutely gorgeous in a lace-trimmed off-the-shoulder dress. The sheer long sleeves add a unique detail to the bodice. As she and Crispin slowly walked down the aisle, her perfectly-shaped leg played peek-a-boo through the thigh-high slit.

I thought about grabbing my phone and snapping some pictures, but decided not to. There are two hired photographers. I decided to just enjoy the moment.

As they passed me, I turned to face the front. Trey's eyes glistened as he watched his bride walk toward him. He stepped down as they reached him and waited as Crispin kissed his wife-to-be on the cheek before taking her hand and stepping back onto the platform. Crispin fixed the back of her dress then took his place on her left-hand side just as the song ended. The officiant told us all to be seated and started the ceremony.

Annita's sniffles sounded through the room as Nori and Trey recited their vows. I'll admit, I teared up once or twice. They're so obviously in love and, even though they're total opposites, they're perfect together.

The officiant pronounced them man and wife and the room sounded with applause as Trey bent his wife over his arm and gave her a kiss that would make Hollywood proud.

LEO and I returned to our table for a much-needed break. We've been on the dance floor since the band started playing and I couldn't handle another fast song. My feet are killing me.

I poured two glasses of water from the pitcher in the middle of the table and handed one to him. After taking a big gulp, I sat back in my chair and looked around the room. His teammates that I met at the golf tournament were all here, along with some other ones. And they've all been on the dance floor most of the night.

"This is a great wedding," I said. "Everyone looks like they're having a good time."

"Yeah, they're a fun crowd."

It still amazes me how normal his friends are. Keera would be in heaven here. Aside from the fact that she always enjoys a room full of man candy, she truly loves baseball. She, Leo, and Trey discussed the game for two hours at his house a couple weeks ago.

I wish there was a way I could bring her to one of these events so she could meet them. But since she's my backup at the studio, that's impossible. Unless we close for a few days.

Would that be so crazy?

"You okay?" Leo asked.

"Yeah, why?"

"You were frowning."

"I was just thinking." I looked around the room again then shifted closer to him. "Keera would love to meet your friends. You know what a big fan she is."

"Maybe we could set something up when we play New York. If there's an afternoon game, we could all go out to dinner afterwards."

"Or maybe she could come down to St. Pete with me," I said before I could think twice about it. His eyes rounded. "I'd have to close the studio, but..." I trailed off and shrugged.

"Whatever you want to do is fine with me. You know I'd love to see you and Keera is always welcome."

"I'm so exhausted." Crispin said as he and Ben joined us at the table. He picked up a napkin and patted his brow and frowned down at it before holding it out for his boyfriend to see. "And look at how much I'm sweating. I must look awful."

He pulled his phone out of his pocket and held it up to look at his face and hair.

"You look as handsome as ever," Ben said.

Crispin flashed a fake smile.

"You're very sweet, but you're a liar. My face is all flush and look at this hair."

His hair looks fine to me, but he's the professional so maybe he sees something I don't.

Nori told me Crispin helped her pick out her dress and I told him how beautiful she looks. He shifted his attention to Nori and Trey out on the dance floor and a real smile crossed his face.

"She does, doesn't she?" He rolled his eyes and looked

back at me. "You should have seen the dress she initially picked out. It was literally a white maxi dress. She looked like she belonged at Woodstock instead of walking down the aisle." He waved his hand. "Although I should be happy she even picked out a dress by herself instead of planning to wear jeans and a graphic tee."

"Speaking of clothes," Leo said. "I'm kind of surprised at what you're wearing."

Crispin looked down at his black tuxedo and tugged at the silk lapel.

"What's wrong with what I'm wearing?"

"I thought for sure you'd wear a kilt à la David Rose."

Crispin's mouth curled into a smile.

"I thought about it, but I'm in a committed relationship now, Leo. I couldn't show up here in a kilt and have all these hot guys wondering what I have on—" He bobbed his eyebrows. "—or don't have on underneath it. Ben would get jealous."

Leo chuckled then shook his head and stood.

"And on that note, I'm going to ask this beautiful woman to accompany me to the dance floor." He held out his hand. "They're playing our song."

I'm moving into his house, thinking about closing the studio to go visit him, and his family has welcomed me with open arms. Now we have a song.

Normally just one of those things would have my brain spiraling into a million different scenarios how this could all go wrong. But I promised Keera I'd enjoy myself instead of over-thinking every little thing. So as Leo pulled me into his arms and we gently swayed to *The Way You Look Tonight*, that's what I'm doing.

Chapter Twenty-Nine

LEO

"You want another one?" Trey yelled from inside his condo.

"Sure."

He came out carrying two bottles of lager, handed one to me, and settled into the other chair out here on the balcony. I stared out at the setting sun shimmering on the water. It was seventy-five and sunny here in St. Pete today and Scranton got six inches of snow dumped on it this morning.

Thankfully I'd hired a guy to plow my driveway and shovel the sidewalks for the whole season. He texted me pictures earlier so I know he'd actually done the job and it's clear for Anjannette.

I took a long draw on my bottle and mentally chuckled. That's what I was doing in between sessions today. Checking texts from the plow guy and worrying about Anjannette driving in the snow.

As if he read my mind, Trey said. "It's gonna be a weird year."

I looked over and saluted him with my bottle.

"That is a true statement."

Pitchers and catchers reported two days ago and that's exactly when Trey and I both arrived in St. Pete. Other years, I'd often come down a few days early just to chill and enjoy the sun. But this year I booked the latest flight possible the night before. I actually thought about taking the earliest flight the day of, but didn't want to risk a delayed or canceled flight and get here late. That wouldn't be a good way to start the season.

"But you looked good today. How's your back feel?"

"Great. The yoga really helped. I'm glad Max suggested it. Even though it kicked my ass at first, it was a pretty easy solution to the problem. I'm glad I stuck with it. Of course, now I just need to make sure I keep up the practice. I may have to get Clay to call me for motivation. Or better yet, do Zoom classes with me."

"Speaking of calls, my father called before."

"Seriously?"

Trey and his father always had a rocky relationship but when Connery "Reg" Reginald Youngman II talked shit about Nori last year, that was it. Trey told him, in no uncertain terms, that he was done with him.

"Yeah." He set his empty bottle on the table between us. "Apparently someone told him about the wedding and he was pissed because he didn't put his game face on fast enough and it was pretty obvious he didn't know anything about it."

"So what'd you say?"

"I reminded him of our last conversation and asked why the fuck he thinks I'd give a shit about the fact that he was embarrassed in front of one of his asshole friends and I hung up then blocked his number."

"That's definitely a healthier reaction than what you used to do."

"*That* is a true statement," he said, throwing my words back at me. "Speaking of parents, how's your mom been since the wedding? She's not bugging you to put a ring on Anjannette's finger, is she?"

"No, she's actually been pretty mellow about our relationship since she met her on Thanksgiving. She's welcomed Anjannette into the family fold with open arms, but even at your wedding, she didn't make one comment about me being next."

"Maybe she's just happy one of her kids is in a committed relationship."

"Maybe."

"Although, with the way Angie was dancing with Clay at the wedding, there may be another Marakis off the market soon."

"Nope." I shook my head and finished my beer in one long gulp. "I'm not going there. I have no idea what's going on and I'm not gonna ask."

"It wouldn't be the worst thing in the world if they got together."

"No it wouldn't. But just like I don't share mine, I don't want to know details about my sisters' dating lives."

Trey's cell chimed and he looked over at me and smiled.

"You know what that text means? It's time to FaceTime my wife."

"At least we can be grateful for technology," I said as we made our way inside. "Cell phones and FaceTime are a definite upgrade from long-distance phone calls once a week like the old-timers had."

I left Trey's condo and took the short walk down the hallway to mine. Anjannette won't be done with classes for another two hours. I grabbed my yoga mat and scrolled to the routines Clay had texted me. Maybe focusing on downward dogs and deep breaths will help settle this feeling of discontent I haven't been able to shake all day.

ANJANNETTE

I LOOKED at the sign I hung on the wall yesterday to let students know the studio will be closed for a week wondering, not for the first time, if I'm sliding back into bad habits. But Keera is so psyched about going to St. Pete in a couple weeks, there's no way I could rescind the offer. Especially since she got official word that the rumor about her company making cutbacks is true and her last day of work is this Friday.

The only other option would be for her to go to St. Pete while I stay behind to run the studio, but that would be more than a little weird.

"What's wrong?" she said from behind me.

"Nothing."

I turned to face her and flashed a forced smile.

"Don't *nothing* me. You've been mopey for three days.

"You know me. I just think too much."

Her eyes shifted over to the sign then back to me.

"Closing the studio for a week to take your best friend in the whole world to St. Pete for spring training is not a sign of backsliding."

"Maybe not, but combined with the fact that I just packed ninety percent of my furniture into a storage unit and moved into Leo's house, it just might be."

Well, I hadn't done the actual packing or moving this

time because Leo hired a company to do it for me, but the end result is the same.

"Oh honey, I'm sorry. I didn't realize moving your stuff would be such a trigger. I would have been there for you more through the process."

"You just found out that you're losing your job and *you're* gonna be there for *me*? God, I am pathetic."

She wrapped her arm around my shoulders and squeezed me tight against her side.

"You're not pathetic. You've just had some bad experiences that have left you scarred." Releasing me, she turned and looked me in the eye. "I'm sorry I didn't realize how bad things were with Travis. I would have been there to help."

"You were going through your own shit with Brian." I shook my head. "We're quite a pair, huh?"

"The important thing is that we're here for each other now and we've learned from our mistakes."

I shifted my eyes toward the sign then back to her.

"That's debatable right now."

"Leo is one of the best guys I've ever met. He'd never treat you the way Travis did."

"The thing is, this isn't about Leo or Travis or any of the other guys I got lost in through the years. It's about me. And I have to make sure I don't go down that rabbit hole again."

"Don't you see how just saying that shows how much you've changed?"

I closed my eyes and shook my head.

"I'm not sure it's that cut and dried."

"You took three whole years to work on yourself. You're not the same person you were back then. Please take my word on that and stop worrying."

"Okay," I said, looking at the poster again. "But you can trust this is going to come up again."

"And I'll be here telling you the same thing."

I wrapped my arms around her and pulled her close for a big hug.

"Thank you for being the best friend in the world."

She pulled back and smiled.

"I'm not done cheering you up yet." She walked over to the iPad and scrolled through a

playlist. "I know this is your happy song. We're going to dance to it over and over again until you're out of your funk."

I wrapped my hand around the closest pole and lost myself to the beat of *Peanut Butter Jelly* by Galantis. Keera is right about the fact that it's my happy song. I'm just not totally convinced she's right about everything else, as much as I might want her to be.

Chapter Thirty

LEO

I SQUATTED behind the plate and Trey went into his windup then delivered a perfect changeup. The second it landed in my glove, I hopped up and threw the ball down to second base and watched Jack Reagan snag it right at the bag.

After two weeks of games, I'm back in the groove and I feel great. My back is loose so every movement behind the plate isn't accompanied by a stabbing pain like it was at the end of last year.

The batter stepped into the box and I settled behind the plate. Trey is a master at painting the corners, so when I gave him the sign for a fastball inside, it skidded right over the edge of the plate, just above the knee, and smacked into my glove. I had him follow that up with the same pitch, but on the outside corner. The hitter fanned at it, but couldn't catch up. After that, I set up right in the middle and slowed things down with a slider. The batter swung way ahead, catching a piece of the ball with the end of his bat, ticking it right into my glove for the first out.

I called a similar pattern for the next two batters. The second guy fouled three pitches off, before popping up to Jimmy Chavez at third base. The third flew out to Dan McMullen in center field.

"You're looking good," I told Trey as we settled onto the edge of the bench in the dugout.

"I feel good." He took a long drink of water then looked at me and smiled. "And I'll be even better when Nori gets here."

"Yeah, tomorrow can't come soon enough."

Anjannette, Keera, Nori, and Angie are all flying in tomorrow, which works out well because Trey and I don't have a game so we'll be able to spend the whole day with them. Some of the guys are coming over for dinner so Keera can have her fangirl moment.

"Well that was a short break," I said as Kasprzyk, Monte, and Chavez got out in quick succession.

"That's better than having a long break that would fuck with my rhythm," Trey said as we headed back onto the field.

The game turned into a pitcher's duel, so the next few innings went by just as fast. We're in the top of the eighth and each team only has one hit and no runs have scored.

Trey is done for the day and Ricky Parrish is next on the mound. A southpaw with a nasty curve, he's a great pitcher to follow Trey because their styles are so different. His warm-up pitches are right on the mark, which is a good sign of how the inning will go.

Ricky stood at the back of the mound rubbing the ball between his hands as the batter walked up to the plate. I squatted into position and he stepped up next to the rubber and waited for my sign. Since the guy in the box is probably expecting a curveball, I went with a fastball. His late swing sent a weak ground ball right back to the mound. Parrish scooped it up and tossed it to Monte for the first out.

We got ahead of the next batter with a four-seam on the outside corner followed by a filthy curve. Unfortunately, the next pitch went a little wild and hit the batter on the thigh putting him on first base with the clean-up hitter up next.

I asked for a time out and jogged out to the mound.

"Skinner has good speed," I said, referring to the guy on first base. "Try to keep his lead short. I'm going with all fastballs so when he does try to steal, I have a chance to shoot him out. And I want to keep the pitches low to draw a ground ball in case they go with a hit and run instead."

"Got it."

Ricky doesn't have the same pinpoint control as Trey or Rusty, but he's usually close enough to be effective. I set up on the inside corner but instead of giving a sign, I pointed toward Skinner, who as predicted, had taken a huge lead. Parrish fired the ball to Monte, who slapped the tag a split-second after the runner's hand hit the bag. The same thing happened for what would have been the next two pitches then Skinner finally took a lead I was comfortable with. It was shortened enough that when the ground ball was hit to second base, Oskar Marquez snagged it and flipped it to Jack Reagan who brushed the bag with his foot before firing the ball to Monte for a perfectly-executed double play.

I jogged back to the dugout and since I'm up second this inning, removed my gear. After taking a quick drink of water, I grabbed my bat and headed onto the on-deck circle. Shawn Riggs stepped up to the plate and I watched him take three balls in a row as I loosened up my shoulders and back, then took a few practice swings. There's a new pitcher on the mound for Houston and it seems he's having trouble finding the plate.

With three balls, Riggs was taking all the way and the pitcher threw a fastball right down the middle for strike one. He followed it up with a curveball that bounced in the dirt, sending Shawn down to first base.

I tightened my batting gloves as I walked over to the plate then stepped into the box. Since four out of five pitches this guy just threw were balls, I won't swing until I see a strike. After throwing two balls high and outside, he managed to put one over the plate. With a count of two and one, I was ready. So when he hung a meatball, I stepped and swung. The bat vibrated in my hands a second before I heard the telltale crack as I made contact and sent the ball flying in a high arc over the left field wall.

Flipping my bat toward the dugout, I started my trot around the bases. Riggs held his hand up for a high-five as I crossed home plate. As I headed toward the dugout, I glanced up into the stands and froze in place then did a double-take, figuring I was hallucinating. When Anjannette stopped clapping to wave down at me, I knew I wasn't.

ANJANNETTE

"WELL, I'd say you surprised them," Angie said.

"Seems that way," I said, not taking my eyes off Leo.

After Trey popped his head out of the dugout and looked up at us, he leaned against the railing in front of it instead of going back inside. Leo joined him a minute later wearing his gear and every once in a while they'd glance up at us.

"You know ladies, the field is out there." Keera pointed. "And there's a game going on."

"I'm good with what I'm looking at," Nori said.

"Yeah, me too."

"With the way Leo is eye fucking our girl here, I think we should make ourselves scarce for a couple hours after the game," Keera said to Angie. "There are just some things I don't want to hear."

"Eewww, that's my brother you're talking about." Angie made a gagging sound then chuckled and said, "But you're right."

Leo glanced back at me.

"In fact, maybe we should get a room for the night. I'm not sure a couple hours will be long enough."

Before Angie could comment, I decided to divert the subject from my sex life.

"So what's happening here?"

"I'm gonna have to get you a *Baseball for Dummies* book. You can't be dating a

ballplayer and not have at least a basic understanding of the game."

"As great as that sounds, it doesn't help me right now."

"Of course, if you were watching the game instead of staring at Leo's ass, you'd probably have a better idea."

"Could we please not talk about my brother's sex life or any of his anatomy?"

The crowd cheered and we looked toward the field.

"Looks like Riddle cleared the bases with a double," Nori said.

There was a short lull in the action while Houston changed pitchers.

"Listen to you speaking baseball," Angie said. "I'm so proud."

"I've learned a lot since last year." She looked at me. "When Trey and I met, I didn't have a clue either. You'll catch on."

The game started again and the first Waves' batter hit the ball but got out. The one after that hit the ball way out in the outfield and made it to second base, but the next two batters struck out.

I watched Leo jog onto the field. He looked over at me and smiled then put his helmet on and squatted behind home plate.

I've really missed him these last three weeks. We spent so much time together leading up to the start of spring training, it was strange coming home to an empty house after he left. Especially since said house is his. We Face-Timed every night which is better than nothing, but it's definitely not the same as waking up with him beside me every day.

I'm still struggling to find the balance in this relationship. As Keera keeps pointing out, Leo isn't Travis, which I understand, but I still never want to be so dependent on another person again. But I really do love Leo. He's so amazing and open and generous, I don't want to hold myself back from experiencing what we can be. Plus holding any part of myself back wouldn't be fair to him.

I'm thinking about making an appointment with my therapist to discuss my feelings and see if she has any suggestions or any strategies for when I get triggered. She was with me though my whole breakup with Travis, so I'm sure she'd have some insight on how I can navigate this.

Keera clapped next to me pulling me out of my thoughts. I looked toward the field and saw the players throwing the ball around the infield. Shifting my attention to the scoreboard, I searched for the word *Outs* and saw the number two glowing beneath it.

A batter stepped up to the plate and the first pitch was a ball. He swung at the next one and I watched as Leo's mask flew off and he fell back onto his ass then stood, holding his jaw.

"What just happened?"

"The batter ticked the ball back and it hit Leo's mask and knocked it off."

Two men walked over to Leo and when he moved his hand, I saw blood on his face.

"Oh God, he's bleeding."

Angie patted my hand.

"It's okay, he'll be fine. He's had worse things happen to him behind the plate. One time the ball hit him square in the throat."

"They're bizarrely resilient," Nori said. "One time Trey got hit in the middle of the shin with a line drive and kept pitching. I would have been on the ground curled up in a ball crying for at least an hour if that happened to me."

The one man had a fanny pack around his waist and pulled out a piece of gauze and sprayed something onto it then dabbed at Leo's face. After inspecting the area he'd just cleaned, he wiped it with a clean piece of gauze then placed a bandage on it. He said something to Leo who then put his mask back on and nodded. And that was it. The men went to the dugout and Leo walked back behind the plate.

The batter got back into the box and I sat on the edge of my seat as the pitcher threw the ball again. Thankfully this time when the batter hit it, the ball went out toward the field instead of in Leo's face. Jack Reagan caught it and threw it to first base for the third out.

So that's it. The game is over and the Waves won.

I watched Leo walk toward the dugout and disappear inside.

"So is there somewhere we can go meet them or should we just call a car and head to the condo?" I asked.

Keera's eyes widened then she pointed toward the field.

"Uh, there's the answer to your question."

The crowd started cheering and I turned my head just in time to see Leo and Trey hop over the wall and run up the steps toward us.

"Oh my God. Can they do that?" I asked.

"I don't think anyone is gonna stop them if they can't," she said with a chuckle.

Trey ran over to the other side where Nori is sitting and Leo stopped at my row and reached out his hand. I took it and he pulled me out onto the step and into his arms. Cupping my face, he flashed a dimple-popping smile then lowered his head and pressed his lips against mine.

God how I missed him.

Everything faded away except for the man kissing me. I dug my fingers into Leo's biceps as his tongue twirled against mine and he added a slight suction that I felt in every erogenous zone in my body. I squeezed my thighs tight to ease the throbbing ache between them and fought the urge to climb him like a tree, wrap my legs around his waist, and grind against him.

Leo slowly ended the kiss and the sounds of the crowd filled my ears once again. They were cat-calling, whistling, and cheering and I should have felt embarrassed at our very public display of affection but my joy at being in his arms again just wouldn't let me.

Chapter Thirty-One

LEO

"SO WHAT MADE you decide to get here early?"

After taking the fastest shower known to man, I ran out to my car with Trey right behind me. He had Nori had taken off in his car and I have the rest of the crew in mine headed to the condo.

"Keera and I got notice a few days ago that our flight was cancelled. They wanted to reschedule us for Saturday, but then we'd only have two days here so I told them that wasn't acceptable. When I pressed, the woman told me she could book us on today's flight so I grabbed it. When I told Nori and Angie, they decided to change their flights too."

"Why didn't you tell me you were coming?"

"We decided it would be more fun to surprise you. At Trey and Nori's wedding, Hannah told me to let her know whenever I wanted to attend a game, home or away, and she'd hook me up with tickets. So I texted her and she left some at will-call."

"How long were you there before I spotted you?"

She shifted to look at Keera and Angie.

"When did we get there?"

"The top of the fifth," Keera said. "Nori was happy she got to see Trey pitch a couple innings."

"I can't believe I didn't spot you for three whole innings."

"Well, you were kind of busy playing your game," she said. "And your attention was probably drawn to those girls in the stands with the *I love you, Leo* and *Marry me, Leo* signs."

"The only person I want holding a sign saying things like that is you," I said and turned to give her a smile.

She placed her hand on my forearm. "Oh I forgot to ask. How's your face?"

I opened my mouth and moved my jaw from side to side.

"A little stiff and sore, but nothing awful." I shrugged. "Goes with the territory."

"I told her about the time you got hit in the throat," Angie said.

"*That* was bad. It hit me right in the Adam's apple and I couldn't breathe. Then it hurt like a bitch for a week whenever I swallowed." I glanced at Anjannette. "I had to come out of the game when that happened. Today's was really no big deal."

I turned into the parking garage of my complex and spotted Trey and Nori getting out of his car. They stepped into the elevator as I pulled into my spot.

We all got out of the car and Angie held out her hand.

"Give me your fob. Keera and I are going somewhere else." I raised my brow. "Anywhere out of hearing distance."

"You're such a brat." I dropped the fob into her hand then leaned down and kissed her cheek. "But thank you."

Anjannette and I headed toward the elevator.

"Have fun, kids," Keera yelled.

It seemed to take forever for the elevator to come back down. When it finally did, we stepped inside and I glanced up at the camera. Everyone at Victory Park saw us make out today, but thoughts of some horny security guard watching us on video gives me the wiggins so I kept my hands to myself.

Once we got to my floor, we walked down to the end of the hallway and I punched the code in and opened the door. We reached for each other at the same time as the door closed behind us. I pulled her against me and sealed our mouths together, thrusting my tongue inside and she met me stroke for stroke. The kiss was wet and wild and I couldn't get enough.

She reached for the waistband of my pants and I pulled back.

"Bedroom."

I grabbed her hand, dragging her through the living room and hallway to my room. Angie and Keera said they were going somewhere but I don't want to take the chance they come back sooner than expected and get an eyeful.

Closing the door behind me, I locked it for good measure. Anjannette was right behind me and she dragged my shirt up, caressing my abs along the way. I reached back and pulled my shirt off and threw it onto the floor. She fanned her fingers out on my chest then circled my nipples with her thumbs. I closed my eyes and groaned when she brushed them with her fingertips then leaned forward and flicked one then the other with her tongue.

I was about to go in for another kiss when she dropped

to her knees in front of me. I watched as she unbuttoned my pants then carefully lowered the zipper over my erection. Circling her hand around to my ass, she squeezed then lowered my pants and briefs just enough to allow my cock to spring free. She caught it in her hand and squeezed, circling the head with her thumb.

"Anjannette," I panted. "You're gonna kill me."

"What a way to go though, right?"

She shifted closer and flicked her tongue against the tip before wrapping her lips around me and sliding them all the way down my shaft. I let out a long, low groan when she reversed the process then swirled her tongue around the head before going down again.

As she came up, she wrapped her hand around the base and slowly moved down until her mouth met her fist. She squeezed and lifted her head then settled into a rhythm designed to make me lose my mind. Down, up, swirl, repeat.

I tangled my fingers into her hair, resisting the urge to hold her in place and fuck her mouth. If I do that, I'll definitely blow, and I don't want that just yet.

Tightening my hold on her hair, I did my best to keep her still. She looked up at me, her lips still wrapped around my dick.

"Stop. You have to stop."

She slowly slid back and let go but not without getting in a few good sucks.

I closed my eyes and took in deep breaths. When I had myself mostly under control, I stepped out of my pants and reached for her.

"Turnabout is fair play," I said.

I pulled her shirt and bra off as I backed her to the bed then pushed her down. She rested on her elbows and watched as I dragged her leggings and panties off. Resting my hands on her waist, I shifted her up until her head rested against the pillows and I settled between her wide-spread thighs.

I reached out to touch her, sliding my finger along her glistening seam.

"Mmm, you're so wet."

I let my tongue follow the path my finger just traced.

"So sweet."

Opening her with my thumbs, I licked at the treasure I revealed, alternately teasing her with the tip of my tongue and tasting her with the flat until she writhed beneath me and her fingers curled into my scalp.

"Leo."

My dick throbbed against the mattress and I pressed against it trying to give him some relief, but that's not what he wants. Before he revolts, I decided to give Anjannette what she's very vocally begging for.

Thrusting two fingers inside her, I curled them and stroked while my tongue circled her clit. She let out a long low moan and I knew she was close. Opening my mouth, I sucked, feasting on her until she spasmed against my fingers and started screaming my name.

I kissed her inner thigh and pulled my fingers out slowly, drawing some aftershocks. I looked up and smiled at her sated glow.

Kneeling, I reached down and pulled her up, settling her thighs on either side of my hips and impaled her with a single thrust. She wrapped her arms around my neck and bit down on my shoulder as she groaned.

"You feel so good," I groaned against her ear and thrust my hips up. "So. Fucking. Good."

She wrapped her legs around my waist and squeezed then relaxed her thighs to shift her hips up and down in tiny increments. The feel of her slick walls pulsing and tightening against me had my balls tingling.

Digging my fingers into her ass, I pulled her forward then back, slamming her against my pelvis over and over again until we both cried out our release.

ANJANNETTE

LEO SAID he was going to invite his friends over so Keera could have a fangirl moment and, if the stunned look on her face when these guys showed up at our door is anything to go by, he totally delivered.

And as if they're mere mortals instead of All-Star ballplayers, Dan McMullen, Jack Reagan, Dale Montgomery, and Phil Riddle are sitting around the table with us eating Chinese food. They've been good sports as Keera asked them question after question about their careers.

"Don't worry, she'll eventually stop staring at you with that fascinated look on her face," Leo said, referring to Keera.

I looked over at the expression on her face and laughed out loud. She looks equal parts stunned and elated, and if I'm being honest, a little manic.

"I'm literally sitting here talking to Jack Reagan about the time he hit a walk-off home run in game seven of the World Series. How am I supposed to look?" Keera asked.

"No worries," Jack said.

"Yeah, it's always nice to meet a fan," Phil added.

Keera smiled and stuck her tongue out at Leo, making the guys laugh.

"But I'm sure as fascinating as it is to me, baseball is

your job, so you probably don't want to sit here talking about it all night," Keera said. "So let's change the subject, shall we?" She folded her hands together and rested them on the table, her formally-worded question and proper pose drawing another chuckle.

"Ooh, ooh, I have one." Angie raised her hand. "I can't believe your kisses ended up on ESPN *and* the MLB network."

"It must be a slow news week," Leo said.

"No, it's just that it was so romantic. Like something out of a movie." Keera placed her hand over her heart and sighed dramatically. "So many people had their phones out recording it, I'm sure it's other places too. Check YouTube."

"Hannah plans on putting it on the Waves website," Jack said. "The fans loved it."

"So did I." Trey bobbed his eyebrows.

"Speaking of Hannah, is she coming down this year?" Leo asked.

"She'll be here for a few days the last week then we'll fly home together. If she came down and worked like she's done the past few years, we would have had to find someone to watch the twins here and she didn't want to do that. So she's taking some vacation days." He nodded his head toward Dan and Dale. "Sabrina and Karen will be here then too so they can help out if she needs it. Oh and Lexi, too. She's a pro after helping out with Gavin."

"Is there a daycare at First Allegiant?" I asked.

"There is, but Aaron and Holly don't go there yet. Hannah is only back part-time at the moment so the Granny Gang watches them."

"Granny Gang?"

"Mrs. Button and her friends," he said. "Considering

their ages, I was a little worried about having them watch the babies, but there are five of them and they're only there a few hours. Plus, it's not like Aaron and Holly are running around."

"I love that name," I said.

"Yeah, they're pretty proud of it," Jack said. "But please, like the lady said, 'let's change

the subject, shall we?' I feel like I've dominated the conversation enough with talk of babies."

"As if that's not our main topic of conversation these days," Phil said.

"Smartass." Jack tossed a balled-up napkin and hit him in the middle of the forehead.

"Children behave," Leo said.

Keera leaned closer to me and stage-whispered. "Did you hear that? Jack Reagan quoted me. I can die a happy woman."

She had a smirk on her face, making light of her words, but I'm pretty sure she's only half kidding.

"Will you be coming down again?" Dale asked. "I know Karen would love to see you

again. She had a great time in Scranton. We both did. She can't stop talking about that hotel you recommended."

"Yeah, I've always loved the Lackawanna Station Hotel. It's so beautiful and has such a

rich history," I said. "And I'd love to see Karen again, but unfortunately, I won't be able to make it back here." I looked over at Keera. "We actually closed the studio this week so we could both be here. I can't do that again."

"Maybe in Myrtle Beach then," he said.

"Yeah, maybe."

I just don't see how that will happen either. I have a few students competing in the Pole Sport Association competition that's being held in Allentown in June. Leading up to that, there will be a lot of private lessons and the studio will be used more often. I can't expect Keera to handle all that so I can run off to visit my boyfriend.

Before I could get too depressed over that fact, I stood. "Who needs another drink?"

Chapter Thirty-Two

LEO

"THESE PAST FIVE days flew by way too fast," I said.

They're flying out later this afternoon and since my game is at night, I'll be able to drop them off at the airport. Anjannette and I woke early, wanting to squeeze as much time together out of our remaining hours as possible. After going out for French toast at a little diner down the block, we decided to take a walk on the beach.

"Way too fast, but I had a great time. Keera did, too. Thank you so much for having us spend time with your friends. And thank them for being such good sports."

"They had fun too, and Keera is already over her fascination. So next time she sees them, it'll just be like they're long-lost friends."

We reached my building but instead of heading up toward the walkway, I stopped. When Anjannette looked up at me, I turned her to face the water. Stepping behind her, I wrapped my arms around her waist and pulled her back against me. After a brief hesitation, she leaned against my chest and we stood there in silence.

After what seemed like forever, she spoke.

"I'm not looking forward to the cold that's waiting for me at home."

"At least it hasn't snowed again. I was worried you'd be flying into a storm."

She didn't comment which wouldn't concern me, but she seemed upset about more than the cold she's facing. Something is off with her the past couple days. Sometimes she's okay but every once in a while, she hesitates or seems distracted. I hate to let her go without finding out what's wrong, especially if we're not going to see each other for a while.

"Is something wrong?"

She didn't say anything at first, but I felt her muscles tighten then she shrugged.

"Did I do something to upset you?"

"No, you're perfect."

While I know that's not true, I think she means it.

"So what's wrong?"

She let out a deep sigh and turned to face me.

"Leo, this trip was great. So was the time we spent together in Myrtle Beach."

When she didn't continue, I said, "Why do I think there's a *but* coming?"

"*But* I can't just pick up and come visit all the time."

I blinked. "I know that. I know you have the studio and can't just run off whenever you want."

"You're right, I *can't*. It doesn't mean I'm not thinking about doing just that."

"I'm really confused."

"I'm sorry, I'm not explaining this very well."

She sat in the sand and dragged her fingers through

her hair. I sat next to her, putting enough space between us so she doesn't feel crowded and waited for her to speak again.

"You know how I told you I wasn't with anyone for three years before we got together?" I nodded. "There's a reason for that."

She bent her knees and wrapped her arms around them as she stared out at the water.

"The last guy I was with—Travis—ended up being not so great."

I curled my hands into fists. If that fucker laid a hand on her, I swear I'll kill him. She rested her hand on my arm and squeezed.

"He didn't hurt me physically." She let go of my arm. "But he was mentally abusive." Shaking her head, she added, "It's so embarrassing to admit this."

I started to put my arm around her but stopped myself. If she wants me to touch her, she'll let me know.

"Anjannette, there's nothing to be embarrassed about. Not with me anyway."

"It is though, and if I could go back and do things differently, I would. Travis was just the last in a long line of losers I changed myself for, and by the time I broke things off with him, I was isolated from my friends, had nowhere to live, and barely knew who I was."

Clay's observation that her inner light was missing makes total sense after hearing her words. I have no idea where this is going or why it's on her mind today. Hopefully her douchebag of an ex hasn't reappeared trying to cause problems.

"When we went through my history, my therapist noticed patterns of things I do when I'm with men. At the time, she recommended I take a year off dating, kind of like they do in twelve-step programs. I didn't think it would be that big of an issue, but the fact that I found it really difficult proved that I had a problem. So after the first year, I decided to do another, and that just naturally led to a third." She looked over at me. "And then you came along."

I'm not even sure what to say to that, so I remained silent. She turned to face the water again and we sat like that for quite some time before she continued.

"I was terrified to go out with you."

"So why did you?"

"I liked you." She shrugged. "But honestly, I figured we'd go out once and that would be it."

"Why would you think that?"

"I don't know exactly, but it's kind of irrelevant. The thing is that we did go out more than once, and here we are."

"Where exactly is *here?*"

"I'm living in your house and I keep trying to figure out how I can rearrange my schedule so I can be with you. So basically I'm falling right back into those patterns. And even though you're not like all those jerks I dated in the past and you'd never take advantage of me the way they did, it's not healthy for me to act like that. Plus, you'd hate that person."

"First of all, you're living in my house because you lost your apartment," I pointed out.

"I moved in with Travis because Keera moved in with her boyfriend and I couldn't afford our apartment on my own."

"And I don't expect you to rearrange your schedule to fit with mine. I'd never ask you to do that. I know you have a business to run."

"I know that, but it doesn't mean I won't." She wiped a tear off her cheek. "It's funny, at

Thanksgiving, Keera's grandmother told me not to be a Miranda, referring to the character in *Sex in the City*."

"I'm familiar with the character, but don't understand what she has to do with us."

"When she started dating Steve, she basically expected the worst based on past relationships. Granny Vi was afraid I was doing that to you." She met and held my gaze. "And I thought maybe she was right, but now I don't. I know how great you are, Leo. Seriously, you're perfect and I love you so much."

"Again, there's a *but*."

"You're not the problem and if I'm being honest, neither were any of my exes. *I'm* the problem, and I don't know how to open myself fully to a relationship without losing myself again."

She stood and brushed sand off her pants. I looked up at her.

"So what exactly are you saying?"

"I don't know. I can't..."

She looked lost and confused. I stood and wrapped my arms around her and she rested her cheek against my chest as she sobbed. At least she's not pushing me away. Not yet anyway.

THE DRIVE to the airport was melancholy. Even Keera and Angie were quiet in the back seat. I'm not sure if they're so sad to be leaving or if they're picking up on the vibe Anjannette and I have had since our walk on the beach.

I'd reassured her the best I could, but honestly, I have no idea what we're going to do.

If she can get away for a day, or even overnight, we

might be able to make it work when we play in New York but that's the best I can figure.

I've told her since we started this relationship that I'll take her however I can get her. If that means FaceTime until October, so be it. I'm not saying it won't be difficult, but if that's what it takes, I'll do it.

All the other stuff she talked about, well as far as I can tell, it's all in her head. But I have three sisters and more female cousins than I can count. I'm not crazy enough to actually say that to her.

I turned onto the airport exit and followed the signs to their airline and pulled up to the curb. Keera and Angie each gave me a big hug and said goodbye then grabbed their bags and walked toward the entrance. I appreciate them giving Anjannette and me time alone to say goodbye.

Pulling her into my arms, I squeezed her tight.

When I pulled back, I said, "We'll make it work. Don't worry."

She offered a wobbly smile, but didn't seem convinced.

"Call me when you get home." I leaned down and gave her a brief but intense kiss. "I love you."

"I love you too, Leo."

My stomach twisted as I watched her walk away and have no idea what the status of our relationship is at this point.

ANJANNETTE

MY PHONE RANG and I turned it off, ignoring Leo's call. It's been ten days since I left St. Pete and I'm still as confused as ever. I've been ignoring his calls because I have no idea what to say to him.

It's not you, it's me is the biggest break-up cliché, but in this case, it's true. It's definitely not him. And while I didn't specifically say the words, breaking up is basically what I did.

I looked around his house knowing what a hypocrite I've been staying here since I got home. My only alternatives would be to get a hotel room or sleep at the studio. I have applications in for three apartments. Hopefully one of them will pan out.

Keera's made it very clear she thinks I'm an idiot and things have been tense between us. I've been trying to keep both that and my bad energy from infecting the studio but there's definitely a palpable tension in the air.

I couldn't stop my groan at the sound of the doorbell. The only person who knows I'm here is Keera and I just don't have the energy to deal with her right now. It's been a long week and the only thing that's kept me going was the thought of spending Sunday alone, on the couch, nursing the ache that's been a permanent fixture in my head since I last saw Leo.

The doorbell rang twice more and I laid down and put the pillow over my head. A few minutes later I heard knocking on the patio doors.

"Let us in, Anjannette."

That's not Keera's voice.

I picked my head up and saw Angie and Keera through the glass.

They're not going to leave so I tossed off my blanket, left the sanctuary of the couch, and opened the door.

"It's freezing out there," Angie said as she stepped inside.

I walked back to the couch, wrapped the blanket around my shoulders, and flopped back down.

They sat in the chairs across from me and looked at each other, seeming to decide who was going to speak first. Angie won, or maybe she lost. Either way, she spoke first.

"What are you doing?"

"I'm trying to relax on my day off."

"Don't be obtuse. What are you doing with Leo?"

"I'm not doing anything."

I blinked back tears as I said that.

"You can't even answer a question about him without tearing up. Is this better than whatever fucked-up reasoning you have for not answering his calls?" Keera asked.

"You know my reasoning isn't fucked up. He deserves better than me."

"I don't have a clue what you're talking about," Angie said. "But it seems to me that Leo should have some say about who and what he deserves."

I wiped tears off my cheeks and tucked my hands back in the blanket.

"Look at me. I'm a mess."

"The thing is, you weren't a mess when you were with Leo," Keera said, raising her voice with each word until she was shouting.

Just hearing his name hurts.

I looked at Angie.

"Does he hate me?"

"I don't know. He won't talk about it."

I frowned.

"He called me to find out if you're okay," Keera said.

"And she called me. Leo didn't tell either of us anything, but Trey told Nori and she told me that he's miserable."

Good Lord, it's like a heartbreak phone chain.

"And obviously you're miserable," Angie said. "So I don't understand."

I gave her the abridged version of my history and where I am now. Her frown grew more pronounced with each word I said. When I was finished, she looked at me like I'd lost my mind.

"Don't take this the wrong way, but that is the stupidest thing I've ever heard."

Keera flashed me an I-told-you-so smirk.

"The two of you just don't understand. I can't lose myself like that again and it's not fair to Leo if I hold a part of myself back from him."

"Honey, why don't you call Rachel Green? I'm sure she'll give you some insight on what you're feeling and help you figure out how to navigate your relationship with Leo."

Angie scrunched her nose.

"Like Jennifer Aniston's character on *Friends*?"

"It's my therapist's name."

When I started seeing Dr. Green, even in my pathetic state, I had a good chuckle about her name. Now, nothing. I'm just sitting here watching Angie and Keera laugh.

Keera sobered when she noticed I wasn't laughing.

"Just call her. Please?"

Since I've been toying with the idea anyway, I agreed.

Chapter Thirty-Three

LEO

I SAT on the couch staring at the TV eating a slice of cold, leftover pizza. Some of the guys were going out to dinner after today's game, but I just wasn't in the mood. I'm not really good company these days and haven't been since Anjannette left St. Pete three weeks ago and cut me off.

She did send me a text telling me she was cutting me off first, so I suppose that's something. Then I got another text telling me she'd be out of my house as soon as she finds an apartment. But that's it. Two texts in three weeks. After everything.

I've been in contact with Keera so at least I know Anjannette is okay, physically anyway. From what I understand she's just as miserable as I am. Keera keeps telling me not to give up and I'm trying not to. But it's not easy.

A knock sounded on my front door and I groaned. The last week in St. Pete the guys were always stopping by, but since we live in the same complex, it's easy. Here in Myrtle Beach, we're scattered all over so random pop-ins are rare.

I peeked out the window and saw Jack Reagan sitting on my front porch.

Opening the door, I said, "Hey Jack, everything okay?"

"You tell me."

How do I answer that? The whole team knows I'm miserable and have an idea why even if they don't know the specifics.

I opened the door and stepped aside, resigned to the fact that Jack doesn't plan on leaving until he says whatever he came here to say.

"I've got cold pizza and cold-ish beer."

"As appealing as that sounds, I'm gonna pass. I actually just ate."

I settled back onto the couch and Jack sat across from me on the loveseat.

"You look like shit."

"Gee, thanks."

"Trey told me a little bit of what's going on. Not specifics, but enough that I have an idea."

"So do you have any solutions for me?"

"No, just a story if you're interested in listening."

"What else have I got to do?"

"Everyone pretty much knows the details about my childhood now, but three years ago, that wasn't the case. You know how I lived my life until I got together with Hannah and that was directly related to my mom dying and my dad basically falling apart." He sat forward, resting his elbows on his knees and continued. "So I start spending time with Hannah and then *spending time with Hannah*. And somewhere along the way, I decided that I needed to pull back so all those nasty feelings interfere with my life, my game, whatever."

"How'd that go over?"

"Not well," he said around a chuckle. "Hannah immediately noticed something was different and called me on it. I told her what I was doing and why. She told me she wanted all of me or none of me. Stupidly, I chose the latter."

"Ouch."

"Yeah, it wasn't good. I looked a lot like you do now, but I convinced myself I was better off. That I was doing something good for Hannah."

"So how did you resolve it?"

"I tracked her and chased her down at the airport. You know, a grand gesture."

"Yeah, women like those."

I thought about what I could do to impress Anjannette and came up blank. Especially since I'm not the one who ended our relationship.

"I'm telling you this to maybe help you understand how no matter how much you love someone, you can royally fuck up doing something you think is best for yourself or them."

"So what can I do to convince her to give us another shot, oh wise one?"

"My recommendation would be to give her some time. I know it's not easy, but I can tell you that the longer I was without Hannah, the more miserable I got. Dan called me on my shit and made me realize I was being a total ass," he said. "And from what I understand, she's as miserable as you *and* her friends are on your side. So the way I see it, it's just a matter of time." He slapped his hands against his thighs and stood. "Hang in there."

"Thanks Jack," I said as I followed him to the door. "I appreciate the talk."

What he told me didn't give me a course of action, but

it did give me hope. And that's more than I had an hour ago.

ANJANNETTE

I LOOKED around the waiting room of Dr. Green's office. Nothing has changed since the last time I was here, not even me, apparently. I took a deep breath in through my nose and let it out slowly the same way trying to clear my head. Getting myself all riled up before going in there won't help anything.

The door to the inner office opened and a patient walked out. Dr. Green looked at me and smiled.

"Anjannette. Come on in." She stepped aside as I entered her inner sanctum. "Have a seat."

One of the couches is different, but I chose to sit in the one I always used when I came here regularly. Dr. Green settled into her big leather chair and picked her iPad up from the table next to her.

When I first started coming here, she used to take notes on a yellow legal pad. Somewhere along the line, she got more technical and started writing on the iPad using a stylus.

"How've you been? How's the studio doing?" she asked.

I decided to answer the easier question first.

"The studio is doing well. It's turning into the space I'd envisioned."

"I've heard good things," she said. "I'm happy it's working out for you."

"Thank you."

"Now for the tougher question. How've you been?"

I twisted my fingers together and tried to remember the answer I'd come up with for that question but drew a blank. So I had to improv.

"For the most part, I'm good. Like I said, the business is going well and I'm okay."

"That's good," she said. "But I don't think you're coming here for the first time in nine months to tell me you're okay. I'm guessing something is bothering you."

"I started seeing someone a few months ago."

"And how's *that* going?"

"For the most part, it's great. He's so different from the other guys I've been with."

"In what way?"

"In *every* way. He's sweet and kind and he treats me well. And he's so supportive of the business and the fact that I pole dance. Super supportive." I paused and collected my thoughts. "The problem isn't him, it's me."

"Why do you say that?"

"He's a baseball player."

"Are we talking about professional baseball?"

I nodded.

"He plays for the Carolina Waves."

"How did you two meet?"

I told her how Leo ended up living in Scranton and why he was at the studio.

"At first I turned him down when he asked me out. I told him it was because I was too

busy, but it was really because I was afraid."

"Of what?"

"At that point, I hadn't dated anyone in three years and I was doing well. So well. I was afraid if I did, I'd backslide."

"So what made you finally say yes?"

"I liked him. But honestly, I figured we'd go out once and that'd be it. Then one date led to two and two to three…" I shrugged. "You get the picture."

"So when did things start going bad?"

"They haven't," I said. "Well not exactly." She frowned and scribbled on the iPad. "Like I said, he's a baseball player. Do you have any idea what their schedules are like?"

"Very hectic during the season, I imagine."

"Extremely hectic. He's been at spring training since mid-February and basically won't be back here until October."

"Are you worried he won't be faithful?"

"Funny enough no, that's not my big fear. Not with him."

"Then what is?"

"That I'll arrange my life to fit into his like I've done before. I'm already living in his house."

She raised her brow.

"So you're living together."

"Not officially."

I told her how I ended up living in Leo's house.

"Well, that sort of makes sense. Are you still looking for an apartment?"

"I found three places I liked and put applications in, but someone got to them ahead of me. So yes, I'm back to searching."

"So your concern is that you're falling into similar patterns as before?"

"Yes."

"And have you talked to—" she gestured.

"Leo."

"Have you talked to Leo about this?"

"I have. The last time we spoke actually."

"And what did he say?"

"He said we'd work it out."

"Do you have a reason to think that's not true?"

I shrugged, unsure what to say.

"How did you feel when you were sharing your story with him?"

"Embarrassed."

"Why?"

"Because I hate the person I was when I was with Travis. I don't ever want to be like her again."

"Anjannette, you have nothing to be embarrassed about. You were in a bad situation and you got out. You've come a long way since the first time we met. The fact that you're even worried about repeating patterns shows how far you've come. I don't think you're acting like that person at all."

"Sometimes I feel like I've come a long way and others it seems like I'm starting to do the same thing I did before."

"Let me ask you something. Do you love this man enough to try to make this work?"

"I do love him," I said. "I just need to know how to navigate a relationship as the new me. How do I open myself up to someone without losing myself again? How do I *know* when I'm losing myself?"

"If Leo is as wonderful as you say, he won't let you lose yourself. Or rather, you'll lose yourself in a different way, a healthy way. When you're in a healthy committed relationship, it's okay to give and take. The problem occurs when, like in your past relationships, you give everything you have and your partner takes it all and still wants more." She studied me as I processed her words. "Does that make sense?"

"It does."

"Just remember to communicate with your partner. Tell him what you need and listen to what he needs then work together so you're both happy in the relationship."

"But you think I can do it?"

"Anjannette, I watched you rebuild your whole life three years ago. So yes, I think you can do it."

"Thank you, Dr. Green."

I left her office feeling more positive than I have in, well ever. Now I just hope it's not too late to mend things with Leo.

Time to call in the troops.

Chapter Thirty-Four

LEO

EVERY ONCE IN A WHILE, you play one a game where everything just falls into place. This is one of those games. Sam Cherry started the on the mound tonight and his pitching was flawless. His velocity was up all the way through the seventh inning, he hit his spots, and his breaking balls were filthy. He allowed one excuse-me hit in the top of the fourth, but other than that, no one got to first base.

Ricky Parrish followed and looked just as good. His curveballs were breaking from twelve to six and guys were screwing themselves into the ground trying to hit them.

The icing on the cake is that I'm really seeing the ball and I've already hit two frozen ropes into the gap. I'm up again in the bottom of the eighth, this time facing a different pitcher. Let's see if the magic is still there.

I stepped into the box and watched the first pitch come in high and outside. The second one was a strike, but it wasn't *my* strike, so I let it go by. The third pitch was my idea of perfect and I saw it from the second it left the pitcher's hand until it sailed right into the zone. I whipped my hands around, swinging the bat at just the right and hit the ball with the sweet spot.

I ran toward first base and as I rounded for second, it was still flying as the left and center fielders chased it. The ball dropped just past the two guys and took one hop to the wall then bounced back past the outfielders. I hit second base and looked to the third-base coach for direction. He was waving me toward him, much to my surprise. Thankfully I didn't slow down at all. Running toward third base as fast as I could, I executed a perfect pop-up slide into the bag a full second before the ball arrived.

Safe at third.

I can count on one hand the number of times I've hit a triple.

There's definitely a shift in the energy tonight. Or maybe the planets are aligned the right way. Whatever it is, for the first time in a month, I just feel *good*. Instead of questioning it, I'm just gonna enjoy the moment.

THE NINTH INNING went just as flawlessly as the rest and we won the game seven to one. After doing a post-game interview, I jumped into the dugout and started to go down the tunnel.

"Leo."

I looked back and spotted Monte.

"Yeah?"

"Could you stick around for a minute?"

"Uh sure."

I looped my chest protector over my head as I walked back to the dugout. Monte was out on the field looking up into the stands and held his finger up, signaling for me to wait. I took the time to remove my shin guards then grab a drink.

"Ready?"

I finished chugging my water and tossed the bottle into the recycling bin then nodded. I have no idea what I'm ready for, but I suppose it doesn't really matter.

Climbing the steps of the dugout, I walked onto the field and turned to look at Dan, Jack, Monte, and Trey, who were standing against the wall smiling at me like four idiots.

"What's up?"

They glanced over their shoulders, directing my attention toward the stands.

My heart stopped. It literally stopped then started pounding so hard, I'm sure it was visible through my shirt.

Anjannette stood on the steps about fifteen rows up holding a sign over her head.

Leo Marakis

I was so wrong

Please give me another chance

I love you!!!!!!!!!!!!!!!!!!!!!!!!!

My teammates separated, and opened the gate. I looked at them then at the gate and shook my head. Walking forward, I closed it and stepped back.

ANJANNETTE

I WATCHED Leo close the gate and step back from the wall and called myself every kind of fool. After not talking to him for over a month, I seriously thought I could just show up here with a sign and everything would be okay. How delusional was that?

Hannah helped me set this whole thing up, complete with a cleared section and security guards ensuring fans wouldn't interrupt us. She even got Leo's friends to help. Now they're all here to witness my fall.

I lowered the sign and rested it on my feet.

The field in front of me blurred as tears filled my eyes. I was about to turn and leave when something caught my eye. I blinked furiously to clear my vision just in time to see Leo jump the wall and sprint up the steps toward me just like he did in St. Pete.

He cupped my face and used his thumbs to clear the tears that had escaped and streaked down my cheeks.

"Hey, what's this about?"

"When—When—" I took a measured breaths to calm myself before I hyperventilated. "When you closed the gate, I thought you were going to leave. I thought you hated me."

He flashed that panty-melting, dimple-popping smile.

"I could never hate you." Leaning down, he gave me a quick kiss then leaned his forehead against mine. "I love you too much.

Tears streamed down my face and I started blubbering.

"Leo, I'm so sorry. I love you. I never should have hurt us like that. I'm so, so sorry. Please forgive me. I swear I'll never do anything like that again."

"Hey."

He kissed my forehead then my nose, then my lips. God love him, the man *must* love me because I'm a tear-streaked snotty mess. And I know from experience that I'm *not* a pretty crier.

"I love you, I forgive you, and we're going to do better moving forward."

"What did I do to deserve you, Leo Marakis?"

"Part of me has known from the first time I laid eyes on you that we belonged together. Even when you slammed the door in my face, I knew you were the one."

Keera had told me that I was the one he wanted months ago. I'd quoted Buffy at the time, but right now, I said the words that are in my heart.

"All I ever want to be is the one."

Leo smiled and pulled me into his arms.

"It's been a while since I've been featured on ESPN. How about you help a guy out?"

"Absolutely."

He placed his mouth on mine and kissed me, long, hard, wet, and deep, bending me over his arm in the process.

Have mercy.

The End

Check out Keera's story in book #1 of my new series,
Peaches & Pole

Chapter 1

Keera

"How did you survive for so long without sex?"

Anjannette looked up and blinked, then raised her right brow.

"When I asked if there was anything else we need to discuss, my sex life isn't what I had in mind."

"I definitely don't want to talk about what your sex life is like now. That would only make my celibacy seem worse, even if it is voluntary. I want to talk about your dry years prior to Leo." I smirked and bobbed my eyebrows. "Pun totally intended."

"I guess we're done with business." She closed her laptop and rested her elbows on the table. "But thankfully everything looks great and it seems like the open house is all set. You don't need me here at all."

"You know that's not true. You're the heart and soul of this place. Everyone misses you when you're gone."

After dedicating herself to the Peaches & Pole for the better part of three years, Anjannette met and fell in love with Leo Marakis, All-Star catcher for the Carolina Waves. When I got downsized by corporate America, she brought me on as a partner, which was definitely a win-win. It gave me enough of a bump in income so I didn't need to find another job and also allowed her the flexibility to travel with Leo throughout the baseball season.

"And don't think you're going to distract me from my question."

She took in a deep breath and let it out on a dramatic sigh.

"All right. What do you want to know?"

"Just what I asked. How did you survive without sex for so long?"

"I remember giving my toys a workout for six months or so, but after that, I just didn't crave it anymore. Plus I was putting all my energy into this place, so that helped shift my focus," she said. "How long has it been?"

"Five months, one week, and three days."

"That's very specific."

"I could probably tell you the hours and minutes too if I really thought about it," I said. "And I've been giving my toys a workout, but they're just not doing it for me anymore. It's much more enjoyable when someone else does the work. Know what I mean?"

"Yeah." Anjannette's mouth curled into a sappy, smitten, and super-satisfied smile. "I know *exactly* what you mean."

"Oh-kay."

The chair scraped against the floor as I pushed back from the table and stood.

"What's wrong?"

"You know that I'm really happy for you, but I'm so freaking jealous right now. I'm ready to jump out of my skin I'm so horny, and you and Leo are fucking like bunnies."

Her eyes widened and she stared at me for a few heartbeats before flashing that satisfied smile again and dramatically nodding her head.

"Yeah we are."

I burst out laughing then leaned down and pulled her into a hug.

"I truly am happy for you." Shifting back, I squeezed her shoulders then let her go and straightened. "I'm just cranky." I stuck my bottom lip out and used my best whiny voice to add, "I really like sex."

Anjannette stood and leaned her hip against the desk.

"The only thing I can suggest is what really helped me. Focus on why you gave it up in the first place."

She raised her voice on the last two words of that sentence turning it into a question. I never really told her why I decided to take a break from men. Initially, I didn't have a concrete answer, it was just something I felt I needed to do. It's a little more clear now, but knowing doesn't make it any easier.

"You're partly to blame for my celibate state."

"Me?" She placed her hand on her chest. "What did I do?"

"You started a healthy relationship with your hottie ballplayer that made me want more than random hookups with dick band-aids. Plus those hookups got old. I realized I was just going through the motions and it became more like a bad habit than something I enjoyed."

Anjannette's image blurred and I blinked several times to push back the tears.

"You okay?"

"Yeah." I dabbed at my eyes. "You know I've never been a crier, but lack of sex must have my hormones all scrambled because the past couple months, the waterworks are never too far off. Sappy movies and sweet commercials have me tearing up and I even got emotional last week after my class perfectly executed a new routine."

"Have you talked to Dr. Green about it?"

When I decided that I finally wanted to deal with some emotional baggage, Anjannette recommended her therapist, Dr. Green. *Dr. Rachel Green.* It's a struggle for me not to make a *Friends* reference everytime I'm with her.

"Yeah, she said that crying is an excellent way of releasing emotions and processing difficult situations." I used air quotes to highlight my therapist's words. "I still don't like it and can't help but wonder if it's worth it. Like seriously, why am I doing this anyway?"

"Change is hard, but it'll be worth it. Honestly, I don't think things would have worked out with Leo if I hadn't focused on myself before we met. I wouldn't have been capable of having a healthy relationship." She squeezed my hand. "You went through a lot with Brian but when you guys broke up, you never really took time to deal with it. Which is exactly what I did for years. I moved from guy to guy, making the same stupid mistakes. The thing is, eventually all that stuff you ignore builds up and tarnishes everything."

My issues didn't start with Brian, but he definitely highlighted all my insecurities. I've always been a bigger girl and I'd be lying if I said that didn't bother me. Pole dance helped me appreciate my body for its strength and even made me feel sexy, but in the back of my mind, I always wish I was smaller.

"When we first got together, Brian said he loved my curves, but once he lost some weight and got obsessed with fitness, the insults started. He complained about what I ate and wore, especially if we were with his Crossfit friends." I snort-laughed. "The sad part is, if I hadn't found out he was cheating, I'd probably still be with him."

"Yeah, same with Travis and me," she said. "And when Dr. Green pointed out my bad pattern and suggested I take a break from men, I hated the idea. Thankfully I'm stubborn and decided to do it just to prove her wrong, because she was totally right."

"I'll admit I thought you were crazy. I couldn't even imagine going cold turkey like that."

"So what changed?"

"Brian isn't the first guy I've dated who ended up commenting on my weight." I blinked away tears as I looked around the studio before meeting her gaze again, then shrugged. "One-night stands with random guys kept me safe from that. Plus the sex was good. In the beginning anyway. I just went through the motions with the last few. But that's not how I want to live my life going forward. I want to spend it with someone who loves me for me and doesn't care about the size of my body."

She pushed away from the table and pulled me into a hug.

"I'm so happy you decided to make a change." Releasing me, she added, "You're beautiful inside and out and some day you'll meet a man who recognizes that and will treat you like the goddess you are."

"Say that louder for the universe to hear."

****

Simon

My phone buzzed and I cringed when I saw my sister's face pop up on the screen. I thought about ignoring the call, but that would only delay the inevitable.

"How's my favorite sister today?"

"I'm your *only* sister and I'm pissed," she said, then added, "At you." As if there was any question.

No use pretending I don't know what she's talking about.

"Shannon, I took Andi out to dinner then dropped her off at the hotel. I don't know what else you expected to happen."

"I *expected* you to give the date a chance. She said you barely spoke and when you did, you gave one or two word answers."

"I did give it a chance," I said.

"By sitting there silent and just nodding like an idiot?"

I closed my laptop and shifted forward to set it on the coffee table. Resting my elbows on my knees, I told her my side of the story.

"I got a few words in at the beginning, but once I asked about her job, she barely stopped talking to breathe. So instead of interrupting, I just listened and nodded."

"It couldn't have been that bad."

"Do you want me to tell you about the designers she's worked with, items of clothing she's worn, and which makeup she prefers?" That question was met with silence so I'm guessing Shannon has experienced similar conversations with Andi. But since she's being quiet, I figured I'd drive my point home. "I could also tell you which photographers are her favorite, although by that point, I was only half listening so I won't be as detailed."

I heard a long sigh and sat back waiting for my sister to speak.

"Did you like her at all?"

"I didn't *dislike* her, but she's not someone I'd want to date."

"Just because of the talking?"

"Honestly, we don't have anything in common."

"Okay, no Andi," she said. "But I do have someone else in mind that I think you'll connect with better."

My sister is a makeup artist for some of the most prestigious photographers in Manhattan so she has a never-ending supply of beautiful women at her disposal.

"I appreciate the thought, but I'm good. Besides, people will start avoiding you if they think you're going to hit them up to go on a date with your nerdy brother."

"My friends think you're adorable and would jump at the chance to date you."

"I seriously doubt that."

"Why not? Nerds are in you know," she added with a chuckle.

Penny and Leonard end up together on *The Big Bang Theory*, but chances are, they'd crash and burn in the real world. There are exceptions of course, but my experience has taught me that the women my sister usually hangs out with and I just aren't a good fit.

"We're too different. Your friends are like you. None of them would be content doing the low-key things I enjoy and I definitely don't fit in their world."

"Relationships are about compromise. Look at mom and dad. They're as opposite as can be and still make it work."

"Mom and dad are the exception," I said. "And besides having nothing in common with your friends, I live in Scranton and they're either in Manhattan or travel all the time. Andi's photo shoot in the Poconos is the only reason we managed to go out."

"I have friends closer to Scranton."

I took off my glasses and rubbed my eyes.

"Shannon, please find another project."

"You and Zoe broke up almost two years ago and aside from the women I've set you up with, you haven't had a date."

"And I'm okay with that."

"Simon, you're a great guy with a lot to offer. I know you'd like to be in a relationship, you just need to meet the right girl. That's not going to happen if you're hiding at mom and dad's playing video games with Andrew and Archer."

My sister and I may be twins, but we're total opposites, in looks, interests, and lifestyle. Where she's like our outgoing, popular father, I take after our more reserved mother. Shannon has made it her life's mission to get me out from behind my computer and make sure I don't end up living in our parents' basement.

"You know I only moved back home because mom and dad took off on their tour of the country. Once they come back, I'll get my own place."

After Zoe and I broke up, I moved into a studio apartment because it was fully furnished and available, but ended up living there longer than I should have. My lease was up, so when mom and dad bought an RV and planned their epic journey, I decided to move back home. Staying here will give me time to find something new and would also make keeping an eye on their house easier. It seems like a win-win to me. Shannon thinks I'm going to stagnate here.

"We'll see."

I swear I heard her eyes roll through the phone line.

"Shan, I went away to college then moved in with Zoe a couple years after I graduated. You make it seem like I've been a hermit."

"Not a hermit exactly. I mean, you go to work and hang out with your friends once in a while," she said. "But let's be honest, you spend more time with your dolls than you do with people."

"They're not dolls, they're collectibles. And I don't play with them. They're on display."

"Okay Andy," she said, referring to Steve Carell's character in *The 40-Year-Old Virgin*.

"On that note, I'm gonna say goodbye."

Her answering laugh should have aggravated me, but for some reason, it made me smile.

"Talk to you later, big brother."

I disconnected the call and picked up my computer, but the game I'd been playing before Shannon called wasn't keeping my attention anymore. Something my sister said kept running through my head. I would like to be in a relationship and if I'm being honest with myself, I know who I want to be in one with. Opening a new browser, I signed onto Facebook and typed in her name.

Keera Jordan.

We worked together for almost a decade before her position was downsized last year. I had a crush on her from day one, but she was dating then engaged. Plus I was with Zoe part of that time. Even if those things weren't true, I'm not sure I would have asked her out. Besides the fact we worked together, we were friends. If things didn't work out or she wasn't interested, that friendship would have been messed up and I'd have to face her every day.

But now that wouldn't be the case. My ego would be bruised if she turned me down, but I'd live.

I scrolled through her feed, which was mostly pictures of classes at the pole dance studio she's working at now. Then something caught my eye. They're having an open house at the studio next weekend. Before I could second-guess myself, I grabbed my phone and dialed Shannon.

"Do you have plans next weekend?" I asked as soon as she answered.

"Nothing that can't be blown off or changed. Why?"

"There's an open house at Keera's pole studio Saturday and I was hoping—"

"I'll be home Friday night."

Sometimes it's not so bad having a pain-in-the-ass sister.